DREAM HEIST:

The Reverie Heist

A Young Adult Fantasy Adventure

BOOK ONE

Copyright

DREAM HEIST: THE REVERIE HEIST
Book One

First Edition: 2026

Cover design by Ken Konet
Interior formatting by Isabella Green

ISBN (Paperback): 978-1-966703-21-1
ISBN (eBook): AMAZON

Published in the United States of America

Content Advisory: This book contains themes of grief, parental abuse, medical trauma, and permanent character transformation. Recommended for ages 13 and up.

For more information, visit: **www.Humbolton.com**
Humbolton; Dallas, TX

Table of Contents

Prologue: The Day Color Died

Twelve Years Ago

The morning sky over New Portside blazed orange and pink, like someone had spilled a bucket of sunrise across the horizon. Elena Finch had almost forgotten what real color looked like. Soon, the whole world would. She paused on the apartment steps, adjusting six-month-old Leo in her arms, just to look at it. "Look," she whispered to her baby, tilting him toward the sky. "See the colors?"

Leo gurgled, reaching pudgy fingers toward the light. His eyes—bright and curious—reflected the dawn. Already he seemed fascinated by everything that moved, everything that shone. Thomas said it meant their son would be an Architect someday. Someone who could navigate the Reverie with skill and purpose.

The Reverie—that's what dreamers called it. The place where consciousness went during sleep. The dimension made of thoughts and imagination and impossible things. For years, people had learned to bring pieces of it back. Small things. Beautiful things. Dream-smugglers had become common as mailmen.

But they'd pushed too far. Taken too much. And now reality was rejecting them. Elena hoped he was wrong. The Reverie was beautiful, yes. But dangerous too. And Thomas spent too much time there, exploring zones that had no names, smuggling things that shouldn't exist in waking hours.

Still. The world was beautiful this morning. New Portside hummed with life. Street vendors set up carts selling fruit so fresh it sparkled—some of it real, some smuggled from dream-orchards where apples tasted like laughter and strawberries sang when you bit them. Music drifted from open windows: jazz from one apartment, classical from another, a kid practicing violin scales. Badly, but enthusiastically.

Children chalk-drew hopscotch squares on sidewalks in every color imaginable. A girl with rainbow ribbons in her hair skipped past, singing a song about flying elephants. Two boys argued cheerfully over which superhero was fastest. An elderly man sat on a bench feeding pigeons, surrounded by flowers he'd smuggled from the Garden Eternal—blooms that never wilted, petals that shifted through the spectrum. This was normal. This was life in a city that had learned to live alongside dreams.

Elena walked toward the park, enjoying the morning sun on her face. Leo babbled happily, watching everything with wide-eyed wonder. She pointed out dogs and birds and clouds shaped like dragons. She sang him the lullaby her mother had sung to her. Everything was perfect. Then the sky flickered. Just for a second. Like a light bulb losing power. The orange and pink dimmed, went flat, then returned.

Elena stopped walking. Around her, other people paused too, looking up with confused expressions. "Did you see that?" someone asked. The sky flickered again. This time longer. The colors drained away like water down a sink, leaving everything pale and washed-out. Then they rushed back, but not quite as bright as before.

Leo started crying. "It's okay, baby," Elena murmured, but her heart was racing. She'd seen smuggles go wrong before—objects from the Reverie losing cohesion, melting into dream-smoke. But this wasn't one object. This was everything.

The singing strawberries at the fruit cart fell silent, mid-note. The never-wilting flowers on the bench began to droop. The chalk on the sidewalk started to fade, bright pinks and yellows turning to pastel, then lighter still. A woman screamed. Elena turned. The screaming woman stood frozen, staring at her hands. They were changing—becoming translucent, dream-like, as if she was half-asleep standing up. Then they solidified again, but her wedding ring had vanished. Just gone. She kept staring at her empty finger, crying.

All around the park, people started shouting. Pointing. Running. Reality was coming undone. Elena ran for home, clutching Leo tight against her chest. Behind her, she heard buildings phase in and out of existence. A grocery store appeared in the middle of the street—fully formed, lights on, shoppers inside—then vanished as quickly as it came. A car drove past with no driver, steering itself according to dream-logic.

The boundary between sleeping and waking was collapsing. Her apartment door stood open. She burst inside to find her neighbor Mrs. Chen sitting on the stairs, speaking in a language that didn't exist. The words flowed smoothly, confidently, but they meant nothing. Dream-babble leaking into her waking mind.

"Mrs. Chen?" Elena tried. The older woman looked at her blankly. Smiled. Continued speaking nonsense.

Elena locked herself in her apartment. The television was on, but every channel showed the same thing: the emergency broadcast signal, then a confused anchor trying to report on events they clearly didn't understand. The crawl at the bottom of the screen read: REALITY DESTABILIZATION EVENT—SEEK SHELTER—AVOID SLEEP—DO NOT PANIC. Her phone rang. Thomas. "Elena." His voice was tight with controlled terror. "Are you home? Is Leo safe?" "Yes. Thomas, what's happening?"

"We pushed too far. The boundary can't hold." Background voices shouted behind him. "We're at the focal point now. There's a way to stop it, but—" He paused. "Someone has to anchor the boundary. Permanently."

Elena's stomach dropped. "What does that mean?" "It means someone has to stay. Between worlds. Holding them apart." His voice cracked. "Forever." "No." Elena gripped the phone so hard it hurt. "No, Thomas, you can't—"

"I have to. I'm the strongest Architect. I understand the Reverie better than anyone." He was crying now. She could hear it. "I'm so sorry, Elena. I wanted to come home. I wanted to watch Leo grow up. I wanted—"

Leo wailed in her arms, as if he understood. "Tell him I love him," Thomas said. "Tell him his father chose to save the world. Tell him—" His voice broke. "Tell him I'm sorry."

"Thomas—" "I love you both. Forever. Remember that." The line went dead. Elena felt it the moment Thomas made his choice. A pulse of energy rippled through reality—not violent, but absolute. Like the universe taking a deep breath and holding it.

Outside her window, the chaos stopped. The phasing buildings solidified. The dream-speaking people blinked, confused, then began talking normally. The translucent hands became flesh again. Reality snapped back into place.

But it snapped back wrong. The colors started to drain. Not all at once. Gradually. Like watching a photograph fade in sunlight.

The orange and pink sunrise dulled to cream, then beige, then grey. The bright blue apartment door across the hall faded to slate, then charcoal, then neutral nothing. The rainbow ribbons in the little girl's hair bled out, strand by strand, until they hung limp and colorless. Elena watched from her window as New Portside transformed. The singing fruit at the cart fell silent and turned grey. The never-wilting flowers crumbled to ash. The chalk drawings washed away in the rain that began to fall—rain that came down the color of dishwater.

Music stopped. Laughter faded. Color leached from everything: buildings, cars, clothes, skin. Even the sky turned flat and empty, a uniform grey dome pressing down on the world. She looked down at Leo. His bright eyes were dimming. His rosy cheeks paling. Even his baby-blue onesie was turning grey.

"No," she whispered. "No, no, no." But there was nothing she could do. The world was becoming monochrome. Becoming safe. Becoming separate from dreams. Thomas had saved reality. But reality had forgotten how to shine. That night, Elena made a choice.

She would never dream again. Never let herself slip into the Reverie. Never risk the boundary that her husband was now holding, alone, forever. More than that: she would raise her children in the grey world. Keep them safe. Keep them grounded. Keep them from ever developing the abilities that might draw them into the Reverie's dangerous beauty.

No art. No music. No wild imagination. No risk. Thomas had sacrificed himself to save the world. She would honor that sacrifice by making sure their children never followed his path. Never paid his price.

She rocked baby Leo, who had finally stopped crying. His grey eyes stared up at her, still curious despite everything. Still seeing wonder in a world that had forgotten color. "I'm sorry," she whispered to him. "I'm so sorry. But this is how it has to be. This is how I keep you safe."

Outside, New Portside settled into its new reality. The government began drafting Conformity Laws. Wellness Centers were designed to help people forget their dreams.

Enforcers started patrolling for signs of creative thinking. The grey world was born.

And in the space between sleeping and waking, in a crystalline structure that would come to be called the Sanctum, Thomas Finch held the boundary and hoped his sacrifice meant something. But he wasn't alone. The Warden—the first and oldest consciousness—watched everything. Always watching. Always waiting.

Hoped the world he'd saved would remember how to live. Hoped his son would forgive him for not coming home. He was wrong about the forgiveness part. Leo would never blame his father. But Thomas was right about something else.

His son would be an Architect. The strongest one yet. And twelve years later, Leo Finch would wake up holding something impossible. A flower. Blue as the sky before it turned grey. Glowing with inner light. Still warm from the dream he'd just left.

Real. Solid. Perfect. And that would be the moment everything changed again. But first, there would be twelve years of grey. Twelve years of Elena trying to control what couldn't be controlled. Twelve years of Leo growing up in a world that had forgotten color.

Twelve years of waiting. And then: the flower. Blue as the sky before it turned grey. Glowing with inner light. Still warm from the dream he'd just left. Real. Solid. Perfect. Twelve-year-old Leo Finch, waking with the impossible in his palm.

And everything would change again.

* * *

Chapter 1: The Grey Morning

Everything in Leo's life was grey. The walls. The food. The clothes. The sky. Even his dreams, when he bothered having them. The government said grey was safe. Grey was orderly. Grey was good. Leo thought grey was death by a thousand paper cuts. The alarm was grey.

Leo knew this because he had checked three times when Mother brought it home from the factory. Regulation Grey-7, the label said. Acceptable for residential use. The numbers glowed a slightly lighter grey—Regulation Grey-4—which meant he could read them in the dark without violating the Illumination Ordinance. 6:00 AM. Monday; the twenty-third week since the accident.

He pressed the button. The alarm stopped. The white noise generator in the corner continued its steady hum, drowning out any sound that might have leaked through the walls from the neighboring apartments. Everyone had them now. Regulation AG-440 generators in every room. To reduce distraction, the government said. To help people focus on what mattered.

Leo sat up. His room was the same as yesterday. The same as the day before. The same as every day for the past twenty-three weeks. Grey walls. Grey floor. Grey ceiling. Grey curtains over the window, though he knew what was outside without looking: grey buildings under grey clouds. The sun was up there somewhere, filtered through the perpetual overcast that hung over New Portside like a wet blanket.

He dressed in his school uniform. Grey pants, regulation length. Grey shirt, regulation buttons. Grey shoes, regulation laces. He checked his hair in the mirror—too messy, as always. If he saw an Enforcer on the street, they might issue a citation. Untidy appearance suggested creative thinking. Creative thinking led to daydreaming. Daydreaming led to... other things.

Things people didn't talk about anymore. He wet his hair down, flattening it as best he could. The graphite smudges on his fingers caught his eye. He'd been sketching again last night. Dangerous. Illegal, actually, since the Art Suppression Act passed two years ago. But he hid the drawings under his mattress, and Mother was too tired to search his room.

Besides, drawing was the only thing that quieted his mind. Breakfast was already on the table when he came downstairs. Grey blocks of compressed nutrients. Technically "food," though that word felt generous. It contained everything a growing body needed: calories, protein, vitamins. It contained nothing a growing person wanted: flavor, texture, joy.

Mother sat across from him, eating mechanically. She wore her factory uniform, grey coveralls with her employee number stitched on the chest. Her shift started at seven. It ended at five. Then she went to her second job at the recycling plant until eleven. Then home for five hours of sleep before starting again.

She didn't look at him. She rarely did anymore. "Hospital day," he said quietly. She nodded. Set down her spoon. Reached into her pocket and pulled out a transit pass. Slid it across the table. "Two hours," she said. Her voice was flat. Tired. "The supervisor said no more than two." "Thank you." She stood. Collected her dish. Paused at the sink with her back to him.

"The doctor might have questions," she said. "Answer honestly." "I will." "Don't mention—" She stopped. Started again. "Just answer what they ask. Nothing more." He understood. Don't mention that Lily had been running.

Don't mention that they'd been arguing about art supplies. Don't mention that Leo had yelled at her, that she'd run into the street without looking, that the car had come so fast—

"I understand," he said. She left without saying goodbye. Leo closed his eyes. Tried not to remember the last time he'd heard her laugh. It had been in this very kitchen. A Tuesday morning. Lily sitting across from him, sneaking bites of his toast because hers had burned. Mother had gone to work early, so it was just them.

"You know what I'm going to do when I grow up?" Lily had asked. "Steal my breakfast forever?" "I'm going to paint the sky." She'd said it so seriously, grey eyes sparkling. "Like, actually paint it. Not in a picture. The real sky. Make it blue and purple and orange all at once." "That's impossible," Leo had said. "The government would never allow it."

"So?" Lily had grinned. The mischievous grin that meant trouble. "I'll do it anyway. You can help me. You're good at planning impossible things." "I'm good at planning **possible** things. There's a difference."

"Nope. You just haven't realized you're impossible yet." She'd taken another bite of his toast. "Besides, someone has to put the color back. Might as well be us." Leo had laughed. Actually laughed. Because Lily made everything sound achievable, even the ridiculous. Even the dangerous.

Then she'd looked at him seriously. "Hey, Leo? You know I love you, right? Even when you're annoying and overprotective and won't let me ride my bike to school alone even though I'm eleven and totally capable?" "I know," he'd said. "I love you too. Even when you steal my toast."

"Good." She'd smiled. "Don't forget that." That was six months and one day ago. The next morning, she'd tried to ride her bike to school anyway. Leo had followed her, worried. She'd turned to wave at him, not watching the intersection. The delivery truck driver didn't see her in time. Leo opened his eyes. The memory hurt like broken glass in his chest.

She'd told him not to forget. And he wouldn't. He'd remember every second of her until he brought her back. Leo finished his breakfast. Rinsed his dish. Put it in the drying rack. The white noise generator hummed steadily, filling the silence where conversation might have been.

He grabbed his backpack and stepped outside. New Portside looked exactly like every other city in the Coastal Conformity Zone. Brutalist architecture, regulation-approved designs. Buildings rose in perfect rectangular blocks, grey concrete and grey metal. No architectural flourishes. No decorative elements. Nothing that might distract the eye or inspire the imagination.

The streets were clean. Obsessively clean. Street cleaners in grey jumpsuits swept constantly, removing any trace of color that might have blown in from... from wherever colors came from. Leo couldn't remember the last time he'd seen anything brighter than Grey-7.

Actually, that wasn't true. He'd seen it in his dreams. But dreams didn't count. The transit station hummed with its own white noise generator, louder than the residential units. People moved through it like grey ghosts, not speaking, not making eye contact. Everyone had somewhere to be. Everyone knew that being late meant citations. Citations meant fines. Fines meant Imagination Wellness Evaluations.

Nobody wanted that. Leo scanned his pass and boarded the 7:15 to St. Grace Hospital. The seats were grey. The windows were tinted grey. Outside, grey buildings slid past in grey morning light. A screen mounted above the doors played the morning news. The anchor—grey suit, grey tie, grey expression—read from the daily bulletin.

"Conformity Council reminds citizens that the twenty-week evaluation period begins next Monday. All residents aged ten to eighteen must report to their designated testing centers. Failure to comply may result in—" Leo stopped listening. He'd heard it before. Tests to measure creativity. Questions designed to catch kids who daydreamed too much. Kids who drew pictures in the margins of their notebooks. Kids who hummed songs that didn't exist yet.

Kids like him. The screen changed to another story. "The search continues for Marcus Harlow, fourteen, who disappeared from his residence in the capital sixteen months ago. Director Harlow asks that anyone with information contact local authorities immediately. The Director reminds citizens that harboring unregistered minors is a Class Three—"

The train stopped. Leo stood. He didn't hear the rest. St. Grace Hospital smelled like cleaning solution and regret. Leo had been coming here every Monday, Wednesday, and Friday for twenty-three weeks. He knew every hallway, every nurse's station, every flickering fluorescent light. He knew which elevator stuck on the fourth floor and which vending machine only dispensed grey protein bars.

He knew the way to Room 447 without thinking. The nurse at the desk—Ms. Reeves, her name tag said—looked up as he approached. "Two hours today, Leo," she said. Not unkindly. Just tired. "Doctor Sato wants to speak with you before you leave."

His stomach tightened. "Is something wrong?" "He'll explain. Room four-forty-seven." He walked down the hall. His footsteps echoed on the linoleum floor. White noise generators hummed in every room, but they couldn't quite cover the beeping of monitors, the hiss of ventilators, the quiet sounds of people who wouldn't wake up.

Lily's room was at the end of the hall. He stopped outside her door. He always stopped here, for just a moment, before going in. Preparing himself. Building the walls that kept his feelings locked away where they couldn't hurt him.

Where they couldn't show. He pushed the door open. She looked like she was sleeping. That was the cruelest part. She looked peaceful. Comfortable. Like she might wake up any second and ask him why he was staring.

But she wouldn't. The monitors beside her bed beeped steadily. Heart rate normal. Blood pressure stable. Brain activity minimal. That last one was the problem. Six months in a coma and her brain showed almost no response to stimuli. The doctors said it was like she'd simply... left. Gone somewhere her body couldn't follow.

Leo pulled a chair up beside her bed. Reached out and took her hand. "Hey, Lily," he said quietly. "It's Monday. I know you hate Mondays." Her hand was warm. That was good. It meant her circulation was fine. Everything physical was fine. It was just her mind that was missing.

"School starts next week," he continued. He always talked to her. The nurses said it might help. He didn't believe them, but he did it anyway because doing nothing felt worse. "You'd be starting seventh grade. Remember how nervous you were about sixth? You thought Mrs. Palmer was going to be terrible, but she ended up being your favorite teacher."

He stopped. His throat was tight. "I'm sorry," he whispered. "I'm so sorry, Lily. I shouldn't have yelled at you. I shouldn't have said—"

The words stuck. He'd said them a thousand times in his head. Why don't you think before you act? He'd been trying to help. Trying to keep her safe. She'd wanted to do an art project for school. Something colorful. Creative. Forbidden by Conformity Laws. He'd been explaining why that was dangerous, why she needed to listen to him, why she could get them both arrested—

And she'd run. Into the street. Into traffic. The impact had sounded like the end of the world. "I should have trusted you," he said. "I should have just... I should have let you choose." The monitor beeped. Her hand didn't squeeze back. A knock on the door made him look up.

Doctor Sato stood in the doorway. He was older, grey-haired, grey coat, grey expression that tried to be kind but mostly looked tired. "Leo," he said. "Can we talk outside?" His stomach dropped. "Is something wrong?" "Just talk."

They stepped into the hallway. The white noise generators hummed. Doctor Sato closed the door behind them and faced Leo with the expression adults got when they were about to say something that would hurt. "I'm afraid we're not seeing the improvement we hoped for," Doctor Sato said. "Lily's brain activity hasn't increased. In fact, it's remained remarkably stable—almost too stable. Like she's..." He hesitated. "Like she's somewhere we can't reach."

"But she's still alive," Leo said. "That's what matters. Right?" "Of course. But we need to discuss long-term care options. Another week without change, and we'll need to have a family meeting with your mother. Decisions will need to be made about—"

"She's going to wake up," Leo said. His voice was sharper than he intended. "She just needs more time." Doctor Sato's expression softened. "Leo, I know this is hard. But we have to be realistic about—"

"More time, please," Leo said politely again. A long pause. Then Doctor Sato nodded slowly. "Two weeks utmost," he said. "But after that, we need to have this conversation. Understood?" Leo nodded. Turned back to Lily's room before the doctor could see his face. Two weeks. Fourteen days to figure out how to fix this. Fourteen days to find a miracle.

He stayed the full two hours. Talked to her about nothing. About school starting. About the grey weather. About how the apartment was too quiet without her music playing, without her terrible jokes, without her laughter.

Without her. When his time was up, he kissed her forehead and left. The transit ride home blurred past. Grey buildings. Grey people. Grey everything. He unlocked the apartment door and stepped inside. The white noise generator greeted him with its steady hum. He dropped his backpack by the door and stood in the kitchen, staring at nothing.

Two weeks. How do you save someone when you don't know what's wrong? How do you fix something when you don't have the tools? His eyes burned. He wouldn't cry. He never cried. Crying was an emotion, and emotions led to creativity, and creativity led to—His sketchbook was where he'd left it, hidden under his mattress. He pulled it out and opened to a blank page.

His hand moved without thinking. Pencil on paper. Lines forming shapes. Shapes forming images. A girl with dark hair. A smile that felt like sunshine. A sister who deserved better than a brother who couldn't save her. He drew until his hand cramped. Until the room grew dark. Until Mother came home from her second shift and went straight to bed without speaking.

He drew until he couldn't draw anymore. Then he closed the sketchbook. Hid it. Changed into grey pajamas and crawled into bed. The white noise generator hummed. Outside, grey night pressed against grey windows.

Leo closed his eyes. "Please," he whispered into the darkness. "Show me how to fix this. Show me anything. Just... help me save her." He hated how desperate he sounded. Hated that he was basically praying when he didn't even believe in anything. But maybe that's what you did when you were this scared. Maybe being scared made everyone sound stupid.

The white noise hummed. Sleep pulled at him. And for the first time in six months, Leo dreamed. He walks through a meadow. That's wrong. He was just in bed. He was just falling asleep. Now he's here, and "here" is impossible. The meadow stretches forever. The grass is green. Not grey-green. Not regulation-approved green. Just green. Pure, bright, impossible green.

The sky is blue. The air smells like flowers. Leo stops walking. His heart pounds. This is a dream. It has to be. But dreams aren't supposed to feel this real. He can feel the grass under his feet. Feel the wind on his face. Feel the warmth of the sun on his skin.

Sun. He can see the sun. When was the last time he saw the sun? He looks at his hands. Counts his fingers. One, two, three, four, five. That's normal. In dreams, people always have the wrong number of fingers. He learned that in school, back when they still taught about dreams before the Suppression Curriculum.

Five fingers. But this still feels like a dream. He looks up. The meadow is real. The sun is real. The flowers are— A single flower grows in front of him. It wasn't there a second ago. Now it is.

It's blue. Not grey-blue. Not regulation blue. Just blue. A blue so bright it almost hurts to look at. It glows with inner light, pulsing like a heartbeat. Leo stares at it. "This is a dream," he says aloud. His voice sounds strange. Clearer than it ever does in the real world. The white noise is gone.

The flower pulses. And then he hears it. A voice. Quiet. Distant. But unmistakable. "Take it," the voice whispers. Leo's breath catches. He knows that voice. It's impossible, but he knows it.

"Take it,"* it says again. *"Hold on. Don't let go."

He kneels down. Reaches for the flower. His hand trembles.

"I'm waiting,"* the voice whispers. *"Come find me."

Leo's fingers close around the stem. The world EXPLODES with light—

[END OF CHAPTER 1]

Chapter 2: The Blue Flower

Leo's fingers close around the stem. The world doesn't just explode with light—it tears open. Pain shoots through his hand, up his arm, into his chest. Not physical pain. Worse. It's the sensation of being pulled in two directions at once, of existing in two places, of reality itself arguing with his presence.

The meadow is still there. The blue flower pulses in his grip, warm and solid and impossibly real. But behind it, through it, Leo can feel his bedroom. His grey sheets. His grey walls. The white noise generator humming in the corner.

He's in both places.

"Hold on,"* the voice whispers. Urgent now. *"Don't let go. Not yet."

The flower fights him. Or maybe reality fights him. It wants to stay in the dream. It wants to remain impossible. His fingers ache with the strain of keeping them closed.

"I don't understand," he says, but his voice cracks between two worlds, echoing strangely.

"You will. Just hold on."

The pulling sensation intensifies. It feels like falling and being yanked backward simultaneously. The meadow blurs. The sky ripples. The grass beneath his feet becomes less solid, more suggestion than substance.

Wake up, some part of his brain screams. This is too much. Too real. Too wrong. But the voice—that impossible, familiar voice—

"Almost there. I believe in you."

Leo holds on. He gasped awake. His bedroom crashed into focus. Grey walls. Grey ceiling. The white noise generator humming its relentless static. Morning light—filtered through grey clouds, grey curtains—leaked into the room.

His hand hurt. Actually hurt. Not dream-hurt. Real hurt. Leo uncurled his fingers. A blue flower lay in his palm. He stopped breathing. The flower was real. Solid. Warm. Its petals glowed with that same inner light, pulsing like a heartbeat. Blue. Impossible, vibrant, beautiful blue. It was here. In his hand. In his bed. In the real world.

"No," he whispered. "No, this is—" "LEO!" His mother's voice cut through the white noise, sharp with anxiety. "You're late! The transport leaves in ten minutes!" He jerked upright. The flower tumbled onto his sheets, that impossible blue against regulation grey fabric. It was real.

He'd pulled something from a dream into reality. That was impossible. Wasn't it? "Leo!" Footsteps on the stairs. "If you miss another day, the school will report us!" He grabbed the flower. It felt warm, alive, like it contained actual sunlight. His fingers tingled where he touched it. "Coming!" he called, his voice cracking.

He heard her footsteps retreat to the kitchen. The white noise hummed. Outside, grey morning pressed against grey windows. And in his hand, a blue flower that shouldn't exist glowed defiantly. Leo's mind raced. This violated everything he'd been taught. Dreams were just electrical impulses. Neurons firing randomly during sleep. That's what the Conformity Education Materials said. Dreams weren't real. They didn't have physical form. They couldn't cross into—

The flower pulsed. His throat tightened. Lily. The voice in the dream. It had sounded like— No. That was impossible too. Lily was in a coma. She couldn't speak, couldn't dream, couldn't call out to him from— From where?

"Get dressed," he told himself firmly. "This is just... you're still dreaming. Or hallucinating. Stress hallucination. That's a thing." He set the flower on his nightstand. Pulled on his school uniform with shaking hands. Checked his reflection—hair too messy again, graphite smudges on his fingers, eyes too wide.

He looked at the flower. It looked back. When he picked it up again, it felt lighter. The glow seemed dimmer. The petals looked less vibrant, more washed-out.

Was it dying? Could dream-flowers die? His backpack lay open on the floor. He grabbed his math notebook—empty except for geometric doodles in the margins—and carefully placed the flower between two blank pages. "Sorry," he whispered to it. "I don't know what else to do with you." He closed the notebook. Shoved it in his backpack. Headed downstairs. Mother was already at the door, factory uniform on, employee badge clipped to her collar. She looked at him with that expression she always wore now—tired, worried, barely holding on.

"Breakfast is on the table," she said. "Eat fast." "I'm not hungry." "Eat anyway. You're getting too thin." He sat. Picked up the grey nutrition block. Took a bite. It tasted like nothing, as always. But this morning, the absence of flavor felt more obvious. More wrong.

Because he'd tasted something in the dream. The air had tasted like flowers. Like possibility. "Did you sleep?" Mother asked. "Yes." "Any dreams?"

His hand froze halfway to his mouth. "What?" "Dreams. The school questionnaire asked if you've been having dreams. They want parents to report unusual sleep patterns." She didn't look at him. Just stared at her own grey block of food. "Have you?"

The notebook in his backpack seemed to burn. The flower hidden between pages. "No," he said. "I never dream." She nodded slowly. "Good. That's good." A pause. "If you did, you'd tell me. Right?" "Of course." Another pause. Longer this time.

"Your father used to dream," she said quietly. "Before the Nightmare. Before the laws. He'd wake up and tell me about impossible things. Flying cities. Talking animals. Worlds that didn't follow any rules." Leo had heard stories about his father, but Mother rarely spoke about him. Not since the Great Nightmare took him when Leo was too young to remember.

He looked at her. Really looked. And for the first time in years, he saw past the grey—saw the woman who'd loved a man who dreamed too much. "Tell me more about Dad," he said quietly. "Just... one story. Please." Mother's expression cracked. For a moment, she looked like she might cry. Then she sat on the edge of his bed.

"Your father," she said slowly, "had a ritual. Every morning, before work, he'd make me coffee. Not grey protein beverage. Real coffee, smuggled from dream cafés where beans grew in impossible colors. He'd pour two cups—one for me, one for him—and we'd sit on the balcony watching sunrise."

She smiled. Barely. A ghost of joy. "He'd say: 'Elena, what are you going to build today?' And I'd tell him about my architecture projects. My designs. My dreams. And he'd listen like I was describing the most important thing in the world. Then he'd say: 'Go build it. I believe in you.'"

Her voice broke. "The morning of the Great Nightmare, he said it one more time. And I said: 'What are you going to build today?' And he said..." She stopped. Breathed. "'A world where our son can dream safely. Even if I'm not there to see it.'"

She stood abruptly. "He lied. There's no safety in dreams. Only loss. Only pain." She looked at Leo with desperate intensity. "Promise me you'll forget this flower. Promise me you'll stay safe. Please." Leo couldn't promise that. But he could understand why she tried so hard to keep him grounded.

"I'll be careful," he said. It wasn't the promise she wanted. But it was the only one he could give. She left without saying goodbye. The flower kept glowing in the dark. Leo finished his breakfast mechanically. Rinsed his dish. The white noise generator hummed its eternal song. He grabbed his backpack and stepped outside. The world was grey, as always. But in his bag, something glowed blue.

School was six hours of regulation education. Mathematics (geometry, because shapes were safe and orderly). Science (chemistry, because mixing compounds followed predictable rules). History (heavily edited, focused on the Great Nightmare and why Conformity saved humanity). Leo sat in the back of every class. Tried to pay attention. Failed. His backpack sat under his desk. The notebook inside seemed to pulse with warmth, though that was probably his imagination. Was the flower still alive? Still blue? Or had it died already, wilted into nothing?

And why had he been able to pull it through? During lunch period—thirty minutes of supervised eating in the cafeteria, grey tables and grey food and grey silence—he snuck into the bathroom. Locked himself in a stall. Pulled out the notebook with shaking hands. The flower lay between the pages. It was grey. Not blue. Not glowing. Just grey. The petals had turned the color of ash, the stem brittle and lifeless. It looked like it had been dead for years.

Leo's chest tightened. "No," he whispered. "No, please—" He touched it gently. The petal crumbled into dust at his fingertips. Within seconds, the entire flower dissolved. Grey sludge spreading across the notebook pages, soaking into the paper, leaving nothing but a stain.

Leo stared at the mess. All that effort. All that pain pulling it through. And for what? Five hours of existence before it died? He closed the notebook. His throat burned. Maybe Mother was right. Maybe dreams were dangerous. Maybe some things weren't meant to cross between worlds.

He shoved the notebook back in his bag and left the stall. In the mirror, his reflection looked hollow. The rest of the day blurred past. Classes. Transit rides. Grey buildings under grey sky. He arrived home to an empty apartment. Mother was at her first job. Wouldn't be back until after eleven.

Leo dropped his backpack by the door. Stared at the grey walls. The grey furniture. The white noise generator humming its mindless tune. The flower was dead. The dream was over. Tomorrow he'd wake up and it would all seem ridiculous—a stress hallucination, nothing more.

Except... A memory rose unbidden. Lily, three months before the accident. Walking home from school together on the approved transport route. Grey buildings, grey sky, grey people moving in approved patterns.

She'd been talking about a project. For art class—except there was no art class anymore. The subject had been eliminated two years ago under the Creative Expression Restriction Act. Too much individualism. Too much chaos. Too much color. But Lily had this idea. She'd found it in an old textbook someone had forgotten to burn.

"It's called painting," she'd said, eyes bright in that way that made Leo nervous because brightness attracted attention. "You use pigments—actual colors, Leo—and you put them on canvas and make... anything. Anything you can imagine." "That's illegal," Leo had said immediately. "Art materials are contraband. Creating unauthorized images is a Class Three violation. If they catch you—"

"They won't catch me," Lily had interrupted. "I'll do it in our apartment. In my room. No one has to know. I just want to make something beautiful. Something that's mine. Don't you ever want that? To make something that isn't grey?" Leo had stopped walking. Turned to face her on that grey sidewalk.

"What I want," he'd said carefully, "is for you to not get arrested. What I want is for you to understand that rules exist for a reason. The Conformity Laws keep us safe. Keep us employed. Keep us alive." "Safe," Lily had repeated. The brightness in her eyes had dimmed. "You mean small. You mean quiet. You mean invisible."

"I mean protected," Leo had insisted. "You're eleven, Lily. You don't understand what happens when you break these laws. I've seen kids get taken away. Families separated. I won't let that happen to you." "So instead you'll just... control me?" Her voice had gotten quiet. Dangerous quiet. "Choose what I eat, where I go, what I think about? When do I get to decide anything for myself, Leo?"

"When you're older. When you understand consequences. When you can be trusted not to—" "Not to what? Not to want things? Not to feel things? Not to be anything except exactly what they tell me to be?"

"Not to make stupid decisions that could destroy our family!" He'd said it too loud. People had looked. He'd lowered his voice. "I'm trying to keep you safe. Why can't you see that?" She'd looked at him with those eyes that could make him feel small and tall at the same time. "You're not my dad," she'd said quietly. "You're my brother. You're supposed to let me try things. Even if I fail. Even if I make mistakes. That's how people grow."

"People who grow get hurt," he'd replied. "I'm keeping you from getting hurt." "You're keeping me in a cage," she'd said. "A grey cage. And you think because the bars are soft, they're not bars at all." Then she'd walked ahead. Put her headphones in. Shut him out for the rest of the walk home.

Leo remembered that now, standing in the grey living room. Remembered dozens of moments just like it. Choosing her breakfast because she'd pick something too sugary, too frivolous, too joyful. Planning her schedule because she'd waste time on things that didn't matter, didn't advance, didn't keep her safe. Correcting her homework because she'd make careless mistakes, creative leaps, dangerous thoughts. Fixing everything because that's what he did. That's who he was. The one who planned. The one who controlled. The one who kept her safe.

Except he hadn't kept her safe. Three months after that conversation, she'd tried to make the art project anyway. In secret. And when he'd found the hidden supplies—the smuggled paints, the illegal canvas—he'd confronted her. Yelled at her. Said words he couldn't take back.

"Why don't you think before you act?" And she'd run. Until he couldn't. Until she ran into traffic because she was angry at him, frustrated by his constant control, tired of being treated like a project instead of a person. "I was trying to help," he whispered to the empty room. The white noise generator hummed its answer: nothing.

He went to his room. Pulled out his sketchbook. Drew her face from memory. The way she smiled when she forgot to be annoyed with him. The way her eyes lit up when she talked about things she loved. The way she looked at the world like it held secrets worth discovering.

He drew until his hand cramped. Then he noticed something. On his shoe. A business card. Grey cardstock with simple black text. He hadn't seen it appear. One second it wasn't there. The next, it was.

He picked it up.

RYLES' PAWN & CURIO

We Buy Impossible Things

14 Salvage Street

Open After Dark

On the back, in handwritten script:

You broke your focus. But I can teach you how to hold it.

Leo turned the card over and over in his hands. This wasn't possible. Business cards didn't just appear. And nobody knew what he'd done. Nobody had seen the flower. Nobody—Unless someone had been watching. Unless someone knew how to do what he'd just done.

Unless he wasn't the only one. The white noise generator hummed. Outside, grey evening settled over grey buildings. Leo looked at the card again.

Open After Dark.

That meant breaking curfew. That meant risking citations. That meant doing something dangerous and unapproved and potentially very, very illegal. He thought about Lily. About the doctor saying they needed to "discuss options." About having fourteen days to find a miracle.

He thought about the flower. How it had felt real in his hands. How the voice had said "I believe in you." How it had sounded like Lily. Leo stood. Grabbed his jacket. Pocketed the business card. Mother wouldn't be home for six more hours.

He had time.

[END OF CHAPTER 2]

Chapter 3: The Pawn Shop

That night, Leo tried again. He lay in bed, grey sheets pulled up to his chin, staring at the grey ceiling. The white noise generator hummed. Outside, darkness pressed against the windows. He closed his eyes.

Focus, he told himself. *Remember the meadow. Remember the flower. Remember the feeling.*

Sleep came slowly. His mind kept circling back to the business card hidden in his pocket, to the grey sludge in his notebook, to Lily's face on the hospital monitors. When sleep finally took him, he fought to stay aware. To keep some part of his mind awake while his body rested. It worked.

He walks through the meadow again. Green grass. Blue sky. Impossible colors that make his eyes ache after years of grey. The sun warms his skin.

But something feels different this time. The meadow seems less solid. More dreamlike. When he looks at the grass, it shifts colors slightly, green to blue to purple and back. That didn't happen before.

He searches for another blue flower. Finds one growing near a twisted tree that definitely wasn't there a second ago. "Okay," he says aloud. His voice echoes strangely. "I can do this. I just need to hold on."

He kneels. Reaches for the flower. His fingers close around the stem. Nothing happens. No tearing sensation. No pain. No pulling between worlds.

The flower sits in his hand, warm and solid, but it doesn't fight him. Doesn't feel like it's anchored to this place. "Come on," he mutters. "Work. Just... work."

He concentrates. Grips tighter. Wills the flower to follow him back to reality. The dream begins to fade. Morning pulls at him. The alarm clock in the real world beeps distantly.

Leo holds on. The meadow dissolves. The flower slips through his fingers like smoke. He wakes up. His hand is empty.

"No," he breathes. He tries again the next night. And the night after. Three more attempts, three more failures. Sometimes he can't even find the meadow. Sometimes he finds it but can't grab anything. Once, he manages to grip a flower but loses concentration halfway through the wake-up, and the pulling sensation stops.

Each morning, he wakes with nothing but frustration and the growing certainty that the first time was a fluke. A lucky accident. Impossible to repeat. By Friday, desperation clawed at his chest. One week had passed since Doctor Sato's ultimatum. Seven days later, they'd have the "conversation" about Lily's long-term care. About options. About giving up.

He couldn't accept that. So Friday night, instead of trying to sleep, Leo opened his grey school-issued tablet and searched.

How to lucid dream.

SEARCH RESTRICTED BY CONFORMITY CONTENT FILTERS

Pulling objects from dreams.

SEARCH RESTRICTED BY CONFORMITY CONTENT FILTERS

Dream control techniques.

SEARCH RESTRICTED BY CONFORMITY CONTENT FILTERS Every query hit the same wall. The government censored everything related to dreams, imagination, creativity. As if information itself could be dangerous. He tried different terms.

Sleep phenomena. REM cycles. Hypnagogic states.

Those searches worked. He found dry, academic papers about brain activity during sleep. Nothing useful. Nothing about pulling matter between dimensions. He was about to give up when he found a buried forum thread, archived from before the Suppression Protocols. Most of the discussion had been redacted—long black bars covering text. But one comment remained:

If you can Grip, find a Curio. They'll teach you. But be careful. The Marshals are watching.

Below it, someone had replied:

Ryles on Salvage is legit. Tell him the flowers sent you.

The rest was redacted. Leo read it three times. The business card in his pocket suddenly felt heavier. He checked the time. 9:47 PM. Mother would be home from her second shift around eleven. That gave him an hour.

Salvage Street was in the industrial district. The bad part of town. Where Enforcers patrolled less often because even they didn't want to go there after dark. He'd never broken curfew before. Never disobeyed in any way that mattered.

But Lily had one day left before the "conversation." Leo grabbed his jacket and slipped out the window. The streets after curfew felt like a different city. Without people, without the hum of transit vehicles, New Portside became hollow. An empty shell of a place. The white noise generators in every building hummed their collective song, creating a low-frequency drone that made his teeth ache.

Leo walked quickly, staying in shadows. His heart hammered. Every corner might hide an Enforcer. Every sound might be boots on pavement, coming to issue a citation. But the streets stayed empty.

He crossed the canal bridge—the same bridge Lily had wanted to walk across three months ago. In the dark, he could almost pretend the water wasn't grey. Almost pretend the world had color hiding somewhere beneath the regulations. The industrial district sprawled ahead. Warehouses and factories, most abandoned after the consolidation protocols. Rust and decay were the only things not colored grey here. They bloomed in orange-brown patches on metal siding, nature's small rebellion.

Salvage Street was a cracked strip of asphalt between two rows of dying buildings. Graffiti covered some walls—grey paint over grey concrete, making shapes that might have been words once. Leo checked the address on the business card. Number 14. Most buildings had no numbers. No lights. No signs of occupation.

Then he saw it. A single window glowing faintly in a three-story brick structure. Not bright. Just a suggestion of light, like someone had covered a lamp with grey fabric. Above the door, a wooden sign hung at an angle:

RYLES' PAWN & CURIO

Leo's mouth went dry. This was real. The card hadn't been a hallucination. Someone actually ran a shop here, in the abandoned district, after curfew. Someone who knew about the flowers.

He climbed three concrete steps and pushed the door. It opened with a bell's soft chime. The shop was chaos. Shelves lined every wall, packed with objects that made no sense. A typewriter that appeared to be growing moss. A compass whose needle pointed up. A jar containing what looked like lightning, frozen mid-strike. Books stacked in impossible towers, defying gravity. A birdcage with no bird but plenty of singing.

The air smelled like old paper and something sharper. Ozone, maybe. Or magic, if magic had a smell. Leo stood in the doorway, unable to process what he was seeing. "Close the door, kid. You're letting the weird out."

The voice came from behind a counter at the back of the shop. Leo couldn't see the speaker—just a mass of grey hair rising above a stack of books. He closed the door. The bell chimed again. "Well?" the voice said. "You coming in or just gawking?"

Leo's feet moved before his brain caught up. He walked between shelves, each one packed with objects that shouldn't exist. A snow globe containing a tiny sun. A mirror that showed him from behind. A music box playing a song he'd never heard but somehow knew.

He reached the counter. An old man sat on a stool, examining a pocket watch through a jeweler's loupe. He had wild grey hair and a wilder grey beard. His left arm ended at the elbow—just a stump where his forearm should have been. His eyes, when he looked up, were wrong. They shifted colors. Grey to blue to green and back.

"You're Leo Finch," he said. It wasn't a question.

Leo's throat closed. "How did you—"

"Your father had the same look. Like a engineer staring at a broken machine, trying to figure out which piece to fix first." The old man set down the pocket watch. "I'm Ryles. And before you ask: yes, I knew Thomas. Yes, I know what you did. And yes, that blue flower turning to sludge is exactly what happens when you break your focus."

Leo pulled out his notebook. Opened it to the pages stained with grey residue. "This was real. For a few hours, it was real. Then it just... died."

"Died?" Ryles snorted. "It went home, kid. Back to where it belonged. Dreams don't like reality much. They're visitors at best." He gestured at his shop. "Everything here? Pulled from the Reverie with proper technique. But it takes practice. And you, apparently, got lucky on your first try."

"The Reverie?"

"Sit down. You're making me nervous looming like that." Leo sat on a stool. His mind raced with questions, but Ryles held up his remaining hand.

"Let me guess what you want to know," the old man said. "One: How did you pull a flower from a dream? Two: Why did it die? Three: Can you do it again? Four: What on earth is happening to you?"

"Yes," Leo breathed. "All of that. And... and can it help my sister?"

Ryles' mismatched eyes studied him. "Lily. The girl in the coma. I heard about the accident." His expression softened. "That's why you're here. That's why you're desperate enough to break curfew and find a shop that technically doesn't exist."

"She has one day," Leo said. His voice cracked. "On Monday, the doctors want to discuss 'options.' I need to help her. If I can pull things from dreams, maybe I can—"

"Save her?" Ryles finished. "Kid, it doesn't work like that."

"But you said—"

"I said you can pull objects. Not people. Not consciousness. And definitely not..." He stopped. Looked at Leo more carefully. "Though there are those who've tried. And failed. And paid for it."

He flexed his missing arm. The stump twitched. "What happened?" Leo asked quietly.

"I got greedy. Tried to Grip something too big. Something too anchored to the Reverie. The universe took payment." Ryles smiled without humor. "Don't be like me."

Silence fell between them. The shop's strange objects hummed and clicked and whispered in the background. Finally, Ryles sighed. "Alright. You want answers. I'll give you the basics. But understand: This information is dangerous. Knowing about Grippers makes you complicit. And the Marshals don't much care for folks who break the rules."

"Marshals?"

"The things that hunt us. But I'm getting ahead of myself." Ryles stood. Walked to a shelf and pulled down a leather-bound journal. "Your father kept records. Him and the rest of us, back before the Nightmare. We called ourselves Explorers then. Now we're just criminals."

He opened the journal. Pages filled with sketches and notes. "The Reverie is real," Ryles said. "A dimension made of dreams, thought, psychic energy—whatever you want to call it. It exists parallel to this world. When you sleep, your consciousness goes there. Most people don't remember. Don't stay aware. But some of us..."

"Can control it," Leo finished.

"We call it Gripping. The ability to pull objects from the Reverie into reality. It requires lucid dreaming—being conscious while you're asleep. There are four types of Grippers, kid. Architects who build and shape. Infiltrators who slip between. Phantoms who phase through. Menders who heal the cost. Your father was the greatest Architect. You might be better. Most people can't do it. But those who can..." He gestured at the shop. "We built an economy."

"An underground economy," Leo said slowly. "That's why this place is hidden. Why the government censors everything about dreams."

"Smart kid. Yeah. See, twelve years ago, there was an incident. We call it the Great Nightmare. Mass Gripping, all at once, nearly merged the dimensions. People died. Reality almost unraveled. Your father and I, along with a few others, we managed to stop it. Barely."

"How?"

"We negotiated. Made a Truce between humans and the things that live in the Reverie. The Lucid Marshals—they're order incarnate, beings whose job is keeping dreams and reality separate. Imagine a human-shaped hole in reality, surrounded by crackling enforcement code. They don't speak. They just... appear. And when they grab you, you're gone. Erased from the Reverie, locked out forever. They agreed to tolerate small-scale Gripping if we stopped the mass exploitation."

Leo's head spun. "So, the government knows about this?"

"Some do. The Conformity Council discovered the Reverie during the Nightmare. They established the laws to suppress creativity, thinking it would prevent people from lucid dreaming. Worked, mostly. Natural Grippers like you are rare now." Ryles closed the journal. "But the council also runs their own black-ops Gripping program. They're breaking the Truce. And the Marshals are getting restless."

Ryles was mid-sentence—something about dimensional stability—when the shop door chimed. He stopped. Went very still. "Get behind the counter," he said quietly. "Now."

Leo didn't argue. He ducked behind the counter. Ryles casually moved to block the back room door. A Conformity Enforcer entered. Grey uniform. Badge number. Clipboard.

"Evening, Ryles," the Enforcer said. Bored voice. Routine inspection.

"Evening, Officer Marks," Ryles replied. Friendly. Easy. Like they did this often.

"Random compliance check. You know how it is." The Enforcer walked the aisles. Checking shelves. Taking notes. "Any unapproved items? Anything that might inspire... creativity?"

"Just junk," Ryles said. "Sell to collectors. You know me." The Enforcer picked up a music box. Wound it. Listened to the melody. Frowned.

"This is a minor key," he said. "Minor keys can induce melancholy. Melancholy can lead to introspection. Introspection leads to—"

"I'll dispose of it," Ryles interrupted. "Thank you for catching that." The Enforcer set it down. Made a note. Looked around once more.

Leo held his breath behind the counter. If they found him here—if they searched the back room— "Alright," the Enforcer finally said. "Approved for another month. Stay compliant, Ryles."

"Always do." The Enforcer left. Door chimed. Silence.

Ryles waited thirty seconds. Then: "He's gone. You can come out."

Leo stood. His legs shook. "Does that happen often?"

"Monthly. They suspect me. Can't prove anything. So they watch." Ryles picked up the music box. Held it gently. "Can't even sell music boxes anymore. This world..."

He shook his head. Set it down. "Where was I? Right. The Truce. That's something you need to know."

"You're saying the government is hypocritical and reality might end again." Leo's voice came out flat. "Great. Perfect. And my sister is still in a coma."

"Your sister," Ryles said carefully, "might be more complicated than you think."

Leo's head snapped up. "What does that mean?"

"It means Lily's coma isn't like the others. Her brain activity is stable. Too stable. Like she's not unconscious—she's somewhere else." Ryles met his eyes. "The Sanctum of Sleep. It's the deepest part of the Reverie. Where the Eternal Sleepers anchor the boundary between worlds."

"The what?"

"Consciousnesses that volunteered—or were taken—to hold the barrier. Without them, the dimensions would merge. They're prisoners and guardians at once." Ryles' voice dropped. "If Lily is there, she's not sick. She's serving."

Leo stood so fast his stool fell over. "That's insane. She's eleven. She can't consent to—to being imprisoned in another dimension!"

"Can't she?" Ryles asked softly. "If the Eternal Sleepers recruited her, they'd have asked. And Lily, from what I knew of her, would've said yes. Especially if she thought it would protect someone she loved." The room tilted. Leo grabbed the counter for support.

Lily volunteered? No. That was impossible. She was just a kid. She wouldn't— Except she would. If she thought it would help. If she thought it was right.

"You're keeping me in a cage," she'd said. What if she'd found her own way out?

"I need to reach her," Leo said. "If she's there, I'll bring her back."

"Kid—"

"Tell me how. Please." His voice broke. "You said you knew my father. He'd help if he were here. So, help me."

Ryles stared at him for a long moment. Then he walked to the far wall and pulled back a grey curtain. Behind it, the wall was covered in impossible things. Weapons that glowed with inner light. Creatures in jars—living shadow, frozen fire, liquid starlight. A miniature sun in a snow globe, burning without consuming itself. A map that showed places that didn't exist. A mirror reflecting a room that wasn't this one.

"This," Ryles said, "is what's possible when you master the Grip. When you learn to navigate the Reverie without breaking. When you understand the cost."

"The cost?"

"Mass conservation. When you Grip something, reality takes payment. Usually something emotionally equivalent. You smuggled a flower—you lost your father's dog tags. Didn't notice, did you? Check your drawer when you get home. They're gone."

Leo's chest tightened. He'd kept those tags by his bed since he was five. A connection to a father he never knew. "That's the Glitch," Ryles continued. "The universe maintains balance. The more you smuggle, the more it takes. And if you're not careful, it takes something you can't afford to lose."

"But you're still doing it," Leo said, gesturing at the shop.

"I'm careful. I know the rules. I pay attention to what vanishes." Ryles turned to face him fully. "Your father didn't. He tried to save the world, and the world took him. Don't make his mistake."

"What was his mistake?"

"Thinking he could control everything." Ryles' eyes stopped shifting. Fixed on Leo with sudden intensity. "Thinking he could fix everything alone. Thinking sacrifice was noble instead of stupid." The words hit like a punch.

"Now you got two choices, kid," Ryles said. "Walk away. Forget this place. Let the doctors do their thing with Lily. Live your grey life and stay safe."

He paused. "Or start learning. Master the Grip. Navigate the Reverie. Find your sister and see if she wants saving. But know this: The Warden watches everything. The Marshals hunt those who break the rules. And reality always collects its debt."

"Who's the Warden?"

"The oldest consciousness in the Reverie. The first Gripper, some say. The embodiment of cosmic law, others claim. All I know is this: Cross him, and you don't come back." Ryles held out his remaining hand.

"So, what's it gonna be, Leo Finch? Safety or truth?" Leo looked at the hand. Looked at the wall of impossibilities. Looked at his own reflection in a mirror that showed him from inside out—heart visible, beating too fast, guilt written in every pulse.

He thought about Lily. About the voice in the dream. About the fourteen days getting closer. He took Ryles' hand. "Teach me," he said.

Ryles smiled. It wasn't a kind smile. It was the smile of someone about to watch a kid jump off a cliff. "Good," he said. "We start tonight."

[END OF CHAPTER 3]

Chapter 4: The Thief in the Night

Leo made it home three minutes before Mother arrived. He climbed through his bedroom window, heart hammering, clothes smelling like the strange ozone of Ryles' shop. He'd just pulled off his jacket when he heard the front door open downstairs. "Leo?" Mother's voice, tired and wary.

"Upstairs!" he called, trying to sound like he'd been here all along. "Doing homework!" A pause. Then footsteps moving toward the kitchen, not upstairs to check on him. She was too exhausted to investigate.

Leo sat on his bed and pulled out the paper Ryles had given him. Techniques for maintaining focus. Exercises for lucid awareness. Tips for the Grip.

Rule One: Reality checks. Count your fingers. Read text twice. Question your surroundings. Doubt trains the mind to recognize dreams.

Rule Two: Physical sensation is the bridge. The more you feel the object—texture, weight, temperature—the easier it is to pull through.

Rule Three: Never rush the wake-up. The transition is delicate. Stay calm. Hold your focus. The universe resists, but it will yield if you're patient.

Rule Four: Accept the Glitch. Something will vanish. Usually something emotionally significant. This is the price. Fighting it makes it worse.

Rule Five: Start small. A coin. A stone. A flower. Master these before attempting anything complex.

Leo read the list three times, memorizing every word. Then he noticed the postscript at the bottom:

P.S. - You're not alone in this. Trust that. Even when it feels like you are.

What did that mean? He folded the paper and hid it with his sketchbook. Changed into grey pajamas. Checked that Mother had gone to her room—she had, door closed, light off. He lay down. Stared at the grey ceiling. The white noise generator hummed.

His dog tags were gone. Ryles had been right. He'd checked his nightstand drawer and found only empty space where they'd been. The universe had taken its payment for the blue flower. What would it take next?

He closed his eyes. Sleep came easier than expected. Maybe because he'd been practicing. Maybe because some part of him was desperate to return to the Reverie. Just before consciousness slipped away, he heard it.

A whisper. Close. Right against his ear.

"First time's always the hardest,"* a girl's voice said. *"But you'll get better."

Leo's eyes snapped open. His room was empty. Dark. The white noise generator hummed its familiar song. Nobody was there.

But he'd heard it. Clear as anything. A voice that shouldn't exist. His heart raced. He turned his head, scanning the shadows.

Nothing moved. "Hello?" he whispered. No answer. He was losing his mind. Stress hallucinations. That's all. Just stress and desperation making him hear things.

He closed his eyes again. This time, sleep took him completely. He stands in the meadow. Immediately, he checks his hands. Counts fingers. One, two, three, four, five. Normal. He looks at the grass. Watches it shift colors. Blue to green to purple. Dream logic.

"I'm dreaming," he says aloud. His voice echoes. "This is the Reverie." The meadow stretches endlessly. Blue sky. Impossible sun. Everything vivid and alive and wrong.

He walks, looking for another flower. Finds one growing near a rock that wasn't there before. Kneels down. Reaches— "You're getting better at this."

Leo jerks upright and spins around. A girl stands behind him. Short. Maybe his age. Athletic build. She wears grey clothes like everyone in New Portside, but her hair is naturally black—he can tell because it's not quite regulation-dyed. She's chewing something. Candy? Her eyes sparkle with mischief.

"Who—" Leo starts.

"Trixie," she says, grinning. "And before you ask: Yes, I'm real. No, I'm not part of your dream. And yes, I've been watching you. Natural Architect like yourself—except you're better at building. I'm better at... other things."

She pops something in her mouth. Chews. Swallows. "Dream Candy," she explains. "Helps me focus. Want one?"

"I want to know how you're in my dream," Leo says.

"Because I walked in." She spreads her arms. "This is a shared dream zone. The meadow. It's shallow Reverie, easy access. Lots of new Grippers start here. I've been checking it nightly for weeks, hoping you'd show up again."

"Why?"

"Because you're Leo Finch. Son of Thomas Finch. The Architect who helped stop the Great Nightmare. And because..." She steps closer, her smile fading slightly.

"Because I've been in your dreams before. The personal ones. The ones where you blame yourself for your sister."

Leo's chest tightens. "You've been spying on me?"

"Protecting you," Trixie corrects. "There are things in the Reverie that hunt new Grippers. Things that would've eaten you alive if I hadn't been running interference. You're welcome, by the way."

"I didn't ask for—"

"No, you didn't. But your sister did." The world stops.

"What?" Leo breathes.

Trixie's expression turns serious. "Look, I can't explain everything right now. It's complicated. But Lily—before the accident, she'd been dreaming here too. We talked. She told me about her annoying brother who loved her so much it felt like suffocation. She made me promise to watch out for you if anything happened to her."

"Lily was a Gripper?"

"The gift runs in families. You know that. Your father, you, her." Trixie pulls out another candy. "She was learning. Getting good. Then the accident happened and she... left. But not the way you think."

"What does that mean?" His voice cracks. "Where is she?"

"I don't know exactly. But I know she's conscious. Active. And I think—I'm pretty sure—she's been calling to you. That blue flower? The voice that told you to take it?" Trixie meets his eyes. "That was her."

Leo can't breathe. Can't think. Lily. Alive. Conscious. Calling to him.

"We need to find her," he says.

"We will. But first, you need to learn control. Master the Grip. And I figured..." Trixie grins again. "Why not team up? You build stuff, I steal stuff. We're a natural pair."

"You're a thief?"

"Infiltrator," she corrects. "I slip into people's dreams uninvited. Steal secrets, memories, items. It's my gift. Everyone's got one. Yours is architecture. Mine is trespassing." She winks. "Wanna see?"

Before Leo can answer, the meadow dissolves. They stand in a bedroom. Not Leo's. Not anyone's he recognizes. An adult man sleeps in the bed, snoring softly. The room is detailed—too detailed for Leo's dream. Every object has weight. Reality.

"This is his dream," Trixie whispers. She moves like a cat, silent and precise. "I pulled us here. Watch." She approaches the dresser. Picks up a set of car keys. Holds them up, showing Leo. Then she closes her eyes.

The same pulling sensation Leo felt with the flower ripples through the air. Trixie grimaces. Her hand shakes. The keys glow faintly. "The trick," she says through gritted teeth, "is feeling the object completely. Not just texture. Emotional weight. This guy loves his car. So these keys carry that. I'm borrowing his love along with the metal."

The glow intensifies. Then fades. Trixie opens her eyes. "Done. They'll be under my pillow when I wake up. And he'll find his keys missing." She grins. "Simple."

"That's theft," Leo says.

"That's practice." Trixie shrugs. "I'll return them eventually. Probably. Point is: I can smuggle from anyone's dream. You can only smuggle from public zones or your own. But together..." She spreads her arms. "We can pull off some interesting heists."

"I'm not stealing," Leo says firmly.

"Not even to save Lily?" Trixie's grin fades. "Look, the Reverie has zones. Shallow ones like the meadow. Deeper ones with better stuff. The Sanctum—where the Eternal Sleepers are—is deepest. You'll never reach it alone. But with a team? With someone who can scout and infiltrate and steal what you need?"

She holds out her hand. "We help each other. You learn to build. I teach you to navigate. We smuggle what we need to reach Lily. Deal?"

Leo looks at her hand. At the mischievous girl who's been in his dreams without permission. Who's been protecting him. Who knows his sister. "One heist," he says. "As a test."

"Perfect!" Trixie's grin returns. "I know just the place. Ever been to the Candy Coast?" The transition is instant. One moment they're in the stranger's bedroom. The next, they're standing on a beach.

But this beach is wrong in the most wonderful way. The sand is sugar. Literally. Leo kneels down and touches it—fine white crystals that sparkle in sunlight. He tastes it. Sweet. Impossibly sweet.

The ocean is soda. Carbonated waves crash against the shore, fizzing and bubbling. The air smells like candy stores and birthday cakes and every dessert he's never tasted because the Grey only serves nutrition blocks. Palm trees made of peppermint sticks rise along the beach. Their leaves are mint candies that rustle in the breeze.

"Welcome to the Candy Coast," Trixie says, spreading her arms. "Shallow Reverie zone. Relatively safe. And full of stuff we can smuggle."

"This is incredible," Leo breathes.

"This is sugar overload. Stay too long and you'll get sick. Also, watch out for the Sugar Golems—they're basically living taffy that tries to trap you. But for a quick smuggle? Perfect."

She starts walking down the beach. Leo follows, his feet crunching on sugar sand. "So what do we take?" he asks.

"Candy that changes flavor based on mood. Super useful. Helps with focus." Trixie points to a tree. "There. See the golden ones?"

Leo looks up. Among the mint-leaf candies, several glow with inner light. "Those are Dream Candies," Trixie explains. "Pull one of those through, and you've got yourself a focus aid. They're valuable. Ryles would trade for them."

"How do I reach them?"

"You're an Architect. Build something." Leo looks at the tree. At the sand. At his hands.

Build something. He closes his eyes. Focuses. This is a dream. The rules are negotiable. If he can reshape dream-matter...

He pictures a platform. Simple. Stable. Rising from the sand. When he opens his eyes, a staircase made of compressed sugar spirals up to the tree.

"Whoa," Trixie breathes. "That was fast." Leo climbs. The stairs hold his weight—they're solid, real in the way dreams pretend to be real. He reaches the golden candies and plucks three. They're warm in his palm, pulsing with that familiar glow.

"Now you just have to hold them while you wake up," Trixie calls from below. "And—oh, crap."

"What?"

"Sugar Golem. We need to go. NOW." Leo looks down the beach. Something massive lumbers toward them. A creature made entirely of taffy—pink and white and stretched in impossible ways. It moves like an avalanche of candy, slow but inevitable.

"Do they attack?" Leo asks.

"They engulf. You get stuck in them, you can't wake up until they let go. Which could be days." Trixie waves frantically. "Come down! We're leaving!"

Leo descends the stairs. Grips the candies tight. Feels their warmth. Their weight. Their—

The Golem reaches them. It towers overhead, taffy arms spreading wide to capture them both. "Wake up!" Trixie shouts. "Just wake up! NOW!"

Leo closes his eyes. Focuses on reality. On his bedroom. On grey sheets and white noise and— The pulling sensation hits him like a truck.

He gasped awake. His bedroom. Dark. The white noise generator humming. His hand hurt.

He opened his palm. Three golden candies lay there, glowing softly in the darkness. Real. Solid. Warm.

He'd done it. Leo sat up, breathing hard. Stared at the candies in disbelief. They pulsed with inner light, beautiful and impossible. A sound from beside his bed made him jump.

Trixie sat on his floor, grinning, holding her own handful of candies. "What—" Leo started. "How are you—"

"Followed you back. It's a trick I learned. Don't worry, I'm just dream-projecting. I'm actually asleep in my own bed across town." She held up the candies. "But these? These are real. We did it. First successful team heist."

Leo couldn't help it. He smiled. They'd actually done it. Then he heard the crack. His bedroom wall split down the middle. Not dramatically. Just a thin line appearing in the plaster, spreading slowly from ceiling to floor.

The Glitch. "Uh oh," Trixie said. At the same moment, across town in her real body, a photo frame in her parents' bedroom shattered. The picture inside—her parents' wedding photo—vanished. Just gone. Leaving only broken glass and empty frame.

"The universe collects," Leo whispered, remembering Ryles' words.

"Yeah," Trixie said quietly. "It does." They sat in silence, both holding their impossible candies, both paying the price for bringing dreams into reality. Then Leo's window exploded. Glass shattered inward. Something grey and humanoid climbed through, moving with eerie, perfect smoothness. Faceless. Geometrically precise. Wrong in every way.

It turned toward Leo. "Lucid Marshal," Trixie breathed. Her projection flickered with fear. "Oh no. Oh no no no—"

The Marshal took a step forward. Its hand reached out. And Leo heard its voice—not spoken, but felt directly in his mind:

CONTRABAND DETECTED. SUBMIT FOR COLLECTION.

"RUN!" Trixie screamed. Leo ran.

[END OF CHAPTER 4]

Chapter 5: The Chase

Leo ran. His feet pounded down the stairs, taking them two at a time. Behind him, the Marshal moved with that horrible smooth precision, not running but gliding, its faceless head turning to track him perfectly. The candies were still in his pocket. They felt hot now, burning through the fabric, calling to the Marshal like a beacon.

"Kitchen!" Trixie's projection flickered beside him, keeping pace. "Go through the kitchen!" Leo burst through the doorway. His mother's bedroom was to the left, door closed. He could hear her breathing, deep and steady. Asleep.

"Mom!" he shouted. "MOM!" The breathing didn't change. She didn't stir.

"She can't hear you," Trixie said. "Marshals control perception when people sleep. To her, you're not here. The Marshal's not here. Everything's normal."

"That's impossible," Leo gasped, but he knew it wasn't. Nothing was impossible anymore. The Marshal reached the bottom of the stairs. Its hand stretched toward him, fingers too long, too perfect, grey and geometrically precise.

SUBMIT FOR COLLECTION, its voice pressed into Leo's mind. *RESISTANCE INCREASES PENALTY.*

"Out!" Trixie yanked at his arm, though her projection-fingers passed through him. "The back door! Go!" Leo grabbed the kitchen counter, used it to pivot, and threw himself at the back door. It was locked. His fingers fumbled with the deadbolt.

The Marshal glided closer. Five feet away. The deadbolt clicked. Leo yanked the door open and stumbled into the tiny backyard. Grey concrete. Grey fence. Grey sky above.

"This way!" Trixie's projection raced ahead, through the fence like it wasn't there. "Follow me to Ryles! His wards will protect you!" Leo climbed the fence. His hands scraped against rough wood. His legs tangled in his pajama pants. He fell hard on the other side, landing on his shoulder in the alley behind the building.

Pain shot through him. Real pain. Physical pain. He looked back. The Marshal stood in his doorway, perfectly still. Watching. Then it took one step forward, through the doorframe, and began gliding toward him again.

Leo scrambled to his feet and ran. The alley was dark. Narrow. Lined with dumpsters and broken crates. His bare feet slapped against cold concrete. He'd forgotten shoes. Forgotten everything except the need to run.

Trixie's projection stayed ahead, a flickering grey ghost leading him through turns he didn't know existed. Left, then right, then through a gap between buildings so narrow his shoulders scraped both walls. "Almost there," she called back. "Just keep—" The Marshal appeared in front of them.

Not behind. In front. It had cut them off somehow, moved through reality like reality was optional. Leo skidded to a stop. His heart hammered. His lungs burned.

The Marshal raised both hands. Its voice pressed into his skull like a migraine.

FINAL WARNING. SUBMIT OR FACE COLLECTION.

"What does that mean?" Leo gasped.

"It means it'll take you instead of the candies," Trixie said. Her projection flickered with something that looked like fear. "It means you'll end up in the Reverie permanently. Lost. Unmade."

The Marshal took a step forward. Trixie's projection suddenly brightened. "Okay. New plan. I'm going to do something really stupid. When I say run, you run to Salvage Street. Number fourteen. Don't stop. Don't look back."

"What are you—"

"Trust me." Her grin was wild, reckless. "And remember: I'm not really here. This is just my projection. So, whatever happens, I'm fine."

"Trixie—"

"RUN!" Her projection exploded. Not literally. But it expanded, filling the alley with grey light that suddenly shifted to blinding white. And within that light, shapes formed. Memories. Dreams. Fragments of thought made solid.

A smoke bomb. Thick, choking, impossible smoke that smelled like birthday cake and terror. The Marshal recoiled. Its smooth glide stuttered. For just a moment, it seemed confused.

Leo ran. He bolted past it, through the smoke, coughing and half-blind. His feet found pavement. His legs pumped. Behind him, he heard the Marshal's voice, but fainter now, more distant.

VIOLATION REGISTERED. ADDITIONAL PENALTY ASSESSED.

Then the smoke cleared and Leo was on Salvage Street, lungs screaming, vision blurring, the grey buildings rising around him like tombstones. Number fourteen. He found it. Stumbled up the steps. Threw himself against the door.

It opened before he could knock. Ryles stood there, eyes shifting colors rapidly. "Get in. Now." Leo fell through the doorway. Ryles slammed it shut behind him and threw three separate locks. Then he pressed his hand against the wood and muttered something Leo couldn't hear.

The door glowed faintly. Just for a second. Then the glow faded. "Wards," Ryles said. "Old magic, dream-made. Marshals can't cross them." He looked at Leo, still sprawled on the floor. "You okay, kid?"

"No," Leo wheezed. "Definitely not okay."

"Fair enough." Ryles offered his remaining hand and helped Leo up. "You got the look of someone who just met their first Marshal. Welcome to the life." Leo's legs felt like jelly. He stumbled to the counter and collapsed onto a stool. His shoulder throbbed where he'd landed. His feet were cut and bleeding. His hands shook.

The Dream Candies were still in his pocket, glowing faintly through the fabric. "I just wanted to help my sister," he said quietly. "That's all. I just wanted to fix things."

Ryles sighed. Walked to a shelf and pulled down a first-aid kit. "That's how it always starts. Someone you love needs help. You discover the Grip. You think you can save them. Then the Marshals come knocking and you realize you're in way over your head."

He set the kit on the counter. Gestured for Leo to show him his feet. "They won't stop hunting me, will they?" Leo asked as Ryles cleaned the cuts with something that stung like fire.

"Not unless you return what you took. Give back the candies, and they'll leave you alone. Probably." Ryles wrapped gauze around Leo's heel. "But you won't do that. Because you're already thinking: If I can smuggle candy, what else can I smuggle? What would help Lily? What could save her?"

Leo said nothing. Because Ryles was right. "That's the trap," Ryles continued. "The Grip gives you power. Power makes you think you can control things. Control makes you reckless. Recklessness gets you killed." He tied off the gauze with more force than necessary. "I lost my arm being reckless."

"What did you try to smuggle?"

Ryles' eyes stopped shifting. Fixed on a memory Leo couldn't see. "My wife. She died during the Great Nightmare. Killed by the dimensional instability. I thought... I thought if I could find her in the Reverie, bring her consciousness back, put it in a new body somehow..."

He didn't finish. Didn't need to. "The universe took my arm," Ryles said quietly. "And it almost took everything else. Reality started unraveling around me. Your father had to pull me out manually. Knocked me unconscious, dragged me back from the edge. I woke up in a hospital, missing my arm, and Thomas was there saying: 'Don't ever be that stupid again.'"

He looked at Leo directly. "But I see that same stupid look in your eyes. That same determination to save someone no matter the cost. Just like him. Just like me. So let me save us both some time: Don't be like me, kid. Don't let love make you reckless."

Leo's throat tightened. He thought about Lily. About their last conversation, six months ago. The day before the accident. She'd confronted him with illegal art supplies hidden in her backpack. Paint tubes. Canvas. Brushes. Contraband that could get them both arrested.

He'd said no. More than no. He'd yelled. "Are you trying to destroy our lives?" he'd demanded. "Do you understand what happens if you're caught with this?"

"I'm willing to take that risk," she'd argued. "It's my risk. My choice. My life."

"Your choices affect me too! Affect Mom! You're not thinking about consequences. You never think before you act!"

She'd looked at him with those eyes that saw too much. "You don't trust me."

"I'm protecting you," he'd said.

"You're suffocating me," she'd replied. Then she'd walked away. Walked out of the apartment. And when he'd followed, still yelling, she'd run. Run into the street. Run into traffic. Run from him. Run from his control.

"I never let her choose anything," Leo said quietly. "I planned everything for her. Breakfast. Routes to school. Homework schedules. Her birthday. I thought I was keeping her safe. I thought I was helping."

"But you were controlling," Ryles finished.

"Yeah." Leo's eyes burned. "And now she's gone. And I can't fix it. Can't plan it away. Can't control it. She's just... gone."

"About that." Ryles stood. Walked to the back of the shop and pulled a folder from a drawer. "There's something you need to see." He opened the folder on the counter. Inside were photographs. Old ones, printed on actual paper, showing places that couldn't exist.

Dream landscapes. The meadow Leo had walked through. The Candy Coast. Other zones he didn't recognize—forests made of shadow, cities built from light, oceans that flowed upward. And then, near the bottom of the stack, one that made Leo's breath stop.

A fortress. Crystalline, impossibly beautiful, glowing with inner light. Built from something that looked like frozen dreams, translucent and perfect. And within the crystal walls, faces. Dozens of them. Maybe hundreds. People suspended in the crystal, eyes closed, expressions peaceful. Like they were sleeping. Like they were waiting.

"The Sanctum of Sleep," Ryles said quietly. "The deepest point in the Reverie. Where the boundary between dimensions is thinnest. Where the Eternal Sleepers anchor reality." Leo's hand shook as he picked up the photograph. Looked closer at the faces. Most were adults. A few were older kids. Teenagers. And there, near the center, in a pod slightly larger than the others—

"Lily," he breathed. She looked exactly as she did in the hospital. Eyes closed. Peaceful. But the crystal around her glowed brighter than the others. Pulsed with rhythmic light. Like a heartbeat.

"That's not possible," Leo said. His voice cracked. "This photo is old. This is from your expedition, years ago. Lily wasn't—she couldn't have been—"

"That photo was taken five days ago," Ryles said. "By someone I trust who went deep on a solo dive. They found your sister there. Conscious. Aware. Trapped in crystal, yes, but not unconscious. Not sick."

"She volunteered?" Leo's hands were shaking so hard he nearly dropped the photo. "She's eleven. She can't consent to being trapped in another dimension!"

"The Eternal Sleepers recruit carefully," Ryles said. "They don't take just anyone. They look for specific traits. Selflessness. Strength. The ability to anchor consciousness in one place while the body stays in another. And..." He paused. "They look for people willing to sacrifice themselves to protect someone they love."

The words hit Leo like a physical blow. Lily had volunteered. Had chosen this. Not because she was sick. Not because of the accident. But because—

"She was protecting me," he whispered. "Wasn't she? She knew I'd discover the Grip eventually. Knew I'd be in danger. So she became an anchor to... to what? Keep the Marshals off me? Keep the boundary stable so I could learn safely?"

"I don't know her specific reasoning," Ryles admitted. "But that sounds like something a younger sister who loved her older brother would do. Especially if that brother had spent her whole life trying to protect her." He closed the folder. "Now she's on the other side. And if you want to bring her back, you're going to need more than good intentions and three Dream Candies."

"What do I need?"

"A team," Ryles said flatly. "The Sanctum is deep. Guarded. Surrounded by nightmare zones that'll kill you if you're not careful. You need scouts. Infiltrators. Healers. People who can watch your back while you're busy building impossible architecture."

"Where do I find a team?"

Ryles smiled slightly. It wasn't a comforting smile. "You already met one of them. The girl who saved you tonight. Trixie Zhang. Best Infiltrator I've ever trained. Incredibly reckless, but loyal."

"She spies on people's dreams without permission."

"She also just sacrificed her projection to save your life. That smoke bomb? That was made from her own memories. Ripping them out and weaponizing them hurts like crazy. She did it anyway." Ryles tapped the counter. "That's the kind of person you want on your team. Someone willing to hurt themselves to protect you."

Leo looked at the photograph again. At Lily's face, peaceful in crystal. "I'll get her back," he said quietly. "Whatever it takes. I'll find a team, reach the Sanctum, and bring her home."

"Even if she doesn't want to come?" Ryles asked. "Even if she chose this? Even if pulling her out means someone else has to take her place?" Leo's hand froze. He hadn't thought about that. About the cost. About what it would mean to wake an Eternal Sleeper.

"The boundary needs anchors," Ryles continued. "That's the whole point of the Truce. The Marshals agreed to tolerate small-scale Gripping because we agreed to maintain the anchors. If you pull Lily out, someone else goes in. Or the boundary destabilizes. Or reality starts unraveling again."

"Then I'll take her place," Leo said immediately.

"There it is." Ryles shook his head. "That martyr complex. Just like your father. Kid, you can't solve everything by sacrificing yourself. That's not noble. That's not love. That's guilt with extra steps."

"What else am I supposed to do?" Leo's voice rose. "Let her stay trapped forever? Accept that she's gone? Just give up?"

"No," Ryles said calmly. "You find a third option. You build something new. You're an Architect, Leo. Stop thinking about rescue and start thinking about engineering. How do you strengthen a boundary without anchors? How do you wake the Sleepers without reality collapsing? How do you fix the system instead of just shuffling prisoners around?"

Leo stared at him. "I don't know."

"Then figure it out. Because if you're really going to do this—if you're really going to assemble a team and dive deep—you better have a plan that doesn't end with you or Lily dead." Ryles pointed at the photo. "She's counting on you. But not to rescue her like some damsel. She's counting on you to be smarter than that. To think. To build. To solve the impossible problem."

The shop fell quiet. The strange objects on the shelves hummed and clicked. Somewhere in the back, something made of glass chimed softly. Leo looked at the photo one more time. At Lily's face. At the crystal around her, glowing like a cage made of light.

"I'll need a team," he said finally.

"Yes."

"And training. I barely know how to smuggle candy without getting killed."

"Yes."

"And information. About the Reverie. About the Sanctum. About everything."

"Yes." Ryles smiled. Actually smiled. "Now you're thinking like an Architect."

He reached under the counter and pulled out a notebook. Leather-bound. Old. The cover was stamped with a symbol Leo didn't recognize—a circle split by a vertical line, with a horizontal line crossing it in the middle. Like a lowercase "t" inside a circle.

"Your father's journal," Ryles said. "He gave it to me before the final dive. Said: 'If anything happens to me, give this to my kids when they're ready.' I've been holding it for twelve years." He pushed it across the counter. "I think you're ready." Leo picked up the journal with shaking hands. The leather was worn smooth. The pages smelled like old paper and smoke and something else. Something that reminded him of the dreams his mother mentioned. Of the father he never knew.

"Start there," Ryles said. "Read everything. Learn what he learned. Then come back tomorrow night. I'll introduce you to the others. Ghost and Yuki. Good kids. Talented. And together?" He grinned. "Together you might just pull off the impossible."

Leo stood. His feet still hurt. His shoulder throbbed. His mind spun with too much information, too many revelations, too many impossible things. But he held the journal tight. And he looked at the photo one more time.

"I'm coming, Lily," he whispered. "I promise. I'm coming." Outside, dawn was breaking. The grey sky lightened to a slightly lighter grey. In a few hours, his mother would wake and find him missing. He'd have to explain. Have to lie. Have to pretend everything was normal.

But nothing was normal anymore. He had a team to build. A dimension to navigate. A sister to save. And for the first time in six months, Leo felt something he'd almost forgotten.

Hope.

[END OF CHAPTER 5]

Chapter 6: Assembling the Crew

Leo climbed back through his bedroom window just as grey morning light began filtering through the curtains. His mother's alarm would sound in twenty minutes. He had time to hide the journal, clean his feet, and pretend he'd been home all night. He shoved his father's journal under the mattress next to his sketchbook. Wrapped his bleeding feet in tissues to avoid leaving trails. Changed out of his torn pajamas into clean ones. By the time Mother knocked on his door, he was in bed, eyes closed, breathing steady.

"Leo. School in thirty minutes."

"I'm up," he called back, voice muffled by his pillow. Her footsteps retreated. He heard her moving through the kitchen, preparing breakfast. The white noise generator hummed its eternal song. Leo sat up. Looked at his hands. They didn't shake anymore. The fear from last night had crystallized into something harder. Something like determination.

He had a team to meet tonight. A father's journal to read. A sister to save. First, though, he had to survive another day pretending everything was normal. School was agony.

Every class felt longer than the last. Mathematics blurred into meaningless equations. Science became incomprehensible elements and reactions. History droned on about the Great Nightmare and the necessity of Conformity, but now Leo knew the truth. The government had caused it. His father had stopped it. And they'd been lying about it for twelve years.

During lunch, he pulled out his father's journal. The cafeteria was loud enough that nobody noticed him reading in the corner. The first entry was dated thirteen years ago:

August 3rd - We found it. Thomas Finch, reporting. After six months of coordinated lucid dreaming, we've confirmed the existence of a stable parallel dimension accessible through REM sleep. We're calling it the Reverie. Ryles thinks it's a collective unconscious. Sarah thinks it's literal psychic space. I think it's both. The architecture alone is impossible—structures that shouldn't stand, zones that defy physics. Today I built a bridge from pure thought. It held my weight. This changes everything.

Leo's breath caught. His father had discovered this. Had been the first to understand what the Reverie was. What it could be. He flipped forward, reading entries about early exploration. The meadow. The Candy Coast. Deeper zones his father had mapped. And then, near the middle, an entry that made his blood run cold:

March 15th - Elena is pregnant. I can't keep doing this. The diving is getting more dangerous. We found the Nightmare Trench yesterday, and Ryles nearly didn't come back. He saw things down there. Things that hunt. I need to stop. But Sarah discovered something in the deep zones. She says there's a Sanctum. A place where consciousness can anchor permanently. If we could study it, understand it, maybe we could—

The entry stopped mid-sentence. The next page was torn out. Leo turned the page. The next entry was six months later, and the handwriting had changed. Shakier. More desperate:

September 8th - The baby is here. Leo. My son. I held him and I thought: I can't do this anymore. I can't risk leaving Elena alone. But the government found out. They're pressuring us. They want to weaponize the Reverie. Turn it into a tool for control. We have to stop them. We have to establish the Truce before they ruin everything.

Leo's hands shook. His father had known he was going to die. Had known and done it anyway because someone had to stop the government. The final entry was dated two days before his father died:

If you're reading this, I'm gone. Leo, Lily—I'm sorry. I tried to make the world safer for you. I tried to stop the nightmare before it consumed everything. Remember: The Reverie is beautiful, but it's also dangerous. Control isn't love. Sacrifice isn't noble. The best thing I can teach you is this: Build with others, not for them. Trust your team. And never, ever try to save the world alone.

Love, Dad

Leo closed the journal. His eyes burned. His father had died trying to protect him. Had died alone, thinking sacrifice was necessary. "Don't be like me," Ryles had said.

"Don't ever try to save the world alone," his father had written. They were both telling him the same thing. Trust the team. Work together. Stop trying to control everything.

The bell rang. Lunch was over. Leo shoved the journal in his backpack and headed to his next class, but his mind was somewhere else entirely. Tonight. He'd meet the team tonight.

Part of him wanted to keep reading the journal. Learn everything alone. Come in prepared. In control. But that's what his father did. And his father died.

So maybe... maybe he'd just show up. Not knowing everything. Not having all the answers. Maybe that's what "letting people help" meant.

It felt wrong. Like showing up to a test without studying. But he'd do it anyway. Ryles' shop looked different at night. The strange objects seemed more alive, humming with energy Leo could almost feel. The air smelled sharper. The shadows moved in ways shadows shouldn't.

Ryles stood behind the counter, sorting through a box of what looked like frozen starlight. He glanced up as Leo entered. "You're early. Good. The others should be here soon." He gestured to a back room Leo hadn't noticed before. "Through there. I've got training space set up."

Leo walked through a doorway that definitely hadn't existed yesterday and found himself in a room that was far too large to fit inside the building. The walls were lined with shelves containing more impossible objects. The floor was covered in chalk circles and strange symbols. "Spatial expansion," Ryles called from the other room. "Smuggled the extra space from a dream. It's unstable, but it works."

Leo was examining a jar containing what looked like liquid darkness when someone spoke directly behind him. "I'm here too, you know. In case you, um..." A pause. "In case you need a phantom of support. Get it?"

Leo spun around so fast he nearly knocked over the jar. A boy stood there. Pale skin. White-blonde hair that seemed to catch light strangely. He was maybe thirteen, thin and wiry, wearing grey clothes that looked too big for him. His eyes were unsettling—not because of their color, but because of how they looked at you. Like he was only half-there. Like he might disappear if you looked away.

"Sorry," the boy said softly. "I do that. Appear without warning. It's kind of my whole thing." He smiled slightly. "I'm Ghost. Well, Marcus technically, but everyone calls me Ghost because I can, well..." He faded. Literally. His edges became transparent. Then solid again. "Do that."

"You're a Phantom," Leo said, remembering Ryles' terminology. "You can phase through things."

"Through dream-matter, yeah. Working on doing it in reality too, but that's harder." Ghost shifted his weight nervously. "Ryles says you're an Architect. That you built stairs out of sugar on your first try. That's... that's really impressive. I can barely build a box."

"I don't know what I'm doing," Leo admitted. "I'm just making it up as I go."

"That's the best way to do it. Making it up. Being spontaneous. Not planning every detail." Ghost's smile faded slightly. "Planning is dangerous. My father always said planning was the key to control. Control was the key to order. Order was the key to—" He stopped. Shook his head. "Sorry. Bad memories. Anyway. I'm here to help. Whatever you need."

Before Leo could respond, the doorway shimmered and Ryles walked through, followed by a girl. She was young. Maybe eleven. Round face, practical bob haircut, dark eyes that seemed to take in everything at once. She wore grey clothes like everyone, but she carried a first-aid kit that looked well-used. There were bandages visible on her own arms, peeking out from under her sleeves.

"Leo, this is Yuki," Ryles said. "Best Mender I've ever trained. She can heal injuries in dreams, sometimes even in reality if the connection is strong enough."

"Everything has a cost," Yuki said. Her voice was matter-of-fact. Practical. "I try to keep the price from being too high." She looked at Leo's feet. "You were running barefoot last night. Ryles patched you up, but the cuts are still fresh. May I?"

Before Leo could answer, she'd opened her kit and pulled out a small flower. It glowed faintly green. She crushed it between her fingers, and the glow spread like liquid light. She touched Leo's feet, and the warmth spread through the cuts. The pain vanished. Just stopped. When Yuki pulled her hand away, the cuts were healed. Not scarred. Not scabbed. Just... gone.

"Whoa," Leo breathed. Yuki winced. Subtly, but Leo noticed. Her hand trembled slightly as she put the flower remnants back in her kit.

"Did that hurt you?" he asked.

"Healing always costs something," Yuki said. She didn't elaborate. Just closed her kit and stood. "But you needed it more than I needed to avoid it. So." She smiled. "Worth it."

"Yuki's been absorbing ambient Glitches for months," Ryles explained. "Every time someone smuggles, reality takes something. She can feel it. Can redirect some of the cost to herself instead of letting it hit randomly. It's killing her slowly, but she does it anyway."

"I'm not dying," Yuki said firmly. "I'm just... tired. There's a difference."

"Right." Ryles didn't sound convinced. He clapped his hands. "Anyway. You three are the core. Trixie makes four when she arrives. Leo's the Architect. Ghost is the Phantom. Yuki is the Mender. Trixie's the Infiltrator. Together, you might just survive a deep dive."

"When does Trixie get here?" Leo asked.

"I'm already here, duh." Trixie's voice came from behind a shelf. She emerged grinning, chewing Dream Candy. "Been here for ten minutes. Wanted to see how you three interacted without me. You're all very polite. It's boring."

"You were spying on us," Ghost said. He didn't sound surprised. Just resigned.

"I'm an Infiltrator. I spy on everyone." Trixie pointed at Ghost. "Did you know you talk in your sleep? You kept saying 'Father, please' over and over last night. Very sad. Very mysterious."

Ghost's face went white. His edges flickered transparent for just a second. "Trixie," Ryles said warningly.

"What? I'm just saying—"

"Don't." Yuki's voice was sharp. "Don't use people's dreams against them. That's not okay."

Trixie's grin faded. "I was just—"

"Being a jerk," Yuki finished. "Apologize."

A long pause. Then Trixie sighed. "Sorry, Ghost. That was... that was mean. I shouldn't have brought it up."

Ghost nodded stiffly. Said nothing. But his edges stayed solid. Leo filed that interaction away. Trixie knew something about Ghost. Something Ghost didn't want shared. And she'd almost revealed it casually, like it didn't matter.

"Alright," Ryles said loudly, breaking the tension. "Now that we've established boundaries—Trixie, don't weaponize people's nightmares—let's talk about training. You four need to learn to work together. Coordinate in dreams. Signal in reality. Move as a unit."

He pulled out a large piece of chalk and began drawing on the floor. Complex symbols. Circles within circles. "This is a Linked Sleep Array," Ryles explained. "Lets you synchronize REM cycles. When you all fall asleep inside this circle, you'll enter the same dream zone at the same time. Good for training. Essential for deep dives."

"Is it dangerous?" Yuki asked.

"Everything about Gripping is dangerous. But this? Less dangerous than most things." Ryles finished the symbol and stood. "Tonight, we start simple. The Test Anxiety Loop. It's a shallow zone. Relatively safe. Good for beginners."

"I've been there," Leo said. "In regular dreams, before I knew about Gripping. It's just school hallways and exams."

"Exactly. Which makes it perfect for smuggling study materials." Ryles grinned. "Notebooks filled with impossible knowledge. Math beyond what's been discovered. Science from dreams of future technologies. History that never happened but feels true. People pay good money for that stuff."

"We're smuggling homework?" Ghost asked.

"You're smuggling practice," Ryles corrected. "Tonight's mission: Each of you pulls out one notebook. Coordinate your smuggles. Watch each other's backs. Don't get caught by the Principal."

"The what?" Leo asked.

"The guardian of the Test Anxiety Loop. It's not human. Not really. Just the manifestation of authority and failure. If it catches you, it expels you to deeper zones. Bad news." Ryles gestured to the circle. "But you'll be fine. You've got a team now."

The four of them looked at each other. Leo, Trixie, Ghost, and Yuki. Four kids who barely knew each other. Four talents that might complement each other or might clash catastrophically. "So," Trixie said, popping another candy in her mouth. "We doing this or what?"

Leo thought about his father's words. Build with others, not for them. Trust your team. "Yeah," he said. "Let's do this."

They sat in the circle. Close enough that their knees touched. Ryles handed each of them a small vial of grey liquid. "Synchronized sleep aid," he explained. "Drink it, and you'll all enter REM at the same time. The array will pull you into the same zone." He paused. "Fair warning: Shared dreams are intense. You'll feel each other's emotions. See each other's memories sometimes. It's amazingly invasive. But it works."

Leo uncorked his vial. The liquid smelled like nothing. He drank it in one gulp. It tasted like grey. Around him, the others did the same.

Within seconds, drowsiness hit him like a truck. His vision blurred. His head felt heavy. "Sweet dreams," Ryles said from somewhere far away. "And remember: Everyone comes home."

Leo's eyes closed. They stand in a hallway. Infinite. Stretching in both directions forever. Lockers line the walls, grey and identical. Fluorescent lights flicker overhead. The floor is linoleum, scuffed and dirty.

Leo checks his hands. Five fingers. He looks at the others. They're here. Real. Solid.

"This is creepy," Ghost whispers.

"This is perfect," Trixie says. She's already moving down the hallway, checking locker doors. "Study materials are in the classrooms. We need to find one that's unlocked." They walk together. The hallway never ends. Doors appear and disappear. Classrooms shift. The fluorescent lights buzz louder and louder.

"I don't like this," Yuki says. She clutches her first-aid kit. "Something's watching us." Leo feels it too. A presence. Authority. Judgment. The weight of expectations and the fear of failure pressing down on all sides.

"There," Trixie points. A classroom door, slightly ajar. Light spills through the crack. They approach carefully. Leo pushes the door open.

Inside, the classroom is perfect. Too perfect. Desks in perfect rows. A chalkboard covered in perfect equations. And on the teacher's desk, a stack of notebooks glowing faintly with inner light.

"Jackpot," Trixie breathes. Leo grabs one notebook. Opens it. Inside, the pages are filled with handwriting that shifts and changes. Mathematics he's never seen. Formulas that make his brain hurt to look at. Knowledge that shouldn't exist.

"Everyone grab one," he says. "Then we run." They each take a notebook. The moment Leo grips his, the weight of it becomes real. Solid. Heavy with impossible information.

The fluorescent lights flicker. A voice echoes through the hallway. Deep. Authoritative. Wrong.

"STUDENTS. RETURN TO YOUR SEATS."

"The Principal," Ghost breathes. "We need to go. Now." They bolt for the door. The hallway stretches longer. The lights flicker faster. Behind them, footsteps. Heavy. Approaching.

"TRUANCY IS UNACCEPTABLE." Leo builds as he runs. Throws up walls behind them, blocking the hallway. The walls are weak, unstable, but they slow the footsteps.

Ghost phases through a locked door, opens it from the other side. "This way!" They tumble through into another hallway. This one curves upward, defying gravity. They run up the wall, holding tight to their notebooks.

"We need to wake up," Yuki gasps. "All at once. On three."

"One," Trixie counts. The Principal crashes through Leo's walls.

"Two," Ghost whispers. The footsteps are right behind them.

"Three!" Leo gasped awake. The others jerked upright simultaneously. They were back in Ryles' shop, in the circle, holding notebooks that glowed faintly in the dim light. Real. Solid. Impossible.

They'd done it. "Wow!" Trixie breathed. She looked at her notebook like it might bite. "We actually did it."

"Team effort," Ghost said quietly. His hands shook slightly. "I couldn't have phased that door without Leo's walls buying us time."

"And I wouldn't have known when to wake up without Yuki counting," Leo added. Yuki smiled. Then winced. Clutched her chest slightly.

"You okay?" Leo asked.

"Glitch," she whispered. "Small one. Someone lost... a memory? Of their first day of school, I think. Reality took payment." She pressed her hand against her ribs. "I redirected some of it. It'll fade."

"You shouldn't do that," Ghost said. "You'll hurt yourself."

"Better me than someone who doesn't understand what's happening," Yuki replied. She straightened. "I'm fine. Really."

Ryles emerged from the shadows, grinning. "Not bad for a first team run. You worked together. Adapted. Survived. That's more than most manage on their first dive." He took the notebooks. "These'll sell for good money. We'll split the profit. Consider it your first paycheck as professional Grippers."

"We're professionals now?" Trixie asked.

"You're not dead. That's professional enough." Ryles stacked the notebooks on the counter. "Same time tomorrow? We'll go deeper. Try something more challenging."

They stood, stretching. Leo's mind still spun from the shared dream. He'd felt them. Trixie's mischief and hidden loneliness. Ghost's fear and determination to prove he existed. Yuki's pain and her conviction that healing others mattered more than protecting herself.

They were a team. Weird. Broken in different ways. But a team. "Hey, Leo," Trixie said as they headed for the door. "You were good in there. Natural leader type. Gave orders without being bossy. Your sister would be proud."

Leo's throat tightened. "Thanks."

"We'll get her back," Trixie said. She said it like a fact. Like there was no other option. "All of us. Together."

"Yeah," Leo said. "Together." They left the shop one by one. Ghost faded into shadows. Yuki walked quickly toward the transit station. Trixie gave Leo a two-finger salute and jogged off into the night.

Leo headed home alone, but for the first time in six months, he didn't feel alone. He had a team. He had a plan. He had hope. He made it home with an hour to spare before Mother's return. Hid the notebook under his mattress with the journal. Changed clothes. Sat at the kitchen table and tried to look like he'd been doing homework.

Mother came home at eleven-fifteen. Exhausted. Grey. Hollow. "Homework done?" she asked.

"Yeah."

"Good." She headed upstairs without another word. Leo waited until he heard her door close. Then he went to his room and pulled out Lily's old backpack from the closet. She'd left it here before the accident. He'd been too heartbroken to look through it.

Now he opened it. School supplies. Grey notebooks. Regulation pencils. And at the bottom, hidden under everything else, her sketchbook.

Leo opened it with shaking hands. The first few pages were normal. Drawings of their apartment. Their mother. Leo himself, captured in pencil, looking too serious.

But near the middle, the drawings changed. A meadow with impossible colors. A blue flower glowing with inner light. A crystal fortress with faces in the walls. And on the last page, a drawing of Leo and Lily holding hands, standing on opposite sides of a door.

Below it, in Lily's handwriting:

If you're reading this, you found it. You know about the Reverie. I'm sorry I didn't tell you. I'm sorry I left. But I'm building my half of the bridge. You just need to build yours. Trust your team. Don't try to save me alone. And Leo? Stop trying to control everything. Let me choose. Let me help.

Love, Lily

Leo's vision blurred. His hands shook. She'd known. Before the accident. Before everything. She'd been learning. Training. Preparing.

And she'd gone to the Sanctum willingly. Not as a victim. As a volunteer. As a builder. "I'll build my half," he whispered to the drawing. "I promise."

He was about to close the sketchbook when Yuki's voice echoed in his memory.

Something huge just Glitched.

Leo looked out his window. Half the city block was flickering. Buildings phasing in and out of existence. The street lamps blinked between there and not-there. The sky above rippled like water.

Scale 2. Maybe approaching Scale 3. Someone was smuggling. A lot. And reality was starting to break.

Leo grabbed his jacket and ran.

[END OF CHAPTER 6]

Chapter 7: The Glitch Storm

Leo woke to sirens. Not the gentle alarm clock beep. Not his mother's footsteps. Actual sirens. Multiple. Cutting through the white noise generator's hum like they were right outside.

He stumbled to the window and looked out. Conformity Enforcers. Three vehicles, grey and angular, parked on the street below. Officers in grey uniforms were entering the building across the street. Leo watched as they emerged minutes later with Mr. Chen from apartment 3B, his hands bound behind his back.

Mr. Chen had always been quiet. Kept to himself. Leo had never noticed anything unusual about him. Except now, as the Enforcers loaded him into their vehicle, Leo saw the flash of color. A red scarf. Illegal. Hidden under Mr. Chen's grey coat.

One of the Enforcers held up what looked like a painting. Even from this distance, Leo could see it was beautiful. Full of colors that shouldn't exist in New Portside. Blues and greens and yellows that hurt to look at after years of grey. The Enforcers threw the painting to the ground and stomped on it. The colors bled into the grey pavement and vanished.

Leo's stomach turned. "They're escalating," Mother's voice said from behind him. He spun. She stood in his doorway, still in her nightclothes, watching the scene with hollow eyes.

"The raids started three days ago," she continued quietly. "They're searching for contraband. For signs of creative thinking. For anyone who might be a..." She stopped. Started again. "Anyone who might be different."

"Mr. Chen was just painting," Leo said.

"Mr. Chen was breaking the law." Mother's voice was flat. Empty. "The laws keep us safe. Keep us from another Nightmare." She looked at Leo. Really looked at him. "You understand that, don't you? Why the rules matter?"

Leo thought about the Dream Candies hidden under his mattress. The journal. The sketchbook. The notebook full of impossible knowledge. "Yes," he lied. "I understand."

Mother nodded slowly. Turned to leave. Paused in the doorway. "If you had something," she said without looking back, "something that broke the rules. You'd get rid of it. Wouldn't you? Before the Enforcers came here?"

Leo's blood ran cold. "Of course." She left. Leo waited until he heard her door close. Then he pulled everything illegal from under his mattress—journal, sketchbook, notebook, candies—and shoved them into his backpack. He'd have to take them to Ryles' shop. Hide them somewhere safer.

He dressed quickly and turned on the grey tablet to check the news. The screen showed a press conference. A stern-faced woman in a grey suit stood at a podium, speaking to cameras. "—structural anomalies reported across New Portside's residential districts. Buildings experiencing foundation issues. Street surfaces developing cracks. Windows shattering without cause." Her expression hardened. "We have reason to believe these incidents are the work of imagination extremists. Individuals deliberately destabilizing reality through illegal dream manipulation."

Leo's hands clenched. They were blaming Grippers for the Glitches. Turning the population against anyone who might be different. "Citizens are encouraged to report suspicious behavior," the woman continued. "Daydreaming. Excessive creativity. Unauthorized art or music. These are warning signs. Early intervention can prevent another Great Nightmare."

The screen cut to footage of the Enforcers raiding homes. People being dragged from their apartments. Paintings and sculptures and musical instruments confiscated and destroyed. Leo turned off the tablet. His hands shook.

This was his fault. His team's fault. They'd smuggled those notebooks, and reality had taken payment. The Glitches were spreading. And now the government was using it as an excuse to crack down on everyone.

He had to get to Ryles. Had to warn the others. School was cancelled. An announcement on the transit screens said: "Emergency compliance inspections. All educational facilities closed until further notice."

Leo took the transit to Salvage Street instead. The streets were emptier than usual. People hurried with their heads down, avoiding eye contact. Enforcer vehicles patrolled every block. Ryles' shop looked closed from the outside. The windows were dark. The door was locked.

Leo knocked anyway. Three times, then twice, then once. The pattern Ryles had taught them. The locks clicked. The door opened a crack.

"Get in," Ryles hissed. "Quick." Leo slipped inside. The shop was darker than usual. Most of the lights were off. The strange objects on the shelves seemed subdued, like they were hiding.

Trixie, Ghost, and Yuki were already there, sitting in the back room around a small table. They all looked exhausted. Scared. "You saw the news," Leo said.

"Hard to miss," Trixie replied. She wasn't chewing candy. Her hands were clasped tight on the table. "My parents left for work at 5 AM. They're part of the raid teams. I heard them talking. They're supposed to check forty homes today. Forty."

"They don't know you're a Gripper?" Ghost asked quietly.

"God, no. They'd turn me in themselves." Trixie's laugh was bitter. "They're true believers. Think the Conformity Laws saved humanity. Think anyone who dreams too much is dangerous."

"They're not wrong about the dangerous part," Ryles said, entering with a pot of something that smelled like tea but probably wasn't. "The Glitches are getting worse. Your little notebook heist? That triggered Scale 2 effects. Buildings cracking. Reality becoming unstable. Do that a few more times and we'll hit Scale 3. Then Scale 4. Then—"

"Another Great Nightmare," Leo finished.

"Exactly." Ryles poured the not-tea into cups. "The government knows it. They're panicking. Hence the raids. Hence the crackdown. They're trying to suppress all Gripping before reality collapses completely."

"But they're the ones causing it," Leo said. "You told me they run black-ops smuggling operations. They're breaking the Truce."

"Course they are. Hypocrites, the lot of them." Ryles sipped his not-tea. "But they've got better control than you kids. Professional Grippers who know how to minimize Glitches. What you four did was amateur hour. Sloppy. Loud. You might as well have painted a target on your backs."

Yuki winced. Her hand went to her ribs. "Another Glitch?" Leo asked.

"Big one," Yuki whispered. "Someone lost... I think someone lost their mother. Not physically. Just forgot she existed. The memory erased. Reality rewrote itself around the absence." She pressed harder against her ribs. "I tried to redirect it but there was too much. It hit someone in the eastern district."

"That's Scale 3," Ryles said grimly. "Memory erasure. Identity deletion. We're approaching the point of no return."

"What happens at Scale 4?" Ghost asked.

"Concepts disappear. Love. Time. Causality. Meaning itself unravels. Reality becomes dream, and dream becomes nothing." Ryles set down his cup. "Your father saw it happen once. During the Great Nightmare. He said it was like watching the universe forget how to exist."

Leo pulled out his father's journal. "I've been reading this. He wrote about the Nightmare. About establishing the Eternal Sleepers. But he didn't explain how it worked. How they stopped it."

"Because it was desperate," Ryles said. "A last-ditch solution that barely worked. The government had been running mass smuggling operations. Trying to weaponize the Reverie. Create dream-weapons, dream-armor, dream-technology. They pulled so much matter across the boundary that reality started collapsing. The Marshals intervened, but even they couldn't stop it alone."

"So my father and his team found the Sanctum," Leo said.

"Found it. Figured out what it was. Realized that conscious anchors could stabilize the boundary." Ryles' eyes shifted through colors rapidly. "We volunteered. Five of us. Me, your father, Sarah, Marcus Sr., and Elena."

Leo's head snapped up. "My mother? My mother was a Gripper?"

"One of the best. Natural Architect like you and your father. She built the initial anchor structures in the Sanctum. Designed the whole system." Ryles smiled sadly. "She gave it up after Thomas died. Swore she'd never dream again. Took suppressants to kill her REM cycles. Raised you and Lily in total Conformity, thinking it would keep you safe."

Leo felt like the floor had dropped away. His mother. The woman who worked three jobs and never smiled and warned him about dreams. She'd been like him once. She'd known about the Reverie.

"Why didn't she tell me?" he whispered.

"Because your father died for this," Ryles said bluntly. "The five of us anchored the boundary temporarily. Held it long enough for the government to stop smuggling, for the Marshals to enforce the Truce. But someone had to stay. Someone had to become the first permanent Eternal Sleeper. Keep the anchor stable."

"Dad volunteered," Leo said.

"Course he did. Martyr complex runs in your family." Ryles' voice cracked slightly. "He said: 'I have kids. They need a world to grow up in. So I'll make sure they have one.' Then he dove deep and never came back."

The shop fell silent. The not-tea steamed. Outside, sirens wailed. "I'm sorry," Ghost said quietly. "That must have been hard. Losing your friend like that."

"Losing a friend who chose to die," Ryles corrected. "That's worse. Because you can't be angry at them for leaving. They did it to save you." He looked at Leo. "Don't make his mistake, kid. Don't think sacrifice is noble."

"But he saved the world," Leo said.

"He saved it alone. That's the mistake. He should have found another way. Should have built a system that didn't require someone to die." Ryles tapped the table. "That's what you need to do. Find the third option. The one where Lily comes home AND reality stays stable AND nobody dies."

"Is that even possible?" Yuki asked.

"I don't know. But if anyone can figure it out, it's an Architect." Ryles looked at Leo. "Your father designed the anchor system. You can redesign it. Make it better. Make it survivable."

Before Leo could respond, Trixie suddenly spoke. "So Ghost, about those nightmares you've been having about your father. The ones where he's—"

Ghost went white. "How do you know about those?"

"I told you. I've been in your dreams." Trixie shrugged. "You keep reliving the same memory. Your dad standing over you, telling you that quiet children are good children. That invisible children are safe children. That the best kids don't—"

"Stop," Ghost said. His voice was barely audible. His edges flickered transparent.

"I'm just saying, it explains a lot about your whole phasing thing. Like, you literally make yourself disappear because—"

"I said STOP!" Ghost's voice cracked. He stood so fast his chair fell over. "You had no right. Those are my memories. My nightmares. You don't get to just... just take them and use them against me!"

"I'm not using them against you!" Trixie looked genuinely confused. "I'm just pointing out—"

"You're violating him," Yuki said coldly. "You're taking private, painful things and making them public. That's not okay, Trixie."

"But I'm trying to help! If he'd just talk about—"

"He doesn't have to talk about anything," Leo said. His voice came out harder than he intended. "Especially not things you stole from his head without permission."

Trixie's face flushed. "I'm an Infiltrator. That's what I do. I see things. I can't help what I see."

"But you can help what you say," Ryles said quietly. "And right now, you're being cruel." Trixie looked around the table. At Ghost, whose edges were barely visible now. At Yuki, whose expression was disappointed. At Leo, who just looked sad.

"I was just—" Trixie started.

"Being mean," Yuki finished. "Again."

Trixie stood abruptly. "Fine. I'll go. Clearly I'm not wanted here." She headed for the door.

"Trixie," Ryles called. She stopped. Didn't turn around.

"Knowing everything doesn't mean understanding anything," Ryles said. "You can see people's secrets, but that doesn't mean you know them. Real intimacy requires vulnerability. Yours. Not theirs."

Trixie said nothing. Just opened the door and left. The shop fell silent again. Ghost slowly solidified. Sat back down. His hands shook.

"I'm sorry," Leo said. "She shouldn't have—"

"It's fine," Ghost whispered. "She's right anyway. My father did say those things. Did make me feel like existing was wrong." He looked up. His eyes were wet. "But those are my nightmares to share. Not hers to take."

"She'll apologize," Yuki said. "Eventually. Once she realizes what she did."

"Will she though?" Ghost asked. Nobody had an answer.

Leo checked the time. Almost noon. "I need to go to the hospital. Check on Lily. After what Yuki said about the Glitches affecting memory, I need to make sure—"

"Go," Ryles said. "But be careful. The Enforcers are watching everyone. If they connect you to the structural anomalies..."

"I'll be careful." Leo grabbed his backpack and headed for the door. As he stepped outside into the grey afternoon, he heard Ghost speak quietly behind him.

"Do you think we're doing the right thing? Trying to save her?"

And Ryles' response: "I think right and wrong stopped mattering the moment reality started breaking. Now we're just trying to survive." St. Grace Hospital was busier than usual. Enforcers in the lobby. Nurses looking nervous. Patients being transferred to other facilities.

Leo kept his head down and headed straight for Lily's floor. Room 447. Nobody stopped him. The room was the same. Grey walls. Grey equipment. Lily on the bed, eyes closed, peaceful.

But something was different. The monitors. They weren't just beeping steadily. They were fluctuating. Heart rate spiking, then normalizing. Blood pressure rising, then falling. Brain activity increasing, then decreasing. Like she was responding to something. Fighting something. Trying to—

Leo pulled out his phone and started recording the monitor displays. The patterns. The timing. Then he looked at the timestamp on the last major Glitch. The one Yuki had felt. The big Scale 2 event.

It had happened at 3:47 AM. Leo checked the hospital logs on the wall chart. At 3:47 AM, Lily's brain activity had spiked. Dramatically. For exactly ninety seconds.

Then it had stabilized again. "She felt it," Leo whispered. "She felt the Glitch. She reacted to it." He pulled out his father's journal and flipped through the pages until he found the entry about Eternal Sleepers.

The anchors aren't passive. They're active participants in maintaining the boundary. When reality destabilizes, they push back. Use their consciousness to reinforce the weak points. It's exhausting. Painful. But necessary.

If an anchor is holding their position during a major Glitch, their vital signs will spike. Heart rate increases. Blood pressure rises. Brain activity surges. They're fighting to keep reality stable.

Leo's hands shook. Lily wasn't just trapped in the Sanctum. She was working. Fighting. Every time he and his team smuggled something, she felt it. Responded to it. Tried to keep reality from collapsing.

And she'd been doing it alone for six months. "I'm so sorry," he whispered. He took her hand. "I didn't know. I didn't understand. But I'm coming. I promise. I'm going to—"

The monitors spiked. All of them. Simultaneously. Heart rate jumping from 70 to 140. Blood pressure skyrocketing. Brain activity exploding across the readout.

Lily's eyelids twitched. Her fingers moved slightly in Leo's hand. And then, impossibly, her lips moved. Forming words without sound. Leo leaned closer. Watched her mouth.

Coming, she seemed to say. *They're coming. Be ready.*

The monitors stabilized. Lily went still again. Peaceful. Like nothing had happened. But Leo's blood ran cold.

They're coming. Who was coming? He checked his phone. A news notification.

BREAKING: Director Vance announces Voluntary Dream Mapping for Coma Recovery Program. Families of comatose patients encouraged to apply.

Below the headline, a photo. A severe woman with silver hair and cold eyes. Director Helena Vance. Head of the Conformity Council. Leo's hand trembled as he opened the article.

"We've developed revolutionary techniques for accessing and mapping dream states," Director Vance was quoted. *"For patients in persistent vegetative states, this technology offers hope. We can reach them. Communicate with them. Potentially wake them."*

The article continued: Applications open Monday. Selected families will receive full treatment free of charge. Director Vance personally oversees the program. Monday. That was in three days.

Leo's phone buzzed. A message from Ryles.

Get back here. Now. Emergency.

Leo kissed Lily's forehead and ran. By the time he reached Salvage Street, the sun was setting. Grey sky darkening to darker grey. The shop's lights were off again. He knocked the pattern. The door opened immediately.

Everyone was there. Trixie had returned, looking chastened. Ghost sat far from her, still flickering slightly. Yuki stood by the window, watching the street. Ryles was at the counter, holding a remote control pointed at a small TV Leo hadn't seen before.

"Watch," Ryles said. He pressed play. The screen showed a press conference. Director Vance at the podium. Same silver hair. Same cold eyes.

"The Dream Mapping program represents a breakthrough in consciousness research," Vance said. *"We can now access the deepest levels of human awareness. Navigate the subconscious. Reach patients trapped in coma states and guide them back to wakefulness."*

A reporter asked: "Director, isn't this the same dream manipulation you've been warning against? The imagination extremism that's causing the structural failures?"

Vance smiled. It didn't reach her eyes. "There's a difference between illegal, uncontrolled Gripping and government-sanctioned medical intervention. We have the training. The technology. The authority. We will use the Reverie to heal, not harm."

"But isn't accessing the Reverie what caused the Great Nightmare?" another reporter asked.

"The Great Nightmare was caused by reckless individuals exploiting the Reverie without understanding the consequences,"* Vance said smoothly. *"We've learned from that tragedy. We have protocols. Safeguards. And most importantly, we have Architects who can navigate the deep zones safely."

The blood drained from Leo's face. "Architects?" the reporter pressed.

"Individuals with natural spatial reasoning abilities in dream states. Rare talents. But essential for reaching the Sanctum of Sleep, where the most deeply comatose patients reside."* Vance looked directly at the camera. *"If you know someone with these abilities, we encourage you to come forward. You could save lives."

Ryles turned off the TV. "She's looking for you," he said quietly. "She knows you exist. Knows you're an Architect. And she's using your sister as bait."

"How does she even know about me?" Leo asked.

"Because someone told her." Ryles gestured to the window. "The Enforcers aren't just raiding homes. They're asking questions. Tracking Glitches. Following the signatures. Your team's little heist? It left traces. And Director Vance is very good at connecting dots."

"So what do we do?" Ghost asked.

"We accelerate the timeline," Ryles said. "You wanted to reach the Sanctum eventually. Train for months. Build your skills. Go in prepared." He looked at Leo. "You don't have months anymore. Vance will find you. Arrest you. Force you to work for her. And if you refuse, she'll let Lily rot while reality collapses."

"We go now," Leo said. It wasn't a question.

"You go tonight," Ryles corrected. "I'll teach you what I can in the next few hours. Give you the gear you need. But understand: You're not ready. The Nightmare Trench will kill you if you're not careful. The Sanctum is guarded by things worse than Marshals. And even if you reach Lily, you'll have to face the fact that she might not want to leave."

"I'll convince her," Leo said.

"What if you can't?" Yuki asked quietly. "What if she chose this? What if pulling her out means someone else takes her place?" Leo thought about his father's journal. About the martyr complex. About the third option.

"Then we find a way to wake all the Sleepers," he said. "We redesign the anchor system. We fix the boundary without requiring prisoners. We do what my father couldn't do."

"In one night?" Trixie asked skeptically.

"We try," Leo said firmly. "Because the alternative is letting Vance win. Letting the government control the Reverie. Letting Lily stay trapped forever. And I'm not doing that."

He looked around at his team. At Trixie, who knew too much. At Ghost, who tried to disappear. At Yuki, who hurt herself to help others. At Ryles, who'd lost everything already.

"I can't do this alone," he said. "I need you. All of you. Even if it's dangerous. Even if it's impossible. Will you help me?"

Silence. Then Ghost stood. His edges solidified completely. "I'm in. I may be scared, but I'm tired of disappearing. Time to be seen."

Yuki nodded. "Someone has to heal you idiots when you inevitably hurt yourselves."

Trixie looked at Ghost. Then at Leo. "I'm sorry. For what I said earlier. For violating your privacy. I was being cruel." She swallowed hard. "But I'm in too. Someone has to scout ahead. Might as well be me."

Ryles sighed. "Your father would hate this plan. But he'd do it anyway. So I guess..." He pulled out a large duffel bag from behind the counter. "I guess I better get you equipped."

He unzipped the bag. Inside, equipment glowed with impossible light. Breathing apparatus for the deep zones. Protective gear woven from dream-matter. Weapons that looked like they'd been pulled from nightmares.

"This is everything I've collected over twelve years," Ryles said. "Use it well. And remember: Everyone comes home. No matter what." Leo looked at the equipment. At his team. At the impossible task ahead.

Then he heard Lily's voice in his memory. Be ready. "We're ready," he whispered. "Tonight, we dive deep." Outside, sirens wailed.

And on the TV screen—still on, just muted—Director Vance smiled her cold smile and said something the camera couldn't quite catch. But Leo could read her lips.

I'm coming for you, little Architect. Run while you can.

[END OF CHAPTER 7]

Chapter 8: The Offer

When Leo got home, his mother was sitting at the kitchen table. Waiting. Not eating. Not working. Just sitting. Hands folded. Expression unreadable.

The white noise generator hummed. "Sit down," she said. Leo's stomach dropped. He sat. Mother slid a piece of paper across the table. Official letterhead. Government seal. Bold text at the top: DREAM MAPPING PROGRAM - PARTICIPANT ACCEPTANCE.

"I enrolled you," Mother said. Her voice was flat. Empty. "Your appointment is tomorrow morning at nine. Director Vance herself will oversee your evaluation."

"Mom, I don't need—"

"The doctor called me today," Mother interrupted. "About Lily. Said we need to discuss long-term options. Said her condition isn't improving. Said—" Her voice cracked. Just slightly. "Said we need to consider letting her go."

Leo's chest tightened. "He gave us two weeks."

"That was four days ago, Leo. We're down to ten days." Mother's hands clenched together.

"This program is our last hope. If Director Vance can reach Lily through dream mapping, if she can wake her up, then—" She stopped. Breathed.

"Then we get our girl back. And you help them. However they need."

"What if I refuse?"

Mother's eyes finally met his. They were hollow. Broken. "Then Lily dies. And I lose both my children to dreams. Just like I lost your father."

The words hit like a punch. "You knew," Leo whispered. "About the Reverie. About Gripping. You were there. Ryles told me."

Mother's face went white. "What did he tell you?"

"That you were an Architect. That you helped stop the Great Nightmare. That you designed the anchor system. That Dad died keeping it stable." Leo's voice rose. "Why didn't you tell me? Why did you let me think dreams were just neural noise? Why did you hide everything?"

"To protect you!" Mother stood abruptly. Her chair scraped against the floor. "Your father died because of dreams. Because he thought he could save the world. Because he couldn't accept that some things are impossible to fix!" Her hands shook. "I wasn't going to lose you too. So I suppressed it. Killed my own gift. Raised you in Conformity. Kept you safe."

"You kept me ignorant," Leo said. "And Lily discovered it anyway. She's in the Sanctum right now, Mom. She's an Eternal Sleeper. She volunteered."

Mother's face crumpled. "No. No, that's—she's just sick. She's just in a coma. She didn't—"

"She chose it. To protect me. Because I was going to discover the Grip eventually and she wanted to be there, anchoring the boundary, keeping me safe." Leo stood. "Just like you tried to keep me safe by lying. Just like Dad tried to keep us safe by dying. Our whole family has a martyr complex."

"Then break the pattern," Mother said quietly. "Go to the appointment tomorrow. Work with Director Vance. Use their resources, their training, their protection. Save Lily the right way. The safe way."

"There is no safe way," Leo said. "That's the point. The Reverie is dangerous. Reality is fragile. And the government caused most of the problems they're now claiming to solve."

"The government is the only thing standing between us and another Nightmare!"

"The government IS the Nightmare!" Leo's voice echoed in the small kitchen. "They're the ones breaking the Truce. Running black-ops smuggling operations. Exploiting the Reverie while telling everyone else to suppress their dreams. They're hypocrites, Mom. And Director Vance is the worst of them."

Mother sank back into her chair. Looked at the acceptance letter. At her son. At the impossible choice between safety and truth. "Go to the appointment," she said finally. "Just... hear what she has to say. Please."

Leo wanted to argue. Wanted to refuse. But he saw the desperation in her eyes. The same desperation he felt every time he thought about Lily. "Fine," he said. "I'll go. But I'm not making any promises."

Mother nodded. Said nothing else. Leo grabbed his backpack and went to his room. Pulled out his phone and texted the group.

Vance wants to meet me tomorrow. Mother signed me up. This is bad.

Responses came immediately.

Trixie: Don't go. It's a trap.

Ghost: Maybe hear her out? Could be valuable intel.

Yuki: Be careful. She's dangerous.

Ryles: Go. Learn what she knows. But don't trust a word she says.

Leo set down the phone. Looked at the acceptance letter his mother had slipped under his door. Tomorrow morning. Nine AM. The Conformity Council building. Room 447.

The same room number as Lily's hospital room. That couldn't be a coincidence. The Conformity Council building was the only structure in New Portside that wasn't grey. It was black. Obsidian and steel and dark glass. It rose thirty stories, a monolith of authority and control.

Leo stood at the entrance at 8:55 AM. His hands were sweating. His heart pounded. The acceptance letter had said to go to the seventh floor. Room 747. (He'd misread it last night—not 447. But still unsettling.)

Security guards in black uniforms checked his ID. Scanned him for contraband. Let him through. The elevator was silent except for soft instrumental music. The kind designed to be calming but just made Leo more anxious.

Seventh floor. The doors opened. A woman waited in the hallway. Not Director Vance. Someone younger. Severe grey suit. Tablet in hand.

"Leo Finch?"

"Yes."

"Follow me. The Director is ready for you." They walked down a hallway that seemed to stretch forever. Doors on either side, all closed. All identical. The lighting was too bright. Clinical. Wrong.

Room 747. The woman opened the door. Gestured for Leo to enter. "The Director will be with you shortly," she said. Then she left, closing the door behind her.

The room was small. A desk. Two chairs. A window overlooking the grey city. On the desk, a folder with Leo's name printed on the cover.

Leo sat. Waited. His leg bounced nervously. The door opened. Director Helena Vance entered. She was exactly as she appeared on TV—severe features, silver hair pulled back tight, cold blue eyes. But in person, she seemed older. Tired. Like she carried a weight that was slowly crushing her.

"Mr. Finch," she said, sitting across from him. "Thank you for coming."

"My mother didn't give me much choice."

"Desperate mothers rarely do." Vance opened the folder. Inside were photos. Of Leo. His school. His apartment building. Ryles' shop. His team. "You've been busy."

Leo's blood ran cold. "You've been watching me."

"I've been watching everyone. It's my job." Vance pulled out a photo of the structural damage from last week's Glitch. "These cracks appeared at 3:47 AM. The same time you and your team successfully smuggled four notebooks from the Test Anxiety Loop. Coincidence?"

"How did you—"

"I have Grippers on my staff. Professional ones. They track signatures. Follow the ripples. You four are amateurs. Loud. Obvious. It's a miracle the Marshals haven't killed you yet." Vance closed the folder. "But that's why you're here. I can offer you something better than hiding in Ryles' dusty shop."

"I'm not interested in joining the government."

"You haven't heard the offer yet." Vance stood. Walked to the window. Looked out at the city. "What do you know about the Sanctum of Sleep?"

"It's where the Eternal Sleepers anchor the boundary. Where Lily is."

"And do you know why we need Eternal Sleepers at all?"

"Because the government broke reality with mass smuggling twelve years ago."

Vance smiled slightly. "Close. We didn't break reality. We discovered how fragile it was. How easily the boundary could collapse. The Eternal Sleeper system was a desperate patch, not a solution. It's been deteriorating for years."

She turned to face him. "The anchors are dying, Leo. Slowly. Consciousness can't hold a boundary indefinitely. The current system gives us maybe five more years. Then the anchors fail. The boundary collapses. Reality and Reverie merge. Billions die in the chaos."

Leo's stomach twisted. "That's not possible. Ryles said—"

"Ryles is optimistic. He wants to believe the Truce will hold. That small-scale Gripping is sustainable. He's wrong." Vance pulled out another photo. This one showed the Sanctum. Crystal walls glowing. Faces inside. "I've been to the deep zones. I've seen the cracks forming. The boundary isn't stable. It's dying. And when it goes, everything goes with it."

"So what's your solution?" Leo asked. "Wake all the Sleepers and let reality collapse faster?"

"No. Replace them with something better." Vance's eyes gleamed. "Technology. Artificial anchors. Machines that can hold the boundary without requiring human consciousness. No more prisoners. No more sacrifice. Just stable, sustainable separation of dimensions."

It sounded too good to be true. "Why hasn't anyone tried that before?"

"Because we couldn't reach the Sanctum to install the technology. The path reshapes itself. Changes based on who's navigating. Only an Architect can build a stable route through the deep zones." Vance leaned forward. "I need an Architect, Leo. Someone who can map the path. Guide my team. Help us replace the failing biological anchors with technological ones."

"And in exchange?"

"You get unlimited access to the Reverie. Proper training from professional Grippers. Safety from the Marshals—we have agreements with them. Resources to help Lily. And most importantly..." Vance pulled out one more photo. "You get to wake your sister and bring her home."

The photo showed Lily. Not in the hospital. In the Sanctum. Conscious. Aware. Looking at the camera with an expression Leo couldn't quite read. Not trapped. Not suffering. Just... waiting.

"This was taken yesterday," Vance said. "By one of my deep divers. I wanted you to see that she's okay. Stable. But she could be home, Leo. Free. If you help us."

Leo stared at the photo. At his sister. At the impossible choice. "Why should I trust you?" he asked quietly. "You're the one who caused the Great Nightmare. Who nearly destroyed reality. Who's been lying to the entire population about dreams."

"Because I understand what you're going through." Vance pulled out one more photo. Not of Lily. Of a young girl. Maybe fourteen. Long brown hair. Bright smile. Wearing clothes that had color. Real color. Red and blue and yellow.

"My daughter, Catherine," Vance said softly. "Before the Conformity Laws. Before the Nightmare. She was creative. Artistic. Full of life."

She set down a second photo. The same girl. Older. Lying in a crystal pod in the Sanctum. Peaceful. Trapped.

"She volunteered to become an Eternal Sleeper five years ago," Vance continued. "The boundary was weakening. We needed more anchors. She said: 'Mother, if I can help save the world, I should.' She was sixteen."

Vance's voice cracked. Just slightly. "I've spent every day since then trying to figure out how to bring her home. How to wake her without killing everyone else. How to fix the system that took my daughter from me."

She looked at Leo directly. "We're the same, you and I. We'll do anything for family. Anything to save the people we love. So work with me. Help me build the technological anchors. Wake the Sleepers. Bring our children home."

Leo's throat was tight. He saw himself in her. Saw the desperation. The determination. The willingness to do whatever it took.

And that terrified him. "I need to think about it," he said.

"You have twenty-four hours." Vance handed him a business card. Actual physical card, rare in the digital age. "My direct line. Call me when you're ready. But Leo?" Her expression hardened. "If you refuse, I move forward anyway. My team will reach the Sanctum with or without your help. And if Lily gets caught in the crossfire of our equipment installation, well..." She didn't finish. Didn't need to.

The threat hung in the air. "You're saying you'll hurt her if I don't cooperate," Leo said flatly.

"I'm saying accidents happen when you're working with experimental technology in unstable dimensional space. Help me, and I'll make sure Lily is prioritized. Protected. Refuse, and..." Vance shrugged. "I can't guarantee anything."

Leo stood. His hands clenched into fists. "That's not an offer. That's coercion."

"That's reality," Vance replied. "Twenty-four hours. Choose wisely." Leo left without another word. Walked down the endless hallway. Took the silent elevator. Emerged into grey morning light feeling sick.

His phone buzzed. A message from Trixie.

We're outside. Get over here. NOW.

Leo crossed the street. Found his team waiting in an alley—Trixie, Ghost, and Yuki, all looking worried. "You were in there for forty minutes," Trixie said. "What did she say?" Leo told them everything. The offer. The technological anchors. The threat. Catherine.

When he finished, they were all silent. "It's a good offer," Ghost said quietly. "Too good."

"It's a trap," Trixie said flatly. "She's using your guilt against you. Offering you the easy solution so you'll trust her."

"What if she's telling the truth?" Leo asked. "What if the boundary really is failing? What if her technology could actually work?"

"Then she'd share it with the world, not weaponize it for government control," Yuki said. "She's not trying to save everyone, Leo. She's trying to save her daughter and forget the consequences."

"That's what I'm trying to do," Leo admitted. "Save Lily and not care about the consequences."

"No," Yuki said firmly. "You're trying to save Lily AND fix the system. There's a difference. Vance wants to replace one broken system with another. You want to build something better."

"Do I?" Leo's voice cracked. "I don't even know what I'm doing. I'm just a kid who can smuggle candy and build sugar stairs. How am I supposed to redesign the entire anchor system? How am I supposed to save everyone?"

"You're not," Ghost said. "Not alone. That's the point."

"Your father tried to save the world by himself," Trixie added. "It killed him. Vance is trying to save her daughter by herself. It's turning her into a monster. You don't have to do that. You have us."

"But what if she's right?" Leo asked desperately. "What if I can't do this? What if I fail and Lily dies and reality collapses anyway? At least with Vance's resources—"

"You'd become her," Yuki interrupted. "Look at yourself, Leo. You're standing here thinking: 'If I just take control, if I just use her power, I can fix everything.' That's exactly what she thought. That's exactly what your father thought. And look where it got them."

Leo closed his eyes. Saw Vance's face. Saw his own reflection in her desperate determination. He was her. The same controlling instinct. The same belief that individual sacrifice could solve systemic problems. The same willingness to hurt others if it meant saving one person he loved.

"I can't work with her," he said quietly. "Can I?"

"No," all three replied simultaneously. Leo opened his eyes. Looked at his team. At the people who'd saved him from himself.

"Then we need to reach the Sanctum first," he said. "Tonight. Before Vance's team can move. Before she can threaten Lily again. We go in, we find a way to wake the Sleepers safely, and we fix this whole broken system."

"That's impossible," Ghost said.

"So was smuggling a flower from a dream," Leo replied. "So was surviving a Marshal. So was assembling a team of broken kids who somehow trust each other. We've done impossible before. We can do it again."

"Together," Yuki added.

"Together," Leo agreed.

Trixie grinned. Popped a Dream Candy in her mouth. "Finally. A proper heist. When do we dive?"

"Tonight. After curfew. We meet at Ryles' shop. Gear up. Coordinate our approach." Leo pulled out his father's journal. "I've been reading Dad's notes. He mapped the route to the Sanctum. It's dangerous. Full of nightmare zones that'll kill us if we're not careful. But it's possible."

"What about the Marshals?" Ghost asked. "They'll try to stop us."

"Let them try," Leo said. "We're not breaking the Truce. We're fixing it. Finding a third option. Building something better than sacrifice."

His phone buzzed. A message from Vance.

I'm waiting for your answer, Leo. Don't make me wait too long.

Leo deleted it. Pocketed the phone. "Let's go tell Ryles," he said. "We have a heist to plan." They headed toward Salvage Street together. Four kids who'd met days ago. Four talents that somehow complemented each other perfectly. Four broken pieces that fit together into something stronger than any of them alone.

Behind them, the Conformity Council building loomed. Inside, Director Vance watched from her window. Watched them leave. Watched them choose defiance over safety. She picked up her phone. Made a call.

"They refused," she said. "Mobilize the team. We move tonight. If they reach the Sanctum first..." She paused. Looked at the photo of Catherine on her desk. "Do whatever it takes to stop them. The anchors must be replaced. Reality depends on it."

She hung up. Looked out at the grey city. "I'm sorry, Leo," she whispered. "But I can't let you save one girl and doom everyone else. Even if it means becoming the villain of your story."

She pressed a button on her desk. On screens across New Portside, her face appeared. Another press conference. Another warning about imagination extremists. But this time, she had photos. Of Leo. Of his team. Of Ryles' shop.

"These individuals are wanted for questioning regarding the structural failures," Vance's voice echoed through every screen, every transit station, every building. "They are considered dangerous. Armed with illegal dream manipulation abilities. Do not approach. Report any sightings immediately."

In the alley near Salvage Street, Leo's phone exploded with notifications. News alerts. Wanted posters. His face everywhere. "We're fugitives now," Trixie said quietly.

"Good," Leo replied. "Means we're doing something right." They disappeared into Ryles' shop. And across the city, Enforcers mobilized. Vance's black-ops team prepared their gear. The Marshals sensed the coming conflict and began gathering in the deep zones.

The race to the Sanctum had begun. And only one team could reach it first.

[END OF CHAPTER 8]

Chapter 9: Preparation

Ryles' shop had transformed into a war room. Maps covered every surface. Not regular maps. Dream maps. Sketches of zones that defied geometry, landscapes that changed based on who viewed them, routes that led everywhere and nowhere simultaneously. Leo's father's journal lay open on the counter, its pages marked with notes in multiple handwritings spanning years.

The team is assembling, Trixie arrived last, slipping through shadows like she was made of them. "Sorry I'm late," she said, not sounding sorry at all. "Had to wait for my parents to fall asleep."

"Enforcer parents must be tough," Yuki said carefully.

"You have no idea." Trixie pulled out Dream Candy, chewed aggressively. "Dinner tonight was a lecture on 'maintaining vigilance against creative deviance.' My mother actually said that. With a straight face. While eating grey protein paste and discussing how many citizens she cited for humming." She laughed, but it sounded wrong.

"Then my dad asked if I'd made any friends at school. And I said yes. And he said: 'Remember, friendship is temporary. Conformity is eternal.' Like that's normal. Like that's how families talk."

Ghost shifted uncomfortably. "That sounds—"

"Awful? Yeah." Trixie's smile didn't reach her eyes. "So I smiled. Nodded. Ate my grey food. Went to my grey room. And the second they went to sleep, I went to the Reverie. Found the brightest, loudest, most colorful zone I could. Just to remember what it's like to FEEL something."

She looked at the team. "That's why I do this. Not for the smuggling money. Not for the thrill. But because somewhere, in some dream, my parents used to be human. And maybe if I can bring enough color back to this world, they'll remember how to be human again."

Silence fell. "Okay," Trixie said briskly, "emotional moment over. Let's go steal some impossible things." But Leo understood her now. Really understood.

The team stood around the central table. Leo, Trixie, Ghost, and Yuki. Four kids about to attempt something that had killed experienced Grippers. Four kids who'd met less than a week ago and now had to trust each other with their lives. "This is insane," Ghost said quietly. He wasn't wrong.

"Insanity is our specialty," Trixie replied, though her usual bravado felt forced. She'd been subdued since the incident with Ghost's nightmare. Guilty. Uncertain. It looked wrong on her.

Ryles spread out the main map. "The route to the Sanctum goes through seven major zones. Some you've been to. Most you haven't." He traced a path with his finger. "Start shallow at the Candy Coast. Stock up, get your bearings. Then deeper into the Toy Box Dimension. That's where it gets dangerous."

"Define dangerous," Yuki said.

"The Toy Box wants you to stay. Forever. It'll show you everything you ever wanted and make you forget why you came." Ryles' eyes shifted colors rapidly. "Kids get trapped there all the time. Lost Children, we call them. Stuck in eternal play. Conscious but unable to wake."

"How do we avoid that?" Leo asked.

"Don't touch anything you don't need. Don't listen to anything that sounds like home. Don't believe any version of reality that's too perfect." Ryles moved his finger along the map. "After the Toy Box comes the Mirror Maze. Then the Clockwork City. Then the Nightmare Trench begins. Three zones of pure fear. Drowned District. Bone Orchard. The Fracture Field. Survive those, and you reach the Sanctum."

"How long?" Leo asked. His stomach was already sinking. "How long does the journey take?"

Ryles' expression was grim. "That's the part most people don't understand about deep diving. The shallow zones—Candy Coast, even the Toy Box—you can visit those in a normal night's sleep. Eight, maybe ten hours, and you wake up fine."

He tapped the deeper zones on the map. "But the Sanctum is beyond the threshold. Past the point where your body can sustain you on a normal sleep cycle. To reach it, you need sustained REM state. Continuous. Uninterrupted."

"How continuous?" Yuki asked.

"Seven days minimum," Ryles said flatly. "You'll enter synchronized sleep and your bodies will remain in that state for a full week. Maybe longer if you encounter delays. Your consciousness will travel through the Reverie while your bodies stay here, maintained in deep sleep."

Leo felt cold. "A week? We'll be unconscious for a week?"

"At minimum. Could be eight or nine days if the zones trap you." Ryles looked at each of them. "This isn't a quick dream. This is committing your bodies to a coma-like state while your minds journey through hell. I'll monitor you, provide hydration through IV, keep you alive. But you'll be completely vulnerable."

"We've already used six days preparing," Ghost said quietly. "If the journey takes seven more..."

"You make the deadline with maybe a day to spare," Ryles finished. "Assuming nothing goes wrong. Assuming I can keep you safe while you're unconscious. Assuming the government doesn't find this shop. Assuming your bodies can survive a week of continuous sleep."

"And if something goes wrong?" Trixie asked.

"Then you die in your sleep," Ryles said. "Or you wake up after the deadline has passed and Lily's already gone. Or the authorities find you mid-dive and pull you out, which would trap your consciousness in the Reverie permanently." The weight of it pressed down on them. Not just the journey. But seven days of vulnerability. Seven days of lying helpless while their minds fought through nightmare zones.

"This is why so few attempt it," Ryles said. "It's not just dangerous in the Reverie. It's dangerous here. Your bodies are targets. Your mother, Leo—she could walk in and find you comatose. The government could raid. Marshals could attack. You'll be defenseless."

"Can you protect us?" Leo asked.

"I'll do my best," Ryles said. "I've got wards on this place. Protections. But for seven days straight?" He shook his head. "That's a long time to hide four unconscious kids."

"We don't have a choice," Yuki said firmly. "If we don't go, Lily dies. If we go and get caught, we might die. But at least we tried."

"At least we tried," Ghost echoed. Leo looked at his team. At three people who were willing to risk a week-long coma to save his sister. Who were willing to trust Ryles to keep their bodies alive while their minds traveled through hell.

"When do we start?" Leo asked.

"Tonight," Ryles said. "Because every day we wait is one less day of margin for error."

"Simple," Trixie muttered.

"You'll need gear," Ryles said. He pulled out the duffel bag from earlier and began extracting items. Each one glowed faintly, impossible light bleeding from dream-matter forced into reality. "Breathing apparatus for underwater zones. Time manipulation devices for the Clockwork City. Protective wards that'll slow the Marshals. Dream Candy for focus. And this."

He held up a crystal. About the size of a fist. It pulsed with rhythmic light. Like a heartbeat. "Linked Sleep Device," Ryles explained. "Keeps your REM cycles synchronized even in deep zones. Without it, you'll drift apart. Get lost. Never find each other again."

Leo took the crystal. It was warm. Alive, somehow. "How does it work?"

"Each of you holds it before sleeping. The crystal imprints your consciousness signature. Then it acts as an anchor, pulling you into the same dream space no matter how deep you go." Ryles' expression darkened. "But there's a cost. Linked Sleep means linked fate. If one of you dies in the Reverie, the others feel it. If one of you gets trapped, you're all pulled toward the same trap. You succeed together or fail together. No middle ground."

Silence fell over the shop. Leo wanted to back out. Text Ryles some excuse. Pretend he was sick. Let them go without him.

But that was the coward option. And Leo wasn't a coward. (He was definitely a coward. But he was going anyway.) "I'm in," Leo said immediately.

"Me too," Yuki said.

Ghost nodded. "Better together than alone." They all looked at Trixie. She'd been quiet. Unusually so. Now she looked at Ghost with an expression Leo had never seen on her face before. Shame. Real, genuine shame.

"Before we do this," Trixie said quietly, "I need to say something." Ghost tensed. His edges flickered.

"I'm sorry," Trixie continued. She wasn't looking at anyone now. Just at her hands. "For what I said earlier. About your nightmares. About your father. I had no right to take those things from your head and just... announce them like they didn't matter. Like they were just information instead of pain."

She took a shaky breath. "I'm an Infiltrator. I see things. I can't help what I see. But I can help what I do with it. And I weaponized your trauma because I thought being clever was more important than being kind. That was wrong. Really, really wrong."

Ghost said nothing. "I don't expect you to forgive me," Trixie said. "But I need you to know: I'll do better. I'll ask before I share. I'll respect your privacy even when I know your secrets. Because..." Her voice cracked. "Because knowing everything about someone doesn't mean I understand anything about them. And I want to understand. I want to be your friend, not your surveillance."

The shop was silent except for the humming of impossible objects on the shelves. Finally, Ghost spoke. "It's okay." Trixie looked up, surprised.

"Just... ask next time?" Ghost said. A small smile. "And maybe don't lead with the traumatic stuff. Work up to it. Give a guy some warning."

Trixie laughed. It sounded wet. "Yeah. I can do that."

"Good." Ghost extended his hand. "Friends?"

"Friends," Trixie agreed, shaking it. Yuki smiled. Leo felt something tight in his chest loosen.

"Now that we've had our feelings," Ryles said, breaking the moment, "let's talk about what you're smuggling." He gestured to a collection of items on the counter. Things that shouldn't exist. A rope made of frozen time. Boots that let you walk on air. A compass that pointed toward whatever you needed most. A knife that cut through dreams themselves.

"Each of you takes what matches your skills," Ryles instructed. "Leo, you get the Architect's Chalk. Lets you draw structures that become real, even in zones where building is restricted. Trixie, the Infiltrator's Mask. Hides your consciousness signature so you can slip between dreams undetected. Ghost, the Phantom Cloak. Enhances your phasing, lets you exist partially in multiple realities simultaneously. Yuki, the Mender's Kit. Flowers that heal anything, even wounds that shouldn't be healable."

He pulled out one more item. A journal identical to Leo's father's, but empty. Blank pages waiting to be filled. "And this is for all of you. Document everything. Draw maps. Write notes. If you succeed, this becomes the guide for the next generation. If you fail..." Ryles didn't finish. "Just write it down. Make sure someone knows what you tried to do."

Leo took the journal. It was heavy. Not physically. Emotionally. The weight of responsibility.

"We'll need to smuggle all this gear," Yuki said. "Each smuggle will cause Glitches. The city's already unstable."

"Can't be helped," Ryles said. "You need the equipment to survive. The alternative is going in unprotected and dying in the first nightmare zone."

"What about the people here?" Ghost asked. "The ones who'll lose things when we smuggle?"

"They'll survive. Reality's resilient. Humans adapt. They'll wake up tomorrow missing memories or objects and they'll build new ones."

Ryles touched his missing arm. 'My wife was a Mender. Best one I ever knew. She died holding the boundary during the Great Nightmare. Burned herself out keeping reality stable.' His voice went flat. 'So yeah. I know what sacrifice looks like. That's the price. That's always been the price. The question is: Are you willing to pay it to save one girl?"

Leo thought about his father. About the journal entries. About the decision to become an Eternal Sleeper to save the world. "It's not just about saving Lily," Leo said. "It's about fixing the system. Waking all the Sleepers. Making sure nobody else has to make this choice."

"Noble," Ryles said. "But you still have to smuggle the gear. Still have to take from others to save your sister. How's that different from what Vance is doing?" The question hit like a punch.

"Because we're trying to fix things for everyone," Yuki said. "Not just for one person."

"Are you?" Ryles challenged. "Or are you telling yourselves that to justify the harm you're causing?" Nobody had an answer.

"I'm not saying don't do it," Ryles continued. "I'm saying be honest about it. You're causing damage. People will suffer because of your choices tonight. Own that. Don't hide behind noble intentions."

He was right. Leo knew he was right. They were about to smuggle equipment, trigger massive Glitches, hurt people who had nothing to do with their quest. All to save Lily. All to reach the Sanctum.

It was selfish. Necessary. Terrible. Just like everything else about Gripping. "I'll own it," Leo said quietly. "We all will. And when we fix the system, when we wake the Sleepers and stabilize reality permanently, maybe it'll be worth it. Maybe the people we hurt tonight will understand."

"Or maybe they'll hate you," Ryles said. "Either way, you'll have to live with it."

He handed each of them their assigned gear. "Smuggle these tonight. One at a time. Space them out by thirty minutes to minimize concentrated Glitches. Meet back here at midnight. Then we synchronize and dive."

They spread out across the shop. Found private corners. Prepared to sleep and pull impossibilities into reality. Leo held the Architect's Chalk. It was white. Pure. Like condensed possibility. He could feel its potential thrumming against his palm.

Before he tried to sleep, he pulled out his father's journal. Flipped to a page near the end. One entry he'd read multiple times but hadn't fully understood until now.

Every Grip is a theft. Every smuggle takes from someone else. There's no such thing as victimless dream manipulation. The universe demands balance. The question isn't whether you'll hurt people. The question is whether what you're trying to accomplish is worth the people you'll hurt along the way.

I don't know the answer to that question. I just know I have to try. Because my children deserve a world worth living in. Even if I'm not there to see it.

Leo closed the journal. Lay down on the floor. Closed his eyes. And pulled the chalk through. The pain was worse this time. Sharper. More insistent. The chalk fought him, didn't want to leave its dream-origin, resisted being forced into reality's rigid rules.

Leo held on. Gripped tighter. Felt the pulling sensation stretch from his hand to his arm to his chest to his entire body. Like reality itself was trying to yank him apart. Then the chalk was in his hand. Real. Solid. Glowing faintly white.

He opened his eyes. Sat up. Checked the wall clock. Outside, somewhere in New Portside, a building's foundation cracked. A family's photo album vanished from their shelf. Someone forgot their grandmother's name for three minutes before remembering again, confused and shaken.

The Glitch had taken payment. Leo looked at the chalk. At the tool that would help him save Lily. "Sorry," he whispered to the people he'd never meet. "I'm so sorry."

One by one, the others completed their smuggles. Trixie pulled through her mask. Ghost phased through his cloak. Yuki extracted her kit with trembling hands. Each time, the Glitches hit. Buildings shook. Streets cracked. Memories flickered. People woke from sleep screaming about things that weren't there anymore, holes in their lives they couldn't quite identify.

By the time they finished, New Portside looked like a city under siege. Emergency sirens wailed. Enforcer vehicles raced through streets. The news broadcasts showed buildings phasing between solid and transparent, reality destabilizing in real-time. "We did that," Ghost whispered, staring out the window.

"We had to," Yuki said. But she looked sick. Her hand pressed against her ribs. "The Glitches are hitting Scale 2 across the whole city. People are losing objects, memories, small things. But it's widespread. Thousands affected."

"Will they be okay?" Trixie asked.

"They'll survive," Yuki said. "But they'll be changed. Incomplete. Something will be missing they can't quite name." Leo thought about his dog tags. About the emotional attachment to his father he'd lost when the blue flower died. About living with holes you couldn't identify.

"We fix this," he said firmly. "We reach the Sanctum, wake the Sleepers, stabilize the boundary permanently. And then nobody else loses anything. That's the deal we're making. Present pain for future stability."

"That's what every tyrant says," Ryles observed from behind the counter. "Present sacrifice for future utopia."

"We're not tyrants," Leo said.

"Not yet." Ryles checked his watch. "It's eleven-thirty. You've got thirty minutes before midnight. Use it to prepare mentally. Because once you take that synchronized sleep aid, there's no backing out. You're committed. Linked. One team, one fate."

Leo looked at his crew. At Trixie, who knew too much and was learning to use it kindly. At Ghost, who was learning to exist visibly. At Yuki, who sacrificed herself for others without thinking. "There's something I need to tell you," Leo said. "Before we do this. Something about the accident. About why Lily ran into traffic."

They turned to him. Waiting. Leo took a breath. Let himself remember. Let himself feel the guilt he'd been carrying for six months.

"She'd hidden art supplies in her room," he said quietly. "Paint. Canvas. Brushes. All illegal under Conformity Laws. When I found them, I lost it. Started yelling about arrests, about consequences, about how she never thought before she acted."

His hands clenched. "I got angry. Frustrated.

I said: 'Why don't you think before you act? Why can't you just trust that I know what's best for you?' And she looked at me with this expression. Like I'd slapped her. And she said: 'You don't want a sister. You want a puppet.'"

The memory burned. "Then she grabbed the supplies and ran. Just ran. Out of the apartment, down the stairs, into the street. I chased her. Still yelling. Still trying to control her.

The car came so fast. The sound—"

His voice broke. "I did that. My need to control everything, to keep her safe by making all her decisions, I pushed her into traffic. I killed her."

"You didn't kill her," Yuki said firmly. "The car hit her. That's not the same thing."

"But if I hadn't—"

"If you hadn't, something else might have happened. You don't control the universe, Leo. You never did. You were just a scared kid trying to protect his sister the only way he knew how." Yuki's expression was gentle. "Your father died trying to control the outcome. Save the world by himself. Vance is trying to control everything to save her daughter. You see the pattern? The Finch family martyr complex isn't about love. It's about fear. Fear of losing control. Fear of trusting others."

"That's why we're here," Trixie added. "To break that pattern. You're not doing this alone. You're doing it with us. And when we reach Lily, you're not going to rescue her like some helpless princess. You're going to ask her what she wants. Let her choose. Even if her choice hurts."

"What if she chooses to stay?" Leo whispered. "What if she's happy as an Eternal Sleeper? What if she doesn't want to come home?"

"Then we respect that," Ghost said. "And we find another way. Build a system where she can rotate out. Where nobody's trapped forever. Where everyone has agency." He smiled slightly. "That's what friends do. They respect each other's choices even when they hurt."

Leo's eyes burned. He nodded. Couldn't speak. "Group hug?" Trixie suggested. "Is this a group hug moment? I feel like this is—"

Yuki pulled them all together. Arms wrapped around each other. Four kids who barely knew each other but understood each other better than most people ever would. "Everyone comes home," Yuki said into the group embrace. "No matter what. That's the pact."

"Everyone comes home," they repeated together. Ryles watched from behind the counter. His eyes were wet. His remaining hand clenched.

"You remind me of your father," he said to Leo. "But you're better. Smarter. You've got something he never had."

"What's that?"

"A team willing to call you on your bullshit." Ryles smiled. "He would've been proud of you. Terrified. But proud." He pulled out four small vials from under the counter. Grey liquid. Synchronized sleep aid.

"Last chance to back out," Ryles said. "Once you drink this, you're committed. The Linked Sleep Device will bind you together. You'll feel each other's fear. Share each other's pain. If one of you breaks, you all break."

"We're not breaking," Leo said. He took a vial. The others followed suit.

"One more thing," Ryles said. His voice dropped. Became heavy. "The raids yesterday. The ones that caught Mr. Chen and the others. That was because of me."

They froze. "What?" Trixie breathed.

"The government's had leverage on me since the Great Nightmare," Ryles admitted. "They know things I did. Things I'm not proud of. They use it to make me feed them information. Names. Locations. Who's Gripping where." His hand trembled. "I've been their informant for twelve years. That's how they knew about you. That's how Vance found your team so quickly."

"You've been spying on us?" Ghost's edges flickered. "Reporting us?"

"Not you specifically. Not at first. But when you started smuggling, when the Glitches became obvious, they pressured me. Said they'd expose me if I didn't help them track you down." Ryles looked at each of them. "I gave them enough to keep them satisfied. Not enough to actually catch you. But I've been walking that line. And yesterday, it cost people their freedom."

"Why are you telling us now?" Yuki asked.

"Because you deserve to know who you're trusting. And because I'm done." Ryles straightened. "After tonight, I'm leaving. Disappearing. They can expose me all they want. I won't help them hunt kids anymore."

"They'll come after you," Leo said.

"Let them." Ryles smiled. "I've been running from consequences for twelve years. Time to face them." Silence fell. The shop's strange objects hummed. Outside, sirens wailed.

"Thank you," Leo said finally. "For telling us. For helping us anyway. For—"

"Don't." Ryles held up his hand. "Don't thank me for doing the bare minimum. I betrayed people. I'm complicit in their capture. The best I can do now is help you succeed so it means something." He gestured to the vials. "Drink. Go save your sister. Fix the broken system. Make my betrayal worth it."

They drank together. The liquid tasted like nothing. Like grey. Within seconds, drowsiness hit. Heavy. Irresistible. They helped each other to the back room, to the Linked Sleep Array Ryles had prepared—a circle of chalk and strange symbols, four sleeping bags arranged in a cross pattern, the crystal device at the center.

They lay down. Held hands. Each person's right hand in the next person's left, forming an unbroken circle with the crystal pulsing in the middle. "Remember the route," Ryles said from the doorway. "Candy Coast. Toy Box. Mirror Maze. Clockwork City. Nightmare Trench. Sanctum. Seven zones. Seven trials. And at the end..." He paused. "At the end, you'll find your sister. And you'll have to choose what kind of person you want to be. Controller or collaborator. Martyr or builder."

"We choose builder," Leo mumbled. Sleep was pulling him down. Hard. "We choose team."

"Good," Ryles said. His voice seemed to come from very far away. "Then maybe you'll succeed where we failed. Maybe you'll build something that lasts." The world faded. The white noise generator's hum became distant. The shop's strange light dimmed.

Leo's last conscious thought was: We're coming, Lily. Hold on. Then he fell into synchronized sleep. And the real heist began.

[END OF CHAPTER 9]

Chapter 10: The Candy Coast

They wake in sugar. That's the first sensation. Not the hardness of Ryles' floor. Not the cold of reality. Sugar. Granulated, white, soft against Leo's back.

He opens his eyes. The sky is impossibly blue. Not grey-blue. Not washed-out. Pure azure, the color of dreams and childhood summers that never existed in New Portside. The sun hangs overhead, golden and warm, not filtered through perpetual clouds.

And the beach— Leo sits up. His hands sink into sugar sand. He tastes it. Sweet. Actually sweet. He hasn't tasted real sugar in years. The Grey only serves synthetic substitutes.

"Holy..." Trixie's voice beside him. They're all here. All four of them. Sitting on a beach made of crystallized sugar, staring at an ocean that fizzes and bubbles like soda. The waves crash in slow motion, carbonation spraying into the air with each impact.

"We're here," Ghost breathes. He's more solid here than in reality. His edges don't flicker. He looks real. Present. Like he's finally allowing himself to fully exist.

"Together," Yuki adds. She checks her kit—still there, strapped to her side. Real in the way dreams pretend to be real. Leo stands. The sugar shifts under his feet. He looks down the beach and sees palm trees. But these trees aren't normal. Their trunks are peppermint sticks, red and white spiraling upward. Their leaves are mint candies that rustle in the breeze, creating a sound like wind chimes.

"The Candy Coast," he says. "We made it."

"It's beautiful," Trixie says. She sounds awed. Vulnerable. "I've been here before in solo dives, but seeing it with you guys... it's different. Better."

Ghost walks to the water's edge. Dips his hand in. The carbonated ocean tickles his fingers. He laughs. Actually laughs. The sound is startling and wonderful.

"I forgot what wonder felt like," he says quietly. "The Wellness Center tried to erase it. Make everything grey and flat and manageable. But this..." He spreads his arms. "This is what they were trying to kill. This feeling."

Yuki kneels and scoops up a handful of sugar. Lets it run through her fingers. "In the real world, we're not allowed to feel this. To experience beauty without purpose. Everything has to be functional, regulated, approved." She looks at them. "But here, we can be ourselves. Fully. Without apologizing."

Leo understands. In reality, they're fugitives. Hunted. Broken. But here, in this impossible place, they're free.

For just a moment, he lets himself feel it. The sun on his face. The sweet smell of candy in the air. The sound of his friends laughing. Then he remembers why they're here.

"We need supplies," he says. "Dad's journal says the deeper zones are hostile. We'll need food, water, defensive items. The Candy Coast is relatively safe, so we stock up here."

"Always the planner," Trixie teases, but there's affection in it. "Can't we enjoy it for five minutes?"

"We can enjoy it while we work," Leo says. "Come on. The journal mentioned Dream Candy grows in the inland groves. We'll need a lot of it for focus in the deep zones."
They walk along the beach. The sugar crunches under their feet. Above them, candy-birds fly—creatures made of spun sugar and food coloring, chirping melodies that taste like nostalgia.

The inland groves are stranger. Trees made of chocolate. Bushes of gumdrops. Flowers that bloom in flavors—strawberry, lemon, mint, flavors that don't have names but taste like specific memories. Happy birthday parties. First kisses. Summer afternoons.

And hanging from the tallest tree, glowing golden against the chocolate bark: Dream Candy. "There," Leo points. But the tree is tall. Twenty feet at least. And the trunk is smooth chocolate, impossible to climb.

"I got this," Leo says. He pulls out the Architect's Chalk. The others watch as he draws on the air itself. White lines appearing in empty space. The lines become real. Solid. A spiral staircase made of compressed light, wrapping around the tree trunk, leading upward to the golden candies.

"Show-off," Trixie grins. They climb. The stairs hold their weight perfectly. Dream-logic made structural. At the top, Leo reaches for the candy.

His fingers close around one. It pulses with warmth. Alive, somehow. Like it contains concentrated awareness. "How many do we need?" Ghost asks.

"At least twenty," Leo says. "Maybe more if—" The tree shakes. Not from wind. From something large moving beneath them. Through the chocolate trunk. Something that shouldn't be possible but is.

"Um," Yuki says. "What was that?" The tree shakes again. Harder. Leo's stairs tremble. Cracks appear in the light-structure.

Then the tree splits open. A creature emerges. Massive. Made entirely of pink and white taffy, stretched and twisted into a vaguely humanoid shape. It has no face. No features. Just a mass of candy-flesh that moves with terrible purpose.

"Sugar Golem," Trixie breathes. "We need to go. NOW." They scramble down the stairs. The Golem reaches for them with taffy arms that stretch impossibly long. One arm wraps around Ghost's ankle.

He phases. His foot becomes transparent, slips through the Golem's grip. "Keep moving!" They hit the ground running. Behind them, the Golem pulls itself fully from the tree. It's at least twelve feet tall. Its taffy body ripples and flows, adapting, pursuing.

"Split up!" Leo shouts. "Confuse it!" They scatter. Leo runs left, toward a grove of lollipop trees. Trixie goes right, into a field of gumdrops. Ghost and Yuki head for the beach.

The Golem hesitates. Can't track multiple targets. Then it splits. Its taffy body divides down the middle, becoming two smaller Golems. They pursue separately. One after Leo and Trixie. One after Ghost and Yuki.

"That's new!" Trixie yells. "They didn't used to do that!"

"Adapt!" Leo calls back. "Trixie, can you steal its core?"

"What core?"

"Every dream-construct has a central point! Something that keeps it cohesive! Find it and take it!" Trixie's eyes go distant. She activates her Infiltrator ability, slipping partially into the Golem's consciousness. Seeing through its eyes. Feeling its structure.

"There!" she points. "In its chest! A candy heart!"

"Ghost!" Leo yells across the beach. "Buy us time!" Ghost understands immediately. He phases completely. Becomes transparent. Then runs straight at his Golem. Passes through it like it's smoke. The creature stumbles, confused. Its taffy body wobbles.

Leo draws with the Architect's Chalk. Fast. Desperate. Lines in the air becoming walls. A barrier between the

Golems and the team. The walls solidify. Sugar compressed into crystal, hard and sharp.

The Golems crash into the walls. Stop. Confused. "Now!" Leo shouts. Trixie closes her eyes. Concentrates. Her Infiltrator power isn't just for minds. It's for anything with structure. Anything with a core.

She reaches into the dream-space. Finds the candy hearts holding the Golems together. And steals them. The sensation is bizarre. Like pulling taffy through her own chest. Painful but possible. She yanks hard.

Two candy hearts pop into her hands. Glowing red. Pulsing. The Golems collapse. Just fall apart. Taffy melting back into formless candy, soaking into the sugar sand.

"Incredible!" Ghost breathes. "That worked."

"Of course it worked," Trixie says, though she's shaking. "I'm amazing."

"You are," Yuki agrees. She's checking everyone for injuries. "Everyone okay? Any wounds?"

"I'm fine," Leo says. His heart pounds. "That was—"

"Incredible?" Trixie suggests.

"Terrifying," Leo finishes. "But yeah. We worked together. We actually worked." They're grinning at each other. Flushed with adrenaline and success. They just defeated dream-constructs through coordination. Through trusting each other.

Then Yuki gasps. Clutches her chest. "What's wrong?" Leo asks.

"Something's wrong with the Coast," she whispers. "It's melting. Destabilizing. Not from us. From someone else. Someone big."

Leo looks around. She's right. The chocolate trees are softening. The sugar sand is becoming slush. The soda ocean is losing its carbonation, going flat.

"Someone else is here," Yuki continues. "Smuggling. Heavily. Taking so much that the zone itself is collapsing."

"Vance," Leo realizes. "Her team is here. They're ahead of us." A sound in the distance. Whistles. Sharp, piercing, wrong. The sound of order being imposed on chaos.

"Marshals," Ghost says. His edges flicker with fear. They appear on the horizon. Not just one or two. Dozens. Marshal Bailiffs, moving in coordinated groups. Grey figures in perfect formation. Hunting.

"They're tracking the Glitches," Trixie says. "Following the signatures. Both ours and Vance's."

"We need to leave," Leo says. "Get deeper. Now." But before they can move, the sky tears. Not metaphorically. Actually tears. A rip in the blue expanse. Something pushes through from the other side. Something dark. Writhing. Wrong.

A rogue nightmare. It spills into the Candy Coast like oil into water. A creature made of shadow and teeth and fear. It's not supposed to be here. This is a shallow zone. Safe. But someone's smuggling has weakened the barriers. Let things through that shouldn't cross.

The nightmare screams. It's the sound of every bad dream compressed into one voice. "RUN!" Leo shouts. They sprint for the water. The nightmare chases. It moves fast. Too fast. Faster than dream-logic should allow.

Leo builds walls. They shatter. Trixie tries to infiltrate its mind. There's nothing there. Just hunger. Just void. Ghost phases. The nightmare's shadow-tendrils pass right through his transparency, find him anyway, yank him back to solidity.

They're not going to make it. The nightmare looms. Opens a mouth full of teeth that look like broken reality. Prepares to consume them. Then something grey steps between them and the nightmare.

A Lucid Marshal. Tall. Faceless. Geometrically perfect. It raises one hand.

The nightmare stops. Actually stops. Frozen mid-lunge. The Marshal's voice presses into their minds. Not words. Concepts.

UNAUTHORIZED BREACH. RETURN.

The nightmare resists. Writhes. Tries to push past. The Marshal doesn't move. Just exists. And its existence is law. Order. Structure. The nightmare is chaos. They cannot coexist.

Slowly, the nightmare begins to unravel. Its shadow-flesh dissolving. Its teeth breaking apart. The scream fading to silence. In seconds, it's gone. Erased. Sent back to whatever deep zone it came from.

The Marshal turns to face them. Leo's blood freezes. They're about to die. The Marshal saved them from the nightmare just to kill them itself. But the Marshal's voice is different this time.

CONTINUE. CAREFULLY. THE BOUNDARY WEAKENS. ALL WHO STABILIZE ARE PERMITTED. GO.

Then it's gone. Just phases away. Back to whatever patrol route it was following. The team stands in stunned silence. "It let us go," Ghost whispers.

"It saved us," Yuki adds.

"The Marshals aren't evil," Leo realizes. "They're just trying to stop reality from collapsing. Just like us."

"But they'll still kill us if we break the Truce," Trixie points out.

"Then we don't break it," Leo says. "We fix it. We show them there's a better way."

Yuki winces again. "We need to move. Now. Vance's team is pulling so much through that the Coast is becoming unstable. If we stay here—"

"We get caught in the collapse," Leo finishes. "Everyone, to the water. We dive deep. Next zone." They run for the beach. The soda ocean is churning now. Unstable. Things move beneath the surface. Shapes that shouldn't exist in a candy-themed zone. Darker things. Deeper things.

"Here!" Trixie points. A whirlpool. Spinning slowly. The water drains down into somewhere else. Another zone. Deeper. More dangerous.

"That's our way forward," Leo says. "Everyone ready?"

"No," Ghost admits. "But let's go anyway." They hold hands. Form a chain. Leo at the front. Trixie, Ghost, Yuki behind him.

"Everyone comes home," Leo says.

"Everyone comes home," they repeat. Then they jump. The whirlpool catches them. Pulls them down. The candy-sweetness of the Coast gives way to something else. Something older. Darker. More primal.

Leo's last view of the Candy Coast shows Marshal Bailiffs arriving in force. Dozens of them. Surrounding something in the distance. Other Grippers. Vance's team.

A battle is starting. Then the water closes over their heads. The whirlpool spins faster. And they fall through layers of sleep. Through REM. Through deep dream. Into zones where childhood memories reign supreme.

Into the Toy Box Dimension. Where the Lost Children wait. And one of them looks exactly like Ghost.

[END OF CHAPTER 10]

Chapter 11: The Toy Box

The whirlpool spits them out. They land hard on something soft. Carpeted. Leo opens his eyes and sees stars. Not real stars. Glow-in-the-dark stickers on a ceiling impossibly far above. The kind that covered his bedroom ceiling when he was six, before the Conformity Laws, before stickers were considered frivolous and removed.

He sits up. Looks around. They're in a child's bedroom. But wrong. The bed is mountain-sized. The dresser towers like a skyscraper. Everything is scaled up, enlarged, from a kid's perspective where furniture is furniture but also mountain ranges to climb.

"Where are we?" Trixie asks.

"The Toy Box Dimension," Leo says. He remembers his father's warnings. "Everything here is from childhood. Toys. Games. Play. It's supposed to be wonderful."

"Supposed to be?" Ghost asks.

"It's also a trap." Leo stands. "This zone wants you to stay. Forever. Playing. Never growing up. Never leaving. It feeds on nostalgia and comfort."

Yuki checks her kit. "How do we avoid getting trapped?"

"We don't touch anything we don't absolutely need. We don't play with anything. We remember why we're here." Leo pulls out his father's journal, flips to the Toy Box section. "Dad wrote: 'The Toy Box offers perfect happiness. That's why it's so dangerous. Who wants to leave when everything you ever wanted is right here?'"

They climb down from the bed. The journey takes minutes—the bed is that huge. At the bottom, they find themselves in a landscape of toys. Building blocks the size of cars. A toy train track that winds through valleys made of stuffed animals. Action figures as tall as humans, frozen in heroic poses. Board games with pieces they could hide inside. Marbles like boulders. Crayons like logs.

And everywhere, the feeling of joy. Simple, pure, childlike joy. The kind that existed before responsibilities, before fear, before the Grey took over everything. "This is incredible," Ghost breathes. He's staring at a robot toy. "I had one of these. Before the Wellness Center. Before Father took it away for being 'unnecessary stimulation.'" He reaches for it.

"Don't," Leo warns. "Remember. Don't touch unless—"

"I'm just looking," Ghost says. But his hand hovers near the robot. Trembling. Wanting. They walk through the toy landscape. It's beautiful. Magical. Everything a child could want. But there's something wrong underneath. A wrongness Leo can't quite identify.

Then he sees them. Children. Dozens of them. Maybe hundreds. Playing in the distance. Building with blocks. Racing toy cars. Laughing.

But they don't age. Don't change. They just play. Eternally. "The Lost Children," Yuki whispers.

Leo approaches one. A girl, maybe eight. She's playing with dolls. Setting up an elaborate tea party. "Hi," Leo says gently.

The girl looks up. Smiles. "Hi! Want to play?"

"What's your name?"

"Sarah. Do you want to be the princess or the knight?"

"Sarah, how long have you been here?"

The girl blinks. Confused. "Here? I don't know. Forever? Does it matter? Look!" She holds up a doll. "She has a real dress! And shoes! Everything's perfect here!"

"Don't you want to go home?" Leo asks.

"Why would I leave? Everything I want is here." Sarah's smile doesn't waver. "You should stay too. It's nice. You'll like it."

Leo backs away slowly. His chest is tight. These kids are trapped. Conscious but unable to leave. Unable to even want to leave because the zone has convinced them this is all they need.

"We need to move," he says to his team. "Before—"

"MARCUS!" The shout comes from deeper in the Toy Box. A man's voice. Familiar.

Ghost freezes. His edges flicker transparent. "No. No, that's not—"

"Marcus, come here! I want to show you something!"

"That's my father's voice," Ghost whispers. "But it can't be. He doesn't know I'm here. He doesn't—"

"It's the zone," Trixie says quickly. "It's showing you what you want most. Don't listen. Don't—" But Ghost is already walking. Drawn. Pulled toward the voice like a string is attached to his chest.

"Ghost!" Leo calls. "Marcus! Stop!" Ghost doesn't stop. They chase him through the toy landscape. Around corners made of building blocks. Past forests of action figures. Through valleys of stuffed animals.

They find him standing in a clearing. And in that clearing, a simulation. A house. A normal house. Not the mansion in the capital where Director Harlow lives. A simple home. Warm. Inviting. Lights in the windows. Laughter inside.

And standing in the doorway, a man. Older. Distinguished. But his expression is wrong. All wrong. It's soft. Kind. Loving.

"Marcus," the simulation says. "There you are. I've been looking for you."

"Dad?" Ghost's voice breaks.

"I'm so sorry," the simulation continues. It steps forward. Opens its arms. "I'm sorry for everything. For making you feel invisible. For praising you only when you were quiet. For sending you to that horrible place. I was wrong. So wrong. Can you forgive me?"

Ghost is crying. "You never apologize. You never—"

"I should have. I love you, son. Not because you're quiet. Not because you're obedient. Just because you're you. Come inside. Let me make it up to you. We'll play games. We'll laugh. I'll listen to your terrible puns. Everything will be perfect."

Ghost takes a step forward. "No!" Trixie grabs his arm. "It's not real! That's not your father!"

"But what if it could be?" Ghost whispers. "What if I stayed here? What if I had the father I always wanted? The family that loved me for existing, not for disappearing?"

"It's fake," Leo says. He's beside Ghost now. "It's the zone feeding you what you want most. But it's not real. Your real father is still out there, still believing quiet children are good children. And you have to face that. Deal with that. Not hide in a fantasy."

"Why?" Ghost asks. Tears stream down his face. "Why do I have to face pain when happiness is right here?"

"Because you're real," Yuki says gently. She's on Ghost's other side. "And real people deserve real relationships. Not simulations. Not fantasies. Real, messy, complicated love from people who choose to love you back."

"I don't have that," Ghost says.

"You have us," Trixie says firmly. "We're real. We see you. The whole you. Not the invisible version. The real Marcus who makes terrible puns and phases through walls and is brave even when he's terrified. We love that person. The real one."

Ghost looks at her. At all of them. Then back at the simulation. The house is so inviting. The father so perfect. Everything he ever wanted.

"I'm sorry," he whispers to the simulation. "But I choose real." He turns away.

The simulation doesn't stop. "Marcus, please. Don't go. I need you. I love you. Come back."

Ghost's edges flicker. Transparent. Almost disappearing. But he keeps walking. The team forms a barrier around him. Physical support. They guide him away from the clearing. Away from the perfect father who never existed.

Behind them, the simulation begins to dissolve. The house fades. The father's voice becomes echoes. Finally, silence. Ghost collapses. Just sits down hard on the toy-strewn ground and sobs.

They sit with him. Don't tell him to stop. Don't rush him. Just sit. Present. Real.

"I saw something else," Ghost says finally, through tears. "Before the simulation. A memory. Me as a little kid. Maybe five. Playing with toys. Laughing. And Father was there. The real Father. And he was smiling. Actually smiling. Because I was happy. Because I was myself."

He looks up. "That existed. Before he decided quiet was better than joyful. Before he started shaping me into something manageable. There was a time when he loved me for being loud."

"What happened?" Yuki asks gently.

"I don't know. The Wellness Center tried to erase those memories. I thought they succeeded. But seeing them here..." Ghost touches his chest. "They're still in me. The happy parts. The parts Father tried to kill. I can remember if I try."

"Then remember," Leo says. "Keep those parts. Don't let him erase you. Don't let anyone erase you."

Ghost nods. Wipes his eyes. "Okay. Okay. I'm done being invisible. I'm done disappearing. I'm Marcus. Marcus Harlow. I ran away because they tried to make me into nothing. But I'm something. I matter."

"You do," they say together. A sound behind them. Voices. Children's voices. The Lost Children have gathered. Dozens of them. Watching. Silent now. Their eternal play paused.

"You're leaving?" Sarah asks. The girl with the dolls.

"Yes," Leo says.

"Can you take us with you?" The question hangs in the air. Heavy. Impossible.

"I..." Leo looks at his team. "I don't know if we can. The Linked Sleep Device only works for four. If we try to add more—"

"We'll all get trapped," Trixie finishes quietly. "The crystal can't handle that many consciousness signatures."

"But we can't just leave them," Yuki says. She's looking at the children. At their frozen-perfect smiles that hide desperate longing. "They're trapped. We could—"

"Could what?" Leo asks. "Carry fifty kids through the Nightmare Trench? Navigate them through zones that'll kill adults? Risk our mission, Lily's life, the stability of reality itself to attempt a rescue we're not equipped for?"

"When you say it like that, it sounds heartless," Yuki says.

"It is heartless," Leo admits. "But it's also realistic. We can't save everyone. Not today. Not with what we have."

"So we just leave them?" Yuki's voice rises. "Tell them 'sorry, you're not important enough'?"

"We tell them we'll come back," Trixie suggests. "After we fix the anchor system. After we stabilize the boundary. We come back with resources, with a plan, and we save them properly."

"And if we fail?" Yuki asks. "If we die in the deep zones? Then they're abandoned forever." No one has an answer.

"I'll try," Yuki says suddenly. She walks toward Sarah. "I'll take one. Just one. Sarah, come here."

"Yuki, no," Leo warns.

But Yuki is already extending her hand. "Sarah, hold on. I'm going to try—" The moment Sarah touches Yuki's hand, the world shifts. Vines erupt from the ground. Not real vines. Toy vines. Made of plastic and bright colors. They wrap around Yuki's legs. Her waist. Her arms.

"No!" Yuki pulls. Tries to break free. Can't. "It's got me!" The Toy Box is fighting back. It doesn't want to let its children go. And it's punishing anyone who tries.

Ghost's edges flickered wildly as he tried to phase through the plastic coils, but they tightened with every second. "I can't slip them!" he choked out. "They're... they're too solid!" Leo's hand flew to the Architect's Chalk. He started to draw a massive steel cage to house the vines, a structure to contain the chaos. It was what he always did—he built boxes to keep things safe. But as the white lines appeared, the vines simply grew through them, shattering the light-structure like glass.

“Leo, stop!” Yuki screamed, pinned against the oversized building blocks. “You’re making it stronger! Every time you try to lock it down, it fights back!”

Leo froze. He looked at the vines, then at Yuki’s terrified face. He realized he was doing it again. He was trying to force the dream to obey his rules, just like he’d tried to force Lily to follow his "safe" routes. He dropped the chalk.

Instead of building, he reached out and touched the plastic vines with his bare hands. He didn't try to pull. He didn't try to break. He just let go of the "Architecture." He imagined the vines not as a threat to be managed, but as a fear to be acknowledged. He let his mind go soft, unravelling the rigid geometric structures he usually relied on.

"I'm not in charge," he whispered, a truth that felt like a physical weight lifting off his chest. "I can't fix everything." The vines didn't break; they simply lost interest. They turned back into harmless plastic toys, clattering to the ground. Leo draws with the chalk. Builds structures to push the vines back. They regrow instantly.

Trixie tries to infiltrate the zone's consciousness. Finds only one command: KEEP. KEEP EVERYTHING. KEEP FOREVER. The vines pull Yuki down. Toward the ground. Toward becoming part of the landscape. Part of the eternal play.

"Help me!" Yuki screams. They grab her arms. All three of them. Pull against the vines with everything they have.

"I can't help you," Sarah says quietly. She's backed away. Apologetic but accepting. "The Toy Box doesn't let go. Ever. You shouldn't have tried."

"LET HER GO!" Leo shouts at the zone itself. "She was trying to help you!" The zone doesn't respond. Just pulls harder. Leo makes a desperate decision. He builds something he's never built before. A structure of pure anti-matter. Not dream-stuff. The opposite. Void. Absence. Nothing made manifest.

The chalk burns in his hand. This shouldn't be possible. Architects build. They don't unbuild. But Leo unbuilds the vines.

They vanish. Simply cease existing. The zone screams—a sound like playground equipment rusting. Like childhood ending. Yuki falls free. They catch her. She's crying. Shaking.

"I'm sorry," she sobs. "I just wanted to help one. Just one."

"You tried," Trixie says. "That's more than most people would do." They look at the Lost Children. At Sarah, who's already returned to her dolls. Already forgotten the attempt. Already lost in play.

"We can't save them today," Leo says. His voice is heavy. "But we can save the system. Fix the boundary. Then come back for everyone. That's the promise. We save everyone or we save no one."

"Everyone or no one," they repeat. A new pact. They move through the Toy Box quickly now. Avoiding temptation. Avoiding the children. Focused.

They find what they need in a toy store zone. Hover-boards that actually work. Defensive tech disguised as superhero gadgets. Protection gear that looks like costumes but functions like armor. They smuggle carefully. Each item pulled through. Each one creating Glitches back in reality.

Leo feels it through the Linked Sleep Device. Feels reality tearing. A playground in New Portside's western district.

It's vanishing. Swings disappearing. Slide dissolving. The entire structure unmade to balance what they're taking.

Children playing there will find empty concrete tomorrow. Will wonder where their playground went. Will never get an answer. "I'm sorry," Leo whispers to people he'll never meet. "I'm so sorry."

They finish. Gather their new gear. Prepare to leave this zone. "There!" Ghost points. An exit. A doorway made of building blocks. It leads somewhere darker. Colder. Less innocent.

They head toward it. Behind them, the Lost Children return to play. Eternal. Trapped. Waiting for rescue that might never come.

The guilt is crushing. But they keep moving. They're almost at the doorway when she appears. A woman. Tall. Geometrically perfect. Faceless like all Marshals. But different. Her grey suit has patterns—mathematical equations flowing across the fabric. Constantly calculating. Constantly computing.

Justice Probability. Her voice presses into their minds. Not words. Pure mathematics. Future possibilities compressed into concept.

I'VE CALCULATED EVERY FUTURE. EXAMINED EVERY POSSIBLE OUTCOME. RUN THE NUMBERS INFINITE TIMES.

She tilts her head. Studying them.

YOU FAIL IN ALL OF THEM.

"That's not true," Leo says. His voice shakes but holds.

PROBABILITY DOESN'T LIE. YOU REACH THE SANCTUM. 0.003% CHANCE. YOU WAKE THE SLEEPERS SAFELY. 0.0001% CHANCE. YOU SURVIVE THE ATTEMPT. 0.00002% CHANCE. THE MATH IS CLEAR. YOU WILL FAIL.

REALITY WILL COLLAPSE. ALL BECAUSE FOUR CHILDREN THOUGHT THEY COULD CHANGE INEVITABILITY.

"We're going to try anyway," Trixie says.

WHY?

"Because math doesn't account for choice," Ghost says. "For will. For people deciding to do impossible things anyway."

CHOICE IS ILLUSION. WILL IS NEUROLOGY. NOTHING IS IMPOSSIBLE. EVERYTHING IS MERELY IMPROBABLE.

"Then we'll be improbable," Yuki says. Justice Probability laughs. It's not a human sound. It's the sound of equations solving themselves. Of certainty.

PROCEED. ATTEMPT YOUR IMPOSSIBLE TASK. I WILL FOLLOW. I WILL DOCUMENT YOUR FAILURE. AND WHEN YOU COLLAPSE, WHEN REALITY UNRAVELS AROUND YOUR HUBRIS, I WILL SAY: THE MATH PREDICTED THIS.

Then she's gone. Phased away. But Leo feels her. Watching. Calculating. Following them through every zone.

"We're being hunted," Trixie says.

"We've always been hunted," Leo replies. "But we're still here. Still moving. Still trying."

"Because we're stubborn," Ghost adds.

"Because we're friends," Yuki corrects. They step through the doorway. The Toy Box dissolves behind them. Childhood fades. Play ends.

And ahead, something worse waits. A maze made of mirrors. Where every reflection shows a different version of yourself. Where truth becomes fractal and identity becomes negotiable. The Mirror Maze.

[END OF CHAPTER 11]

Chapter 12: The Mirror Maze

The Mirror Maze doesn't have walls. It has reflections. Infinite reflections. Surfaces that show Leo himself, but not quite right. Different angles. Different lighting. Different versions.

In one mirror, he's smiling. In another, crying. In a third, his eyes are hollow. Empty. "Stay close," he says to the team. "Don't trust anything you see."

"Too late," Trixie mutters. She's stopped in front of a mirror. Staring. Her reflection stares back but it's wrong. The reflection is older. Harder. Alone. No friends beside her. No team behind her. Just empty space where people used to be.

"Trixie?" Leo approaches carefully. The reflection speaks. Not with Trixie's voice. With something colder.

"This is what you become," the reflection says. "You push everyone away. You use their secrets like weapons. You make them hate you because you're scared they'll leave first. So you leave. You're always alone. Always watching. Never participating."

"That's not true," Trixie whispers.

"Isn't it?" The reflection leans forward. "You violated Ghost's privacy. You hurt him. You'll do it again. That's who you are. A spy. A thief. Someone who steals intimacy instead of earning it."

Trixie's hands clench. "I apologized. I'm changing."

"For how long? Until the next time you're scared? Until the next time being clever seems more important than being kind?" The reflection smiles. "You'll always be alone, Trixie Zhang. Because you make yourself impossible to love."

"Stop," Leo says. He steps between Trixie and the mirror. "Don't listen to it." But Trixie can't look away. She's frozen. Trapped by the reflection of her worst self.

"Leo!" Ghost's voice, urgent. Leo spins. Ghost is standing in front of a different mirror. But this one isn't showing the present. It's showing the past.

The Wellness Center. White walls. White floors. White everything. And a younger Ghost—younger Marcus—strapped to a chair. Electrodes on his temples. A doctor in a white coat holding a device.

"This treatment will help you," the doctor says in the reflection. "You dream too much. You imagine too much. We can fix that. Remove the excess. Make you normal."

"I don't want to be normal," the reflection-Marcus says. "I want to dream. I want to imagine. Please don't—"

"The treatment begins now." The machine activates. Marcus feels something pulling at his thoughts. His happiest memories—birthdays, laughter, joy—being taken away like books removed from a shelf. But then the reflection shifts. Shows something else. Something worse.

A choice. Marcus is older now. Thirteen. He's been in the Center for months. And a different doctor appears. Younger. Kinder.

"I can offer you something," this doctor says. "A smuggled item. Memory-wipe. Use it on yourself, and you can erase the pain. Forget the treatments. Forget your father. Forget everything that hurts. Start fresh."

And in the reflection, Marcus takes it. Takes the memory-wipe. Uses it on himself willingly. Choosing to erase rather than endure. The real Ghost stares at the reflection. His face is white. "No. I didn't. I thought they did it to me. I thought—"

"You chose," the mirror says. It's Ghost's voice but colder. "You erased yourself because existing hurt too much. You're a coward. You always have been. That's why you phase. Why you disappear. Because deep down, you want to not exist. You chose nothing over pain."

Ghost's edges flicker. Transparent. Almost gone. "Ghost!" Yuki runs to him. But she's stopped by her own mirror.

In it, she's stone. Literally. Turned to grey marble. Frozen mid-motion. Her expression is agony. Her hands reach out for something she can never touch.

"This is your future," the mirror says. "You absorb too much. Take too much pain. Eventually, the Glitches will fossilize you. Turn your flesh to stone. Your blood to crystal. Your heart to rock. You'll be alive but unable to move. Unable to help. A statue of good intentions."

"I have to help people," Yuki says. Her voice trembles. "I have to—"

"You have to destroy yourself to feel worthy?" the mirror asks. "You have to martyr yourself to prove you matter? That's not healing. That's suicide with extra steps." Yuki touches her chest. Where the tremor lives. Where the absorbed pain collects.

"You're already turning," the mirror says. "Feel it. The hardness. The coldness. Soon you won't feel anything at all."

And Leo. Leo stands in front of his mirror. And sees Director Vance. Not himself. Her. Silver hair. Cold eyes. Severe suit. Standing over a button. A red button labeled WAKE ALL SLEEPERS.

But then the reflection shifts. The face changes. Becomes Leo's. Older. Harder. But still him.

"This is what you become," the reflection says in Leo's voice. "You reach the Sanctum. You wake Lily. But you don't stop there. You wake all the Sleepers. Not because you fixed the anchor system. But because you couldn't. Because you failed to find the third option. So you choose destruction over imprisonment. You let reality collapse. Kill millions. All to save one person you love."

The reflection presses the button. In the mirror, reality shatters. People scream. Buildings crumble. The boundary between Reverie and reality disappears. Chaos. Horror. Death.

"You become her," the reflection says. "You become Vance. Because you both believe the same thing: that individual love justifies collective harm. That saving one person matters more than saving everyone."

"No," Leo breathes. "I wouldn't. I'm trying to fix—"

"You're trying to control," the reflection interrupts. "Just like always. You controlled Lily's life. Now you're trying to control her death. Her choice. Her sacrifice. You can't accept that she chose something different than what you wanted. So you'll destroy the world to prove you know better."

The mirror shows more. Shows Leo as a tyrant. As a monster. As someone who believed love justified any atrocity. "That's not me," Leo says. But his voice shakes.

The reflections begin to move. To step out of their mirrors. Solid. Real. Hostile.

Trixie's reflection emerges. Eyes cold. Smile cruel. It has knives made of stolen secrets. Ghost's reflection emerges. Barely visible. A coward made of absence. It phases and attacks simultaneously.

Yuki's reflection emerges. Stone already. A statue that moves with grinding sounds. Heavy. Unstoppable.

Leo's reflection emerges. It's Vance. It's him. It's both. A tyrant wearing his face.

"Fight!" Leo shouts. They fight. But how do you fight yourself? How do you defeat the reflection that knows everything you know? Thinks everything you think?

Leo builds structures with the chalk. His reflection builds counter-structures that perfectly neutralize his. They're evenly matched. Exactly evenly matched. Because they're the same person.

Trixie infiltrates. Her reflection infiltrates back. They wrestle in mindspace. Both trying to steal the other's consciousness. Neither winning.

Ghost phases. His reflection phases with him. They exist in the same impossible space. Transparent together. Fighting while barely present.

Yuki heals. Her reflection absorbs. They cancel each other. Light and dark. Creation and entropy.

"We can't win!" Trixie gasps. "They're us! We can't beat ourselves!"

"Then stop fighting!" Yuki shouts. She lowers her hands. Stops attacking. Faces her stone reflection directly. "You're right. I do absorb too much. I do sacrifice myself because I think that's what makes me valuable. And you're right that it's killing me."

The stone reflection stops. Waits. "But I'm not going to stop," Yuki continues. "Because helping people matters more than protecting myself. Yes, it's slowly turning me to stone. Yes, it'll probably kill me eventually. But that's my choice. My sacrifice. And I accept it."

The stone reflection stares at her. Then nods. And dissolves. Not destroyed. Accepted.

"She's right!" Ghost says. He stops phasing. Stands solid in front of his coward-reflection. "I did erase myself. I chose the memory-wipe because existing hurt too much. I chose nothing over pain. And you know what? That makes sense. I was thirteen. I was terrified. I was being tortured."

His reflection says nothing. "But I can choose differently now," Ghost continues. His voice grows stronger. "I erased myself. But I can remember again. I can reclaim what I deleted. I can choose presence over absence. I can choose to exist even when it hurts. I CHOOSE to remember. I choose to be Marcus Harlow. I choose to matter."

The coward-reflection smiles. Slightly. Sadly. Then dissolves. Trixie faces her lonely reflection. "You're right too. I do push people away. I do use secrets like weapons. I'm terrified of being vulnerable." She takes a shaky breath. "But I'm trying. I apologized to Ghost. I'm learning to ask permission. I'm choosing intimacy over surveillance. Even when it's scary. Even when I might get hurt."

Her reflection nods. "Good luck," it says. Then dissolves. Leo stands in front of his Vance-reflection. It stares at him with cold calculation.

"I could become you," Leo admits. "I have the same controlling instinct. The same belief that I know what's best for everyone. The same willingness to hurt others to save one person I love." He swallows hard. "But I won't. Because I have something you don't."

"What?" the reflection asks.

"A team who calls me on my bullshit." Leo looks at his friends. "People who stop me from making terrible decisions. Who remind me that collaboration is stronger than control. Who pull me back from the edge."

The Vance-reflection studies him. "What if they're not enough? What if you still become me?"

"Then they'll stop me," Leo says simply. "And I'll let them. Because I trust them more than I trust myself."

The reflection smiles. Not cruelly. Almost proudly. "Good," it says. "That's the difference between us. I never learned to trust." It dissolves.

The team stands in the empty maze. The mirrors are clear now. Showing only their real reflections. No alternates. No futures. Just themselves as they are.

"We did it," Trixie breathes.

"We accepted ourselves," Yuki corrects. "The good and bad. The potential for heroism and monstrosity."

"So now what?" Ghost asks. A sound. Footsteps. Mathematical. Precise.

Justice Probability appears. She's been watching. Calculating.

IMPRESSIVE. YOU DEFEATED YOURSELVES. PROBABILITY OF SUCCESS INCREASED TO 0.005%. STILL FAILURE. BUT LESS CERTAIN FAILURE.

"We'll take it," Leo says.

YOUR FUTURES STILL COLLAPSE TO ONE ENDING. I SEE THE PATTERNS. YOU REACH THE SANCTUM. ATTEMPT TO WAKE THE SLEEPERS. FAIL CATASTROPHICALLY. REALITY UNRAVELS. ALL BECAUSE FOUR CHILDREN THOUGHT THEY COULD CHANGE MATHEMATICS.

"Math doesn't account for free will," Ghost says.

FREE WILL IS DETERMINISTIC NEUROLOGY. I'VE CALCULATED IT. YOU WILL MAKE PREDICTABLE CHOICES LEADING TO PREDICTABLE OUTCOMES.

"Then we'll surprise you," Leo says. He looks at the mirrors. At the central one. The biggest. It shows the entire maze reflected infinitely.

His father's journal mentioned this. The central mirror is a nexus. A hub. A connection point to everywhere and nowhere. "Everyone hold hands," Leo says. "Trust me."

They form a chain. Leo at the front. He raises the Architect's Chalk. Draws not on air but on the mirror itself. Lines of pure light. Cracks spreading through the glass.

WHAT ARE YOU DOING? Probability demands. "Something unpredictable," Leo says. He shatters the central mirror. It explodes. Not violently. Quietly. The glass becomes light becomes portals. Thousands of portals. Each leading somewhere different. Some to zones they know. Many to zones that shouldn't exist.

WHICH PORTAL WILL YOU CHOOSE?* Probability's voice is almost panicked. *I CAN'T CALCULATE WITHOUT VARIABLES. WHICH ONE? WHICH ONE?

"I don't know," Leo admits. He looks at his team. "Pick one. Any one. Don't think. Just choose."

"That's insane," Trixie says.

"That's unpredictable," Leo replies. "She can't follow what she can't calculate. We choose chaos. We embrace uncertainty. We become impossible to predict."

Ghost points at a portal. "That one. It feels right."

"Good enough for me," Yuki says.

NO! WAIT! I NEED MORE INFORMATION! I NEED VARIABLES! I CAN'T CALCULATE RANDOMNESS!

"That's the point," Leo says. They jump. Through the portal. Into uncertainty. Into a zone that might kill them or save them. They have no idea which.

That's what makes it impossible to predict. Behind them, Justice Probability stands in the shattered maze. Surrounded by infinite portals. Unable to choose. Unable to calculate. Unable to follow.

THIS IS NOT HOW PROBABILITY WORKS,* she says to the empty maze. *THIS IS NOT—

But they're already gone. Falling through dream-space. Through layers of sleep. Toward something older. Something that moves wrong. Something where time itself becomes negotiable.

Toward the Clockwork City. And Probability, for the first time in her existence, doesn't know what happens next.

[END OF CHAPTER 12]

Chapter 13: The Clockwork City

They fall through the portal and land in gears. Not on gears. In them. The city is gears. Buildings made of spinning cogs. Streets paved with clock faces. The sky ticks. Actually ticks. Each second marked by a visible shift in the atmosphere, like reality itself has a second hand.

Leo stands. Tries to speak. But something's wrong with his voice. It comes out too fast. High-pitched. Sped up like an old recording on fast-forward.

"—isisthis—" He can't control it. Can't slow down. His movements are jerky. Quick. Everything happening too fast.

Trixie moves beside him but wrong. Slow. Too slow. Like she's underwater. Her voice drags out across seconds. "Wheeeeeere aaaare weeeeee?"

Ghost doesn't move at all. He's frozen. Mid-step. One foot raised. Expression caught between fear and wonder. Locked in a single moment that won't progress.

And Yuki— Yuki is walking backwards. Her steps reverse. Her head turns in the wrong direction. When she opens her mouth to speak, the words come out reversed. "?siht si tahW"

They're all experiencing time differently. Displaced. Desynchronized. The Clockwork City has separated their timestreams. Leo tries to think fast enough to match his accelerated perception. The journal. His father's journal. What did it say about the Clockwork City?

Time is negotiable here. Every person moves at their own pace. The only way to navigate is to trust that your team is experiencing the same moment, just differently. You must coordinate blind.

But how? How do they coordinate when Leo is moving at triple speed, Trixie at half, Ghost frozen, and Yuki backwards? A figure approaches. Tall. Made entirely of clock parts. A body of gears and springs. A head that's a clock face showing no specific time—all the hands spin at different speeds. When it speaks, its voice ticks.

"Tick. Travelers. Tock. You are. Tick. Displaced. Tock. The Clockwork City. Tick. Requires temporal. Tock. Synchronization."

"Time Shepherd," Leo says. At least he thinks he says. It comes out too fast. A blur of sound.

The Shepherd's clock-face head tilts. "Tick. You move. Tock. Too quickly. Tick. You must. Tock. Slow."

"How?" Leo asks. But it's already too fast. The word is gone before the Shepherd can process it. The Shepherd reaches into its chest. Pulls out a pocket watch. Not a normal one. This watch has four faces. Four sets of hands. Each moving at different speeds.

"Tick. For you. Tock. Four Grippers. Tick. Four timestreams. Tock. Four paths." It hands the watch to Leo. "Tick. Reunite them. Tock. Restore synchronization. Tick. Or remain. Tock. Displaced forever."

The Shepherd walks away. Its footsteps tick against the clock-face ground. Leaving Leo holding an impossible watch and three team members experiencing time wrong. Leo looks at the watch. Studies it. Each face corresponds to a person. His face shows hands spinning rapidly. Trixie's face shows hands moving slowly. Ghost's face shows hands frozen at twelve. Yuki's face shows hands moving counter-clockwise.

There's a dial in the center. Four settings. He can adjust one person's time at once. But only one. And he doesn't know what each adjustment does. Trial and error in a place where time itself is broken.

Leo closes his eyes. Thinks. His father would plan this. Calculate every possibility. Choose the optimal path.

But Leo isn't his father. Leo trusts his team. He adjusts the dial to Trixie's setting. Pulls it gently. The watch vibrates. Somewhere in the slowed timestream, Trixie's perception shifts.

From Trixie's perspective, the world suddenly speeds up. Buildings that were barely rotating now spin visibly. Leo, who was a blur before, becomes recognizable. Still too fast but close enough to see. And she understands. Leo is trying to sync them. He's adjusting her time to match his frequency. She needs to help.

She reaches for her Infiltrator abilities. Normally she infiltrates minds. But consciousness is temporal. It exists in moments. If she can slip into the city's temporal flow, find the stream where she and Leo intersect—

She pushes. Harder than she's ever pushed. Feels herself moving between moments. Skipping seconds. Fast-forwarding through slowed time.

And suddenly she's there. In Leo's timestream. Moving at his speed. Jerky and too-fast but together. "You did it!" Leo's voice is still high-pitched but comprehensible.

"We did it," Trixie corrects. "What about Ghost and Yuki?" They look at Ghost. Still frozen. Stuck in a single moment that won't end.

"We need to reach him," Leo says. "Pull him into our timestream."

"How? He's not moving. He can't help himself." Leo looks at the watch. Ghost's face shows frozen hands. No movement. No progression. He's trapped between seconds. In the space where time doesn't flow.

"I have an idea," Leo says. "But it's going to be weird."

"Everything here is weird."

"Weirder." Leo adjusts the dial. Points it at himself. Turns it backwards. His timestream reverses. Suddenly he's moving through moments he already experienced. Walking backwards. Speaking in reverse. But conscious. Aware. Moving against time's flow.

He reaches the moment when they first arrived. When they were all still together. Before the displacement. And there's Ghost. Before the freeze. Still moving. Still present.

Leo grabs him. Physically grabs Ghost's arm. Then he reverses the reversal. Pulls the dial forward. Fast-forwards through all the moments he just rewound. Dragging Ghost with him. Pulling him forward through the freeze. Through the stuck moment. Into the present where Trixie waits.

Ghost gasps. Unfrozen. "What—what happened?"

"You were stuck," Leo explains. "I pulled you out."

"By time-traveling?"

"By trusting the watch." They look at Yuki. Still walking backwards. Speaking in reverse. Experiencing everything in the wrong direction.

"She's the hardest," Trixie says. "She's not just displaced. She's inverted. Moving opposite to time's flow."

"Then we go backwards to meet her," Leo says. He adjusts all three of their dials. Points them at Yuki's setting. Counter-clockwise. The world reverses. Buildings un-spin. Events un-happen. They walk backwards while thinking forwards. It's disorienting. Wrong. But it works.

They reach Yuki's timestream. Move beside her. Match her backwards pace. "!uoy ees nac I" Yuki says. Her face lights up. "!em dnif uoY"

"We found you," Leo says. But it comes out reversed too. "!uoy dnuof eW" They understand each other now. Speaking the same temporal language. Moving in the same inverted flow.

Leo shows Yuki the watch. Points to her face. Shows her the counter-clockwise hands. Then he mimes turning the dial forward. Bringing her hands clockwise. Reuniting all four timestreams.

Yuki nods. Understands. But she hesitates. Points to her chest. To something Leo can't see but she can feel.

The Glitches. She's been absorbing them. And in reversed time, absorption becomes expulsion. She's not taking pain. She's releasing it. Backwards through time. Undoing some of the damage.

"!pleh I lleW" she says. "!dniwer I elihw"

"She wants to help while she's rewound," Trixie translates. "Undo some of the temporal damage."

"There's no time," Leo says. Then realizes how absurd that sounds in the Clockwork City. But Yuki is already moving. Backwards through the city. Toward something she sensed. Following a trail of temporal distortion.

They follow her. Moving through reversed streets. Past unspinning gears. Until they reach a plaza. And there, frozen in time, stuck in a temporal loop: Vance's team.

Four Grippers. Adults. Professionals. Wearing government-issued gear. They're trapped in a moment. Trying to smuggle something massive. A chunk of the Clockwork City itself. A gear the size of a house. They grabbed it. Started pulling it through to reality. And the city fought back. Froze them in the attempt.

But the freeze is leaking. Spreading. Creating a time loop that extends beyond the Reverie. Leo can feel it through the Linked Sleep Device. Somewhere in New Portside, people are stuck. Repeating the same ten seconds over and over. Unable to progress. Trapped in frozen time because Vance's team tried to smuggle something too big.

"!meht eerf teG" Yuki says. "!epacse yeht ro ,pooL"

"She's right," Ghost says. He can understand reversed speech now. They all can. "If we don't free them, the loop will spread. Freeze more people. Maybe freeze all of reality."

"Why should we help them?" Trixie asks. "They're hunting us. They want to reach the Sanctum first."

"Because people are suffering," Leo says. "Because we're better than leaving enemies trapped. Because this is what Grippers are supposed to do: fix what's broken." He approaches the frozen team. Studies the temporal distortion. The loop is tight. Recursive. They're stuck in the moment of grabbing the gear. Pulling it. Feeling the city resist. They loop back. Grab again. Pull again. Resist again. Forever.

Leo studies the frozen moment. Vance's team had been trying to smuggle a massive gear—house-sized, made of crystallized time itself. The Clockwork City had fought back, trapping them in the instant of theft. 'If we can reverse their timestream to before they touched it,' Leo explains, 'the loop should break. But we need to be precise. One second too early, they're still approaching. One second too late, they're already trapped.'

Trixie infiltrates the loop's structure. 'I can see the exact moment. It's when their leader gave the order to grab. If we rewind to two seconds before that—' 'Do it,' Leo says. Together, they manipulate the pocket watch.

There. A fraction of a second. Right when they realize the city is fighting back. Before they fully commit. Before the trap closes.

He turns the dial. Locks onto that moment. Then reverses it. Forces their timestream backwards. Away from the grab. Away from the smuggle. Back to before they touched the gear.

The loop shatters. The team unfreezes. But displaced. Moving wrong. Too slow or too fast. Temporally scattered.

They don't recognize Leo and his team. They're too disoriented. They just run. Stumble through the Clockwork City. Seeking escape. Leaving the massive gear behind. Leaving their ambition behind.

"They'll recover," Leo says. "Reach the Time Shepherds. Get synchronized again. But they've lost time."

"We've gained time," Trixie corrects. "While they were frozen, we progressed." Yuki moves back to them. Still reversed. Still walking backwards. She points to herself. To the watch. Ready.

Leo adjusts all four dials. Brings them all forward. Synchronizes them to standard time. The city time. The flow that matches the ticking sky.

The world stabilizes. They move normally. Speak normally. Experience moments in proper sequence. "We're together," Ghost says. He's solid. Present. Fully here. "Actually together."

Leo noticed Ghost's hands were shaking. Subtle, but there. "You okay?"

Ghost looked at his hands. They flickered slightly at the edges. "Being frozen like that... it reminded me of something."

"You don't have to—" Yuki started.

"No. I—I think I need to." Ghost took a breath. "You've all probably wondered why I'm running. Why Director Harlow is searching for me." The team went quiet. Listening.

"He's my father," Ghost said. "Director of the Imagination Wellness Initiative. He runs the Centers. Designs the 'treatments.'" The word came out bitter.

Leo's stomach dropped. "Ghost—"

"When I was twelve, I started phasing. In real life, not just dreams. Couldn't control it. Would go transparent during dinner, at school, randomly. My father said it was 'dangerous creative deviation.'" Ghost's voice was barely audible. "He put me in his own Center. For six months."

"That's—" Trixie's voice cracked. "That's his own kid."

"He said he was helping me. Teaching me to 'suppress the aberration.'" Ghost looked at them, eyes wet. "It wasn't help. It was cruel. Disguised as therapy, but it was abuse. And the whole time, he'd say: 'This hurts me more than it hurts you, Marcus. I'm doing this because I love you.'"

Yuki stepped closer. "That's not love."

"I know." Ghost's edges flickered more strongly. "So I ran. Sixteen months ago. And I've been invisible ever since. Because if they find me—if he finds me—" His voice broke. "I can't go back there. I'd rather fade completely."

Silence fell. The Clockwork City ticked around them. Then Trixie put her hand on Ghost's shoulder. "We won't let them take you."

"Never," Yuki agreed.

Leo met Ghost's eyes directly. "You're part of this team. And we protect our own. That's a promise." Ghost nodded. Didn't phase away from their touch. Stayed solid. Present. With them.

"Thank you," he whispered. "For pulling me out. For... all of it." They walked in silence for a while. The Clockwork City's ticking seemed quieter now, respectful of what had been shared. Sometimes words weren't necessary. Sometimes just walking together was enough.

"The city is still displaced. We need to keep moving before we get separated again." Leo says. They walk through the Clockwork City. Past buildings that spin at different speeds. Through streets that lead to different moments. The temporal mechanics are beautiful but wrong. Fascinating but dangerous.

Time Shepherds watch from alleys. Clock-faced beings maintaining order. Ensuring travelers don't break too many temporal rules. They nod to Leo's team. Acknowledging their synchronization. Their success where Vance's team failed.

"The exit should be ahead," Leo says, consulting the journal. "Dad marked it as a clock tower. The biggest one. It leads down. Into the nightmare zones."

"Are we ready for that?" Yuki asks. She looks tired. Absorbing Glitches backwards took a toll. "The nightmares are supposed to be—"

"Worse than anything we've seen," Trixie finishes. "Fear made solid. Trauma given form. The things that keep Grippers from reaching the Sanctum."

"We've come this far," Ghost says. "We can't stop now." They find the clock tower. Massive. Impossibly tall. Its face shows four different times simultaneously. The door at its base is open. Dark. Leading down into something colder. Darker. More primal.

Before they enter, Leo checks the watch. All four faces show synchronized time now. Same speed. Same moment. Together.

"Everyone comes home," he says.

"Everyone comes home," they repeat. They step through the doorway. The Clockwork City's ticking fades behind them. The mechanical precision gives way to something raw. Organic. Wet.

They descend stairs that weren't there a moment ago. Down. Down. Down into depths that shouldn't exist. The air grows colder. Damper. The smell changes. Not oil and metal anymore. Water. Salt. Decay.

They reach the bottom. Step into water. Ankle-deep. Black water that reflects nothing. Water that feels wrong. Not cold. Not warm. Just wrong.

Above them, impossibly far away now, the last tick of the Clockwork City echoes. Then silence. They're standing in a street. An underwater street. Buildings rise around them, drowned and dark. Windows glow faintly with lights that shouldn't work underwater. And in the distance, shapes move. Floating. Drifting. Bodies that aren't quite dead.

"The Drowned District," Leo whispers. The first nightmare zone. The water ripples. Not from their movement. From something else. Something approaching.

And Leo hears it. Faint at first. Then louder. A voice he recognizes. Lily's voice. Coming from the dark water. Calling to him.

"Leo? Leo, where are you? I'm scared. I'm so scared. Please help me."

It's not real. It can't be real. This is the nightmare zone. It shows you fears. It lies.

But it sounds exactly like her. "Don't listen," Trixie says. Her voice shakes. "It's the zone. It's trying to trap us."

But Leo is already walking. Toward the voice. Toward the fear. Into the black water that's rising. That's pulling him down.

Into the nightmare.

[END OF CHAPTER 13]

Chapter 14: The Drowned District

They fall through the whirlpool. Spinning. Dropping. The Clockwork City's mechanical precision gives way to something organic. Wet. Ancient.

When they land, it's not on solid ground. It's in water. Leo gasps, disoriented. His feet find no purchase. He's sinking. The others surface around him, coughing, struggling.

The water is wrong. Leo knows this immediately. Water should be cold or warm. Wet. Tangible. This water is none of those things. It's liquid absence. Liquid fear. It touches his skin and he feels it seeping inward. Into his pores. Into his mind.

"Breathing apparatus," Trixie gasps. She's already pulling hers from her pack. The masks Ryles gave them. Dream-tech that filters nightmare substance. Keeps you breathing in zones where air becomes hostile.

They pull on their masks. Seal them. Leo inhales and tastes something like relief. The fear-water can't get in through his lungs anymore. Just his skin. Just his mind.

"Stay together," he says. His voice is muffled through the mask. "Don't let the zone separate us." They walk through the drowned street. Buildings loom on either side. Grey stone. Crumbling. Windows dark except for those faint glows. Leo peers into one. Sees furniture. A drowned living room. A couch floating near the ceiling. A table turned sideways. Everything preserved in liquid fear.

And sitting at the table, a figure. A woman. Middle-aged. She's not moving. Just sitting. Staring at nothing.

Drowned but not dead. Trapped in whatever memory the water is forcing her to relive.

"Don't look at them," Trixie says. "The Drowned. They're the ones who gave up. Who let the water consume them. If you stare too long, you start thinking maybe they have the right idea. Maybe drowning would be easier."

Leo looks away. Focuses forward. The street continues. The water rises. Now knee-deep. Now waist-deep. The breathing apparatus keeps working but Leo can feel pressure building. The zone pressing in. Testing his fears. Looking for weaknesses.

Ghost's mask starts beeping. A warning light flashes red. "What's wrong?" Yuki asks.

"It's failing," Ghost says. His voice is tight with panic. "The seal is breaking. The water's getting in."

"Switch to backup," Leo says. "Everyone has a backup mask." Ghost fumbles with his pack. Pulls out the second mask. But his hands shake. The fear-water is already affecting him. Making him clumsy. Uncertain. The second mask slips. Falls into the water. Sinks.

"No!" Ghost reaches for it. But it's gone. Already dissolving. Dream-tech corroding in nightmare substance.

"Share mine," Trixie says. She pulls her mask partially off. Creates a gap for Ghost to breathe through. They press close. Sharing air. Sharing space. Intimate and desperate.

The water rises. Chest-deep now. Leo builds platforms with the chalk. Floating structures they can rest on. But the platforms sink. The water dissolves them. Everything dissolves eventually. Everything drowns.

They keep moving. The street opens into a plaza. In the center, a fountain. But the fountain flows upward. Black water shooting into the dark above. And around the fountain, bodies. Dozens of them. The Drowned. Floating.

Circling. Their eyes open but unseeing. Their mouths moving but making no sound.

"They're speaking," Yuki says. She's listening. Somehow hearing what the others can't. "They're saying: Give up. Let go. The water is kinder than the trying."

"Don't listen," Leo says. But he's already hearing other voices. Lily's voice. His mother's. His father's. All coming from the black water. All saying the same thing: Why keep fighting? Why keep swimming? Everyone drowns eventually. Everyone gives up. Everyone fails.

The water rises to his neck. Leo tilts his head back. Keeps his mask above the surface. But barely. The pressure is enormous. The fear is crushing.

Then the water shows him. The accident. Not as he remembers it. As it really happened. Every detail. Nothing hidden. Exactly how it happened.

He's walking home from school with Lily. She's eleven. Happy. Talking about a project she wants to do. An art project. Forbidden by Conformity Laws but she doesn't care. She wants to paint. Wants to create. Wants to be herself.

"No," Leo says. Exactly as he said six months ago. "Art is illegal. You'll get caught. You'll get us both in trouble. You need to think before you act."

"I am thinking," Lily argues. "I'm thinking about what makes me happy. About what matters to me. You never let me choose anything, Leo. You plan everything. Control everything. When do I get to decide for myself?"

"When you're older. When you understand consequences. When you can be trusted not to make stupid decisions."

"So never?" Lily's eyes flash. "You'll never trust me. You'll never let me grow up. You want me to stay small and manageable and safe forever."

"I want you alive!"

"This isn't living! This is existing! There's a difference!" And then she runs. Not away from danger. Away from him. Away from his control. Into the street. Into traffic. The car comes so fast. The sound is worse than Leo remembered. The impact. The scream. The moment where everything breaks.

Leo watches it happen. Again. And again. The water forces him to loop. To relive. To drown in the memory.

"Leo!" Trixie's voice. Distant. Muffled. "Leo, it's not real! It's the water! Fight it!"

But it is real. That's the worst part. This happened. He said those words. He pushed her away. He caused this.

The water rises over his head. Leo inhales liquid fear. His mask has failed. When did it fail? He can't remember. Can't think. Can only drown in the truth.

Then hands grab him. Pull him up. Yuki and Ghost. They've abandoned their own masks. Breathing the nightmare water directly. Suffering so Leo doesn't have to suffer alone.

"We've got you," Yuki gasps. Black water pours from her mouth. She's absorbing it. Taking Leo's fear into herself. Filtering it through her Mender's gift. "We've got you."

They drag him to a platform. Not one Leo built. One that Yuki created. Made of healing light compressed into solid matter. It holds them above the water. Barely.

Leo coughs. Vomits black liquid. His throat burns. His mind burns worse. The memory is still there. Still looping. Still true.

"I killed her," he sobs. "I pushed her away. I made her run. It's my fault."

"No," Ghost says firmly. He's dripping. Shaking. But present. "She made her choice. She ran. You didn't push her into traffic. You were trying to protect her. You were scared. And yeah, you were controlling. But that doesn't make you a murderer. It makes you human."

"Ghost's right," Trixie adds. She's helping Yuki hold the platform stable. Both of them are suffering. Taking the zone's torture so Leo can breathe. "You made mistakes. You need to forgive yourself. Because drowning in guilt doesn't help Lily. Moving forward does."

Leo looks at them. At his team. At the people suffering for him. Sacrificing for him. "Your turn," he says to Trixie. "The water's going to show you next. What are you afraid of?"

"Everything," Trixie admits. "But mostly..." She trails off. The water rises around her. Into her. The zone finding her fear. Extracting it. Making it real.

She's in her apartment. Real apartment back in New Portside. Her parents are there. Both Conformity Enforcers. Both believers in the system. They're looking at her with expressions she's never seen on their faces but has always feared: Disappointment. Disgust. Rejection.

"You're one of them," her father says. His voice is cold. "An imagination extremist. A threat to society. Our daughter is a criminal."

"I trusted you," her mother adds. "We raised you properly. Taught you the rules. How could you betray us like this?"

"I didn't," Trixie says. But she did. She is. She's a Gripper. She breaks their laws. She violates everything they believe in.

"You're coming with us," her father says. He pulls out restraints. The ones he uses on criminals. "You'll be evaluated. Processed. Corrected. One way or another."

"No," Trixie backs away. "I'm your daughter. You love me. You have to—"

"We loved the daughter we thought you were," her mother says. "Not the criminal you became. That person died. This person needs to be stopped." The restraints close around Trixie's wrists. She's being arrested. By her own parents. For being herself.

The water pulls her down. She's drowning in the knowledge that love is conditional. That acceptance has limits. That being real means being rejected. Leo pulls her up. Returns the favor. "It's not real! It's the water! Your parents don't know!"

"But they would reject me," Trixie gasps. "If they knew. If they ever found out. I'd lose them. I'd lose everything."

"Then they don't deserve you," Yuki says. "Real love doesn't require you to be someone you're not. Real love accepts all of you. Even the scary parts."

"We accept you," Ghost adds. "All of you. The spy. The thief. The friend. The human. We see you and we stay. That's what matters."

The water shifts. Finds Ghost. He tenses. Knows what's coming. The Wellness Center. White walls. White floors. White everything. He's strapped to a chair. Electrodes on his temples. His father standing beside the doctor. Watching. Approving.

"This will help you," the doctor says. "Remove the excessive imagination. Make you normal. Make you good."

"I don't want to be normal," Ghost—Marcus—says. "I want to be me."

"You want to be sick," his father corrects. "You want to indulge in fantasies. That's weakness. We're making you strong." The machine activates. Pain shoots through Marcus's head. Not physical pain. Worse. The sensation of being erased. Of having parts of yourself deleted. Memories. Dreams. Hopes. Everything creative. Everything joyful. Everything that makes him himself.

He screams. His father watches. Unmoved. "Louder," his father says. "Scream louder. Get it out of your system. Then be quiet. Be good. Be nothing."

The water drowns Ghost in the memory. In the knowledge that his father chose erasure. Chose to delete his son. Chose nothing over who Marcus really was. The team pulls him up together. All three holding him. Anchoring him.

"You survived," Leo says. "You're still here. Still yourself. He couldn't erase you."

"We see you," Trixie adds. "The real you. The one who makes terrible puns and phases through walls and is brave even when he's terrified."

"You chose to remember," Yuki finishes. "In the Mirror Maze. You chose to reclaim what was taken. That's stronger than any erasure."

Ghost nods. Crying. "Thank you. All of you. Thank you for—"

The water takes Yuki. She's younger. Maybe eight. Standing in a bedroom. Her grandmother is on the bed. Dying. Cancer. Terminal. Nothing medical science can do.

But young Yuki has just discovered her gift. She can heal. She's healed cuts. Bruises. Small things. Why not big things? Why not cancer?

She places her hands on her grandmother's chest. Channels everything she has. Every ounce of healing energy. Every desperate wish. Every prayer that this will work.

Her grandmother's eyes open. She smiles. "My sweet Yuki. You're trying to save me."

"I can do it," young Yuki says. "I can heal you. I can make the cancer go away."

"No, darling. You can't. Some things are too big. Some things are meant to happen."

"Then I'll take it!" Yuki doesn't understand what she's saying. Doesn't understand the cost. "I'll take the cancer from you. Put it in me. Then you'll be okay."

She pulls. Tries to absorb the sickness. And it works. For a moment, it works. The cancer transfers. Yuki feels it entering her body. Dark. Cold. Wrong.

Her grandmother gasps. Relief. The pain eases. For just a moment, she's free. Then Yuki's eight-year-old body starts shutting down. She's taken something too big. Something that will kill her. The cancer spreads through her small frame instantly.

Her grandmother realizes what's happening. Yanks her hand away. "No! Give it back! Take it back! You can't—"

But it's too late. Young Yuki collapses. Dying. The cancer she took is killing her. Her parents rush in. Call emergency services. The healers come. They save her. Barely. But they can't remove the cancer completely. Just suppress it. Push it down into dormancy. Tell her: Never do this again. Never take something this big. It will kill you.

Young Yuki learns the truth: Healing costs. And sometimes the cost is your life. The water drowns adult Yuki in this memory. In the knowledge that she's been doing the same thing ever since. Taking pain. Absorbing damage. Slowly killing herself to help others.

The team tries to pull her up. But she's too heavy. The water clings to her. She's been absorbing their fear-water. Their nightmares. Their pain. Now it's dragging her down.

"Yuki!" Leo reaches for her. "Let it go! Release the water! You don't have to carry it!"

"Yes I do," Yuki says. Her voice is calm. Accepting. "If I release it, you'll drown. All of you. The water will take you instead of me. I won't let that happen."

"We won't let you drown!" Trixie grabs Yuki's arm. But the water pulls harder. Yuki sinks deeper. Her head goes under. Black water covers her face.

"Build something!" Ghost shouts at Leo. "You're an Architect! Build something that floats! Something that saves her!" Leo's hands shake. He pulls out the chalk. But what can he build? The platforms sink. The structures dissolve. Everything drowns in the fear-water.

Unless— Unless he builds something that doesn't fight the water. Something that accepts it. Moves with it. Uses it.

Leo draws. Not a platform. A vessel. A submarine. Made of compressed dream-matter reinforced with their combined will. A structure that doesn't float above the water but moves through it. Navigates it. Accepts the fear and processes it and transforms it into propulsion.

The submarine manifests. Small. Cramped. But solid. Real. It doesn't sink.

They pull Yuki into it. Seal the hatch. The submarine descends. Leo at the controls. The others supporting. The vessel moves through the fear-water. Through the nightmare. Through the district.

Inside, Yuki coughs. Vomits black liquid. But breathing. Alive. "I almost gave up," she whispers. "I almost let the water take me. It would've been easier. Would've stopped the pain."

"But you didn't," Leo says. "You held on. You trusted us to save you."

"We're a team," Ghost says. "That's what teams do. We save each other. No martyrs. No heroes. Just people who refuse to let each other drown."

The submarine pushes forward. Through streets. Past the Drowned floating in eternal surrender. Past buildings that whisper temptation. Past the plaza where the fountain flows upward into darkness.

And at the bottom of the darkness, Leo sees something. A presence. Ancient. Vast. Waiting.

"The Warden," he breathes.

"You feel him too?" Trixie asks.

"Everyone feels him," Yuki says. "He's the reason the nightmare zones exist. The reason this is all so hard. He's testing us. Making sure only the worthy reach the Sanctum."

"What happens if he decides we're not worthy?" Ghost asks. No one answers. The submarine rises. Leo navigates toward a light in the distance. An exit. The surface. They're leaving the Drowned District. Escaping the liquid fear.

They break through. The submarine surfaces in air. Real air. They open the hatch. Climb out. Collapse on solid ground.

They're in a forest. But wrong. The trees are white. Skeletal. Made of bone. The ground is carpeted with skulls. Thousands of them. Millions maybe. Stretching as far as they can see.

"The Bone Orchard," Trixie says. She sounds hollow. Exhausted. "Second nightmare zone."

"We're halfway through," Leo says. "Three more zones. Then the Sanctum."

"If we survive," Ghost adds.

"We'll survive," Yuki says. But she's clutching her chest. Where the absorbed cancer lives dormant. Where the fear-water she took is settling. Slowly killing her. "We have to."

They stand. Look at the forest of bones. At the memorials to everyone who died trying to reach the Sanctum. At the impossible task ahead. And somewhere in the distance, deep in the Orchard, Leo hears laughter. Not human laughter. Something older. Crueler.

The Warden is watching.

[END OF CHAPTER 14]

Chapter 15: The Bone Orchard

The forest is silent. That's the first thing Leo notices. No wind. No birds. No insects. Just silence pressing down like weight. Like the absence of everything that makes a forest alive.

The trees are bone. Literally. Femurs rising from the ground like trunks. Ribs branching outward like limbs. Skulls nested where fruit should grow. Everything is white. Calcium white. Death white.

And each bone pulses faintly. Like it contains something. A heartbeat. A memory. A trapped soul.

"Don't touch them," Yuki says. Her voice is barely a whisper. Like speaking louder would wake something. "Each bone is a person. A Gripper who died trying to reach the Sanctum. If you touch them, you'll experience their death. Feel what they felt. It can kill you."

"How do we navigate without touching?" Trixie asks. The trees are dense. Packed close. Bones everywhere. It's impossible to walk through without contact.

"Carefully," Leo says. He pulls out his father's journal. Flips to the Bone Orchard section. His father's handwriting is shakier here. Like writing about this place physically hurt him.

The Bone Orchard is a memorial and a warning. Every Gripper who failed becomes part of it. Their bones integrate into the forest. Their memories soak into the structure. Walk carefully. Touch nothing. And if you must touch, prepare to die.

"Great advice, Dad," Leo mutters. They move forward. Single file. Leo at the front. He steps around a femur protruding from the ground. Ducks under a ribcage arch. The bones are everywhere. Unavoidable. He grazes one with his elbow.

The memory hits him instantly. A woman. Maybe thirty. She's running through this same forest. Panicked. Being chased. Behind her, something made of bones moves. The Guardian. Massive. Relentless. She can't outrun it. She knows this. But she tries anyway.

The Guardian catches her. Its bone hands close around her consciousness. Pulls her from her body. She screams. Not pain. Worse. The sound of someone being unmade. Her bones detach. Float away. Become part of the forest. She joins the Orchard. Forever.

Leo gasps. Yanks his elbow away. The memory fades. But the sensation remains. The knowledge of what it feels like to die in the Reverie. To have your consciousness extracted and trapped. To become memorial instead of memory.

"You okay?" Ghost asks.

"No," Leo admits. "But keep moving." They continue. Each step is calculated. Each movement precise. But the forest is too dense. They all touch bones eventually. All experience flashes of death.

Trixie touches a skull. Sees a man drowning in the Drowned District. Giving up. Accepting the water. His last thought: At least it's over.

Yuki brushes against a spine. Experiences a teenager freezing in the Clockwork City. Time stopping. Consciousness caught between seconds. Never progressing. Never ending. Eternal moment of terror.

Ghost steps on a finger bone. Small. Almost invisible. The death is quick. A child. Maybe nine. Lost in the Toy Box.

Chose to stay. Chose eternal play. Then the zone consumed them anyway. Broke the promise. Turned play into prison into death.

They're all shaking now. All contaminated by death memories. All closer to becoming part of the Orchard themselves. "We need to move faster," Leo says. But faster means less careful. Less careful means more contact. More contact means more death.

They're trapped in an impossible choice. Then Ghost sees something ahead. A clearing. Open space. No bones. "There! If we can reach that—"

He runs. Desperate for the safety. His foot catches. He falls. Lands hard. His hands slam into the ground. Into a ribcage. His fingers close around the bones.

The death memory doesn't just flash. It consumes. Ghost's consciousness is yanked from his body. He experiences the death completely. Not a glimpse. The full thing.

He's a man. Older. Experienced Gripper. He's reached the Bone Orchard with his team. They're navigating carefully. Then the Guardian appears. Massive. Made of all the previous victims. It attacks. His team runs. He stays behind. Sacrifices himself. Buys them time.

The Guardian reaches for him. Ghost feels himself coming apart—like he's made of mist and the Guardian is wind, scattering him. He becomes bones. Becomes trees. Becomes part of the hunting ground.

His last thought: I hope they make it. Ghost lives this. Feels this. Dies this. And then he's dying for real. His body back in reality—back in Ryles' shop—is convulsing. The Linked Sleep Device can't handle death. It's trying to wake him. But his consciousness is trapped in the bone. In the death memory. He can't leave.

"GHOST!" Leo grabs him. Tries to pull him away from the ribcage. Ghost's hands are locked. Frozen. He's not letting go. He's not there to let go. He's in the death. Experiencing it. Becoming it.

"He's dying," Yuki says. She's checking his pulse. Barely there. Fading. "We're losing him."

"No we're not," Trixie says. She activates her Infiltrator ability. Not on minds. On death itself. She slips into the bone memory. Into the death Ghost is experiencing. She's never done this. Never infiltrated something that isn't conscious. But she tries anyway.

She finds Ghost. His consciousness fragmenting. Scattering. Becoming part of the Orchard. She grabs hold. Anchors him. Won't let him disperse.

"Come back!" she shouts into the death-space. "Marcus, come back! You're not dead! You're not bone! You're real! You're here! You're—"

"A friend," Yuki adds. She's placed her healing hands on Ghost's chest. Can't heal death. But can heal the dying. Can give him strength. Can make the choice to live easier.

"We need you," Leo says. He's holding Ghost's hand. The one not touching the bone. "We can't do this without you. Please. Don't give up. Don't join the Orchard. Stay with us."

Ghost's consciousness wavers. Caught between life and death. Between body and bone. Between his team and the memorial. Then he chooses. Pulls himself together. Refuses to scatter. Yanks his hands away from the ribcage with everything he has.

He falls backward. Into Leo's arms. Gasping. Alive. Barely.

"I died," he whispers. "I felt myself die. I was gone. I was bones. I was—"

"But you're not," Trixie says. She's crying. "You're here. You're alive. You're Marcus."

"I'm Marcus," Ghost repeats. Like a mantra. Like proof. "I'm Marcus Harlow. I exist. I'm real. I'm not dead."

They hold him. All three. Anchoring him in life. Reminding him he's more than bone. More than memory. More than death.

A sound. Movement. Something large approaching through the forest. The Guardian. It emerges from the trees. Massive. Made of bones from thousands of victims. Hundreds of thousands maybe. Skulls form its head. Femurs its arms. Ribs its chest. It moves with grinding sounds. Calcium scraping. Death walking.

"You touched the bones," it says. Its voice is many voices. All the dead speaking together. "You experienced death. Now you must join us. Become part of the Orchard. That is the law."

"We're leaving," Leo says. He helps Ghost stand. "We're not joining anything."

"All who touch the bones join the Orchard. All who fail the nightmare trials become memorial. That is how it has always been. That is how it must be."

"We didn't fail," Trixie says. "We're still alive. Still moving. Still trying."

"You touched death. That is failure." The Guardian takes a step forward. Its bone feet crack the ground. "The Warden established this law. I enforce it. You will join the Orchard."

"Then the Warden is wrong," Leo says. He's drawing with the chalk. Building structures. Barriers. Anything to slow the Guardian. "Touching death isn't failure. Giving up is failure. We haven't given up."

"You will." The Guardian advances. Ignores Leo's structures. Walks through them. "Everyone gives up eventually. Everyone becomes bone."

It reaches for Ghost. The newest victim. The one who touched deepest. The one closest to death. Ghost phases. His body becomes transparent. The Guardian's bone hand passes through him. Can't grab what isn't solid.

"I'm not becoming bone," Ghost says. His voice is stronger now. Certain. "I chose to exist. I chose to be real. I'm not letting death unmake that choice."

The Guardian pauses. Its skull-head tilts. "You are unusual. Most who experience death want to surrender. Want to stop fighting. You want to continue."

"Because I have something to live for," Ghost says. He looks at his team. "I have friends. I have purpose. I have myself. That's worth fighting death for."

The Guardian considers this. Its many voices whisper to each other. Debating. Calculating. "You may pass," it says finally. "But know this: The Screaming Gallery ahead is worse. And beyond that, the Warden himself waits. He will test you in ways death cannot. He will show you that joining the Orchard is mercy compared to what comes next."

"We'll take our chances," Leo says. The Guardian steps aside. Gestures toward a path through the forest. A route where the bones are slightly less dense. Slightly more navigable.

"Before you go," the Guardian says, "you should see something. Your father, Thomas Finch. He has a memorial here. A tree made from his bones. His sacrifice is honored. His death is remembered. You should pay respects."

Leo's chest tightens. "Show me." The Guardian leads them deeper. To a clearing where a single tree stands. Larger than the others. More elaborate. Made from bones that glow faintly with residual consciousness.

Thomas Finch's memorial. Leo approaches slowly. Touches the tree. "Dad?" Leo touched the bone-tree.

And heard: "Hello, Leo." Not a memory. Not imagination. His father's actual voice, preserved in the Bone Orchard memorial.

"You're here? You're really here?"

"Part of me. The part that still dreams. The part that couldn't let go completely." Warmth in the voice. Pride. "You're doing it, son. Building what I couldn't build. I'm sorry I wasn't there to teach you."

"You taught me anyway. Through the journal. Through the example. Through—" Leo's voice cracked. "Through leaving. I learned what NOT to do."

Gentle laughter. "The best lesson. Don't sacrifice yourself alone. Don't try to save the world without help. Don't leave your family." A pause. "I was wrong, Leo. I thought being the hero meant dying alone. But you? You're building with others. That's real heroism."

"I miss you."

"I know. But I'm here. Part of the network. Part of the system we're building. When you finish this—when you wake all the Sleepers—I'll finally be free too. We all will."

"I promise," Leo said. "I'll finish it."

"I know you will. Because you're my son. And you're better than I ever was." Then the memory comes. But not death. Something else. His father's final thoughts before becoming an Eternal Sleeper. Before sacrificing himself to anchor the boundary.

I'm scared. I don't want to die. Don't want to leave Elena and my children. But someone has to do this. Someone has to anchor reality. If not me, then who? I have the skills. I have the knowledge. I have the martyr complex that makes me think I'm the only one who can save the world.

That last part is the problem, isn't it? Believing I'm special. Believing I'm necessary. Believing I'm the only one who can fix this.

I should have trained others. Should have built a team that could continue without me. Should have designed a system that didn't require permanent sacrifice.

But I didn't. So now I'm here. Making the choice. Becoming the anchor. Dying so others can live.

Leo, Lily—if you're reading this somehow—learn from my mistake. Don't try to save the world alone. Don't believe you're the only one who can fix things. Build with others. Trust others. Let others help.

And forgive me. For being absent. For choosing death. For believing martyrdom was noble instead of stupid.

The memory fades. Leo is crying. His hand still on the tree. On his father's bones. "I forgive you," he whispers. "And I promise. I won't make your mistake. I won't die alone. I won't become another memorial. I'll live. I'll build. I'll finish what you started. But with my team. Together."

He steps back. Looks at the memorial one last time. Then at his friends. "Let's go," he says. "Let's reach the Sanctum. Let's wake the Sleepers. Let's build the system my father couldn't build. Let's make his death mean something."

"Everyone comes home," Yuki says.

"Everyone comes home," they repeat. The Guardian watches them leave. Its bone body creaking. Its many voices whispering. It has seen thousands try to reach the Sanctum. Seen thousands fail. Seen thousands join the Orchard.

These four might be different. Or they might become the next trees. Time will tell. The team walks through the designated path. Careful. Deliberate. Avoiding bones where possible. Accepting death-flashes where necessary.

The forest thins. The bones spread farther apart. They're reaching the edge. The exit. And beyond the exit, they hear it.

Screaming. Not one voice. Thousands. Millions. An infinite chorus of agony. Psychological torture made audible. The sound of every fear vocalized. Every trauma spoken. Every nightmare given voice.

The Screaming Gallery. The third and final nightmare zone. "I don't know if I can do this," Ghost says. He's still shaking from his near-death. "I don't know if—"

"You can," Trixie says firmly. "Because we'll do it together. That's how this works. We share the burden. We split the pain. None of us carries it alone."

"What if the screaming breaks us?" Yuki asks. "What if we can't endure it?"

"Then we endure until we can't," Leo says. "And when we can't anymore, we endure anyway. Because Lily is beyond that gallery. The Sanctum is beyond that gallery. Everything we've fought for is beyond that gallery."

He looks at each of them. "One more nightmare zone. Then we face the Warden. Then we reach Lily. Then we fix everything. We're so close. We can't stop now."

"One more," Trixie agrees.

"One more," Ghost echoes.

"One more," Yuki finishes. They step out of the Bone Orchard. The skeletal trees fade behind them. Ahead, a corridor. Long. Dark. Endless.

Day eleven. Real-world time. Ryles sat in his darkened pawn shop, watching four unconscious children and wondering if he'd killed them. The IVs dripped steadily.

Saline. Nutrients. The bare minimum to keep their bodies alive while their minds traveled through hell. Leo on the couch. Trixie on the floor, wrapped in blankets. Ghost phased partially through the wall—even unconscious, his body couldn't fully commit to existence. And Yuki against the window, stone already creeping up to her elbows.

Five days so far. Five days of continuous sleep. And the Linked Sleep Device on the counter pulsed with rhythms that made Ryles' stomach turn. Something had gone wrong an hour ago. The crystal had flared red. All four of their heart rates had spiked simultaneously. Ghost's body had convulsed so hard the IVs nearly tore from his arm. For three minutes—three eternal, impossible minutes—Ryles had been certain they were dying.

Then the crystal calmed. Their vitals stabilized. The crisis passed. But Ryles couldn't shake the certainty that he'd just watched them barely survive something in the Reverie. Something he couldn't protect them from. Something he could only witness through fluctuating lights and erratic heartbeats.

He checked the IVs again. For the hundredth time today. Leo's needed adjusting. The tape had come loose during the night. Ryles fixed it with his one hand—the right hand, the only one he had left—and tried not to remember the day he lost the other.

The Toy Box. Fourteen years ago. He'd been greedy. Stupid. Convinced he could smuggle something big. Something worth the risk. A whole carousel, spinning and golden and perfect. He'd gripped it. Pulled. Forced it through the boundary.

The Glitch had been catastrophic. Seven buildings collapsed. Forty-three people injured. And Ryles' left arm had simply... ceased to exist. Not torn off. Not cut. Just gone. Reality's payment for his greed.

Sarah had healed him. His wife. The best Mender in their generation. She'd closed the wound, stopped the phantom pain, made his body accept the absence. She'd held him while he cried. Told him he was still whole. Still worthy. Still loved.

And then, two years later, the Great Nightmare had come. And Sarah had volunteered to hold the boundary with Thomas. Had used every ounce of her gift trying to keep reality stable while Thomas anchored the Sanctum. It hadn't been enough. The strain had killed her. Burned her out from the inside. Her last words had been to Ryles: "Make sure the kids are okay. Make sure Thomas' children know he loved them."

Ryles looked at Leo now. Thomas' son. Twelve years old. Unconscious for five days. Traveling through zones that had killed experienced Grippers.

"I'm sorry, Sarah," Ryles whispered to the empty shop. "I don't think I kept them okay." Outside, footsteps. Ryles' head snapped up. The wards on the shop would alert him to any Marshals, any government agents. But they didn't protect against civilians. Against someone like—

A knock on the door. "Ryles? I know you're in there. I can see the lights." Elena's voice. Leo's mother. Former Architect. Woman who'd suppressed her gift for twelve years and now stood outside, demanding answers.

Ryles moved to the door. Didn't open it. "Elena. Go home."

"Where's my son?"

"On a camping trip. I told you this."

"For eleven days? Without telling me where?" Her voice cracked. "I'm his mother, Ryles. I have a right to know."

Ryles pressed his forehead against the door. Felt the weight of every lie he'd told. Every secret he'd kept. "He's safe. That's all I can tell you."

"Let me in. Let me see him."

"I can't."

"Because he's not on a camping trip." Statement, not question. "He's diving. Isn't he? He found out about the Reverie and you helped him dive deep." Pause. "Is he going for Lily?"

Ryles said nothing. Silence was confirmation enough. " I can't forgive you, Ryles." Elena's voice turned sharp. Cold. "You know what happened to Thomas. You were there. You saw what the deep zones cost. And you still let a twelve-year-old—"

"He was going with or without me!" Ryles snapped. "At least this way I could give him gear. Train him. Stack the odds in his favor."

"The odds are always against them! The Reverie doesn't care about training or gear or good intentions. It takes what it wants and leaves bodies behind. Or worse—leaves them alive and broken, like Thomas, trapped forever holding reality together." Her fist hit the door. "Let me in. If my son is dying in there, I deserve to see him."

Ryles looked back at the four unconscious kids. At the IVs keeping them hydrated. At the Linked Sleep Device showing their shared heartbeats. At Ghost's half-phased body and Yuki's spreading stone. If he let Elena in, she'd see all of it. See what he'd facilitated. See four children on the edge of death.

She'd pull the IVs. Wake them forcibly. Trap their consciousness in the Reverie forever. "They're alive," Ryles said. "They're fighting. And in two more days, they'll either wake up or they won't. But if you interrupt the process now, you guarantee they die. So go home, Elena. Trust me. Trust your son. And let them finish what they started."

Long silence. Then: "If he dies, I'm killing you."

"If he dies, you won't have to. I'll do it myself." Footsteps retreating. Elena leaving. Ryles exhaled and returned to his vigil.

The shop was cold. He'd turned off the heat to conserve energy—the wards were draining the building's power faster than usual. Too many protections layered on top of each other. Scrambling surveillance. Deflecting Marshal attention. Hiding four impossibly valuable targets.

He pulled his coat tighter with his one arm and checked the time. 3:47 AM. Day eleven. They'd been asleep for almost 264 hours. Their bodies were weakening despite the IVs. Muscles atrophying. Bones becoming brittle. If they stayed much longer, they'd wake up needing weeks of physical therapy. If they stayed too long, they wouldn't wake up at all.

The Linked Sleep Device pulsed. Steady. But underneath, Ryles could sense something. A tension. A wrongness. They were approaching something big. Something dangerous. The device couldn't show details—just emotions bleeding through the connection. Fear. Determination. And underneath it all, love.

They loved each other. These four kids who'd met less than two weeks ago. They'd bonded in ways that took most people years. And that love was keeping them alive when skill alone would have failed. Ryles thought about Thomas. About Sarah. About the team they'd assembled twelve years ago to stop the Great Nightmare. They'd loved each other too. Had fought together. Sacrificed together.

Half of them hadn't come back. "Please," Ryles whispered to gods he didn't believe in. "Please let these kids be smarter than we were. Please let them all come home." He moved to Yuki's unconscious form. Stone had crept past her elbows now. Up to her shoulders. Her transformation was happening even in sleep—her body knew what she'd chosen, knew what she'd become. By the time she woke, she'd be monument instead of girl.

If she woke. Ryles placed his hand on her stone arm. It was cold. Smooth. Already harder than human flesh should be. "You didn't have to do this," he said quietly. "You're fourteen. You should be worried about school, about friends, about first crushes. Not about becoming an anchor. Not about sacrificing your humanity to save the world."

But even as he said it, he knew it was a lie. Kids like Yuki didn't choose normal lives. They chose meaning. Purpose. Mattering. And if that meant turning to stone to save reality, they'd do it without hesitation.

Just like Sarah had. The crystal flared again. Not red this time. Gold. Bright and sudden and—

All four kids gasped simultaneously. Their bodies arched. The IVs rattled. Ghost solidified completely for three seconds—the longest Ryles had ever seen him fully present while unconscious. Then they settled. Breathing hard. Hearts racing. But alive. Still alive.

Ryles checked the monitors. Vitals elevated but stable. Whatever they'd just survived—whatever trial the Reverie had thrown at them—they'd passed. "Good," Ryles breathed. "Good. Keep fighting. Keep surviving. You're so close."

He didn't know how close. Didn't know they'd just navigated the Fracture Field. Didn't know they'd faced their flawed selves and chosen truth over perfection. Didn't know they were about to meet the Warden. He only knew their heartbeats were synchronized. Their breathing matched. They were still together.

Still a team. Day eleven became day twelve. The sun rose grey outside. New Portside woke to another morning of structural cracks and reality glitches. Another morning closer to the doctor's deadline.

Ryles made coffee with his one hand. Checked the IVs. Adjusted blankets. Monitored the crystal. And waited.

This was all he could do. Wait. Watch. Hope. Pray to gods he didn't believe in that these kids were stronger than the adults who'd gone before them.

That they'd learned from his generation's mistakes. That they'd come home. All of them. He looked at his missing arm. At the space where it should be. Payment for greed. For pushing too far. For thinking he could control the Reverie instead of respecting it.

These kids weren't making his mistakes. They were building instead of taking. Collaborating instead of controlling. They were better than he'd been. Better than Thomas had been. Better than any of them.

If anyone could reach the Sanctum and return alive, it was them. "Two more days," Ryles said to the unconscious children. "Two more days and you'll be home. I'll keep you safe until then. I promise."

He'd broken promises before. Lost Sarah. Lost half his team. Lost his arm and his pride and his certainty that he understood the Reverie. But this promise—keeping these four kids alive—this one he would keep.

Even if it cost him everything he had left. The crystal pulsed. Steady. Strong. Four heartbeats synchronized.

Ryles settled into his chair and resumed his vigil. Day twelve. Forty-three hours until deadline. And four children fighting through hell, unaware that in the real world, a one-armed man sat guard over their bodies and refused to let them die alone.

[END OF CHAPTER 15]

Chapter 16: The Fracture Field

They step into the third nightmare zone holding hands. The transition is instant. Violent. Reality tears. One moment they're together, four people linked in a chain. The next, the world splits. Fragments. Multiplies. Leo sees the corridor ahead fracture like a shattered mirror—each shard reflecting a different version of the same space.

And in each reflection, his team exists. But wrong. Multiplied. Divided. Leo's hand suddenly grips nothing. He's alone.

He spins. Calls out. "Trixie? Ghost? Yuki?"

Three voices answer. No—nine voices. Multiple versions overlapping. "Leo!" That's Trixie. But which Trixie? He sees her ahead. No—two of her. No—*three* versions standing in different fractured reflections of reality.

The first Trixie waves enthusiastically. Smiling. Cheerful. She's vibrant, energetic, everything dialed up to maximum brightness. "Leo! Thank goodness! I found you!"

The second Trixie stands farther back. Quiet. Reserved. She doesn't wave. Doesn't smile. Just watches him with careful, distant eyes. Professional. Controlled.

The third Trixie sits on the fractured ground, crying. Makeup smeared. Hair disheveled. She looks broken. Lost. Vulnerable in a way that makes Leo's chest ache.

"Which—" Leo starts. Then stops. Because he sees Ghost now. And there are *four* versions of him. One Ghost is completely solid. Fully present. No transparency, no phasing. He stands confidently, visibly, taking up space without apology.

Another Ghost is entirely invisible. Leo can only perceive his outline—a shimmer in the air, the suggestion of a person without the substance. The third Ghost flickers. Solid, transparent, solid, transparent. Caught between states. Struggling to maintain existence.

The fourth Ghost is partially phased. Half his body visible, half transparent. Like he can't decide whether to exist or disappear. "Leo?" Yuki's voice. He turns.

Two versions of her stand nearby. Just two, but the contrast is stark. The first Yuki glows with power. Radiant. Healthy. Her skin is clear, her eyes bright. She looks strong, capable, like she could heal the world without breaking a sweat.

The second Yuki looks exhausted. Her hands are already turning grey—stone creeping up her fingers. She's hunched, clearly in pain, clearly dying. Absorbing damage that's killing her slowly. Leo's breath catches. He doesn't understand. None of this makes sense.

Then the space around him speaks. Not a voice. A presence. The zone itself communicating directly into his mind.

REALITY HAS FRACTURED. YOUR TEAM EXISTS IN MULTIPLE STATES. ONLY ONE VERSION OF EACH PERSON IS REAL. CHOOSE CORRECTLY, AND YOU REUNITE. CHOOSE INCORRECTLY, AND THAT PERSON DISAPPEARS FROM YOUR TEAM FOREVER.

Leo's stomach drops. "How do I know which is real?"

YOU KNOW THEM. PROVE IT.

Trixie stands in a different fractured shard, seeing her own impossible choices. Four versions of Ghost surround her. She studies them frantically. Which is real? The fully visible one? That's what she wants. What she's been pushing him toward. But—

The zone's voice whispers to her mind: *THE REAL VERSION IS NEVER THE IDEAL. IT IS THE TRUTH.* Trixie's breath shakes. Not the ideal. The truth.

She looks at the four Ghosts again. The fully solid one smiles at her. Confident. Present. Perfect.

But that's not Ghost. That's who she *wants* Ghost to be. The invisible one doesn't acknowledge her at all. That's who Ghost was trying to be. Erased. Gone.

The flickering one looks terrified. Unstable. Barely holding on. The partially-phased one... Trixie's eyes lock on him. He's watching her with those careful eyes. Half-visible, half-transparent. Not hiding completely. Not forcing himself to be fully present. Just... existing in the uncomfortable in-between.

That's Ghost. The real one. Struggling to be seen but not ready to be fully visible. Honest about his uncertainty instead of pretending confidence or disappearing entirely. But to choose him, she needs to... what? Call him out? Prove she knows him?

Trixie's throat tightens. She needs to say something true. Something that acknowledges his failure, his flaw, his most vulnerable moment. "Ghost," she says to the half-phased version. Her voice shakes. "You erased yourself. You chose the memory wipe because you couldn't handle being your father's son. You ran from your pain instead of facing it."

The other three Ghosts flicker. Start to fade. "But you came back," Trixie continues. "You're choosing to remember now. And I know you're not all the way visible yet. I know you're still scared. But that's real. That's you. The real you."

The partially-phased Ghost solidifies slightly. Not completely. But more present than before. He nods. Once.

CORRECT, the zone confirms.

Two of the Ghost versions vanish entirely. The flickering one and the invisible one dissolve like mist. But the fully-solid Ghost remains. Trixie's heart sinks. She got it wrong. She—

No. Wait. The fully-solid Ghost is dissolving too. Slower. He's fighting it. Reaching for her. "Trixie, you were so close. I could have been perfect for you. I could have been—"

"You could have been a lie," Trixie says firmly. "And I don't want lies." The perfect Ghost vanishes. Only the half-phased one remains. The real one. He's watching her with something like respect.

"Thank you," he says quietly. "For choosing the truth." Ghost faces his own trial. Three versions of Yuki stand before him. The first glows with impossible health. Strong. Powerful. The healer who never suffers, never sacrifices, never pays the price.

The second looks normal. Pleasant. Smiling. The teammate who helps without complaint, who serves without acknowledgment, who exists to support others. The third is dying. Visibly. Stone spreading up her arms. Face tight with pain. Every breath is effort. She's absorbing damage and it's killing her and she keeps doing it anyway.

Ghost stares at them. The zone's rule echoes in his mind: *The real version is never the ideal.* He wants the healthy one to be real. Desperately. Wants Yuki to be okay, to not be suffering, to not be sacrificing herself.

But that's not the truth. The normal one—the pleasant, smiling teammate—that's who Yuki pretends to be. The mask she wears so no one worries. But the dying one. The one in visible pain. The one whose sacrifice is written on her body in spreading stone.

That's real. Ghost's voice cracks. "Yuki. You're killing yourself. You've been absorbing everyone's pain—mine, Leo's, Trixie's—and you never tell us how much it costs. You never ask us to stop hurting so you can stop healing. You just... take it. All of it. Until you turn to stone."

The dying Yuki meets his eyes. Nods slowly. "You're a martyr," Ghost continues. Pain in every word. "And you think that makes you valuable. You think your worth comes from how much you suffer for others. But that's... god, Yuki, that's the most broken thing about you. You don't know how to exist without pain."

Tears stream down the dying Yuki's face. But she's smiling. "You see me," she whispers. "The real me."

CORRECT.

The healthy Yuki and the normal Yuki dissolve. Only the dying one remains. She's still turning to stone. Still suffering. But she's real. And Ghost chose her anyway.

"We need to fix this," Ghost says urgently. "We need to stop you from—"

"Not yet," Yuki interrupts. "First we finish the trial. Then we fix me. Together." Yuki sees three versions of Leo. The choice should be easy. But it's not.

The first Leo stands tall. Confident. The leader who knows all the answers, who makes perfect plans, who controls every outcome. He radiates certainty. The second Leo is broken. On his knees. Sobbing. Consumed by guilt so completely he can barely function. Destroyed by the weight of his failures.

The third Leo... he's standing, but barely. His expression is tired. Guilty. Scared. He's trying to be strong but you can see the cracks. The uncertainty. The fear that he's not enough, that he'll fail again, that his need to control comes from terror of losing control.

Yuki's heart aches. The ideal would be the confident leader. But that's not Leo. That's who he pretends to be. The broken one is dramatic. Appealing to her healer instinct. Someone she could fix, could save. But that's not real either. That's Leo's fear of what he might become, not who he actually is.

The third one. Tired. Guilty. Scared but still standing. That's Leo.

"You pushed Lily into traffic," Yuki says. Her voice is gentle but firm. "You controlled her so much that she ran from you. You made her feel like she had to sacrifice herself to matter because you never let her make her own choices. That's on you, Leo. That's your failure."

The confident Leo flickers. Starts to argue. "I was protecting her—"

"You were suffocating her," Yuki interrupts. "And you know it. The real you knows it."

The broken Leo sobs harder. "I killed her. I destroyed everything. I'm a monster—"

"You're not a monster," Yuki says. "You're just scared. And you made mistakes because you were scared. That's human. That's real."

Both false Leos begin to dissolve. Yuki turns to the third Leo. The tired, guilty, scared-but-standing one. "You failed her. But you're here. You're trying to fix it. You're learning to let go of control. You're not perfect. You're not fixed. But you're trying. And that's the real you."

The third Leo—the real Leo—meets her eyes. Nods. "I'm so tired of pretending I know what I'm doing."

"I know," Yuki says. "We all are."

CORRECT.

The false Leos vanish. Only the real one remains. Leo sees them now. The real versions. Trixie—crying, broken, vulnerable. Ghost—half-phased, uncertain, in-between. Yuki—dying, stone-skinned, sacrificing.

They're all flawed. All broken in some way. None of them are the ideal versions. But they're real. The fractured realities begin to merge. The shattered mirror pieces sliding back together. Leo, Trixie, Ghost, and Yuki stand in a restored corridor. Whole. Together. Real.

But Leo realizes with cold certainty: He hasn't completed his trial yet. The zone speaks again: *ONE TEST REMAINS. YOU HAVE CHOSEN YOUR TEAM. NOW THEY MUST CHOOSE YOU.* Leo's stomach drops. He sees it happening. His own form fracturing. Splitting into versions of himself.

And his team must choose which is real. Leo sees three versions of himself standing before his friends: One Leo is confident. The leader. The one with all the answers.

Another Leo is broken. Consumed by guilt. Barely functional. The third Leo is exhausted. Trying so hard. Scared but standing.

His team studies him. Studies all three versions. Trixie speaks first. "The confident one isn't real. Leo's never been certain. He just pretends really well."

Ghost nods. "The broken one is appealing. Dramatic. But that's not who he is either. That's his fear, not his reality."

Yuki steps toward the third Leo. The exhausted one. "You're terrified you're not enough. You think if you stop controlling everything, it'll all fall apart. You carry so much guilt you can barely breathe. But you keep going. Keep trying. Keep hoping that maybe this time you won't fail the people you love."

She touches his face. Gentle. Knowing. "That's the real you," Yuki says. "Tired. Scared. Trying anyway."

CORRECT.

The false Leos dissolve. The real one remains. They stand together in the now-unified corridor. All four of them. Real. Flawed. Known.

Leo's voice shakes when he speaks. "You chose the worst versions of us."

"We chose the real versions," Trixie corrects. "There's a difference."

"We know each other's failures," Ghost adds. "We know each other's flaws. And we choose each other anyway. That's what makes us a team."

"Not perfection," Yuki finishes. "Truth." The corridor ahead opens. Beyond it, light. Crystalline. Beautiful.

And a presence. Massive. Ancient. Waiting. The Warden.

They hold hands again. But this time it's different. They're not holding idealized versions of each other. They're holding the real versions. The broken ones. The flawed ones.

The honest ones. "Together?" Leo asks.

"Together," they answer. And they step forward to face the Warden. Not as perfect heroes. But as four scared, flawed, real kids who know each other's failures and choose each other anyway. That, the zone seems to whisper as they pass through, is the kind of bond that can change the world.

[END OF CHAPTER 16]

Chapter 17: The Warden's Test

They stand before the Warden. He is massive. Ancient. Made of light and shadow intertwined in patterns that hurt to perceive. He has no face but infinite eyes. Each one watching. Judging. Knowing.

His voice is the first sound. The original word. The first sound that ever existed. "Welcome, little builders," the Warden says. "You have passed through my trials. Survived my tests. Arrived at my threshold. But now comes the real question."

The ground beneath them shifts. Becomes transparent. Shows the Sanctum below—rows and rows of crystal pods containing sleeping figures. Each one glowing faintly. Each one conscious. Each one trapped.

"Why should I let you pass?" the Warden asks.

Leo steps forward. Heart pounding. "Because my sister is down there. Because she didn't choose this. Because it's wrong."

"Wrong?" The Warden's infinite eyes focus on Leo. "I have maintained the boundary between reality and Reverie for twelve thousand years. Prevented apocalypses. Kept humanity safe. The Eternal Sleepers are necessary. Their sacrifice protects billions. How is that wrong?"

"Because they didn't volunteer," Leo says. "Because you're using people as tools. Because there has to be another way."

"There isn't." The Warden's voice is sad. Ancient grief. "I have searched. Calculated. Tested. This is the only solution that works. Reality needs anchors. The Reverie needs walls between it and the real world. Someone has to hold those walls. Forever"

"Then let me serve," Leo says immediately. "Take me instead. Free Lily. I'll be your anchor."

"No," Trixie interrupts. "That's just trading one prisoner for another. That doesn't solve anything."

"Then what do you suggest?" the Warden asks. He turns his infinite gaze to Trixie. "You, Infiltrator. You who steals secrets and violates boundaries. Why should I trust you with the most important boundary of all?"

Trixie flinches. But she holds her ground. "Because I know what it's like to be used. To have people take things from you without permission. I would never do that to the Sleepers. Never. I steal secrets. I don't steal lives."

The Warden studies her. Then turns to Ghost. "And you, Phantom. You who exists between states. Who disappeared himself. Why give power to someone who disappears?"

Ghost is silent for a long moment. Then he solidifies completely. Becomes fully present. Fully visible. "Because I learned. I disappeared because I was afraid. Afraid of being hurt. Afraid of being erased. But I came back. I chose to exist. I chose to matter. And I'll never hide again."

The Warden nods slowly. Turns to Yuki. "And you, Mender. You who absorbs pain. You who is dying to heal others. Why should I choose death over life?"

Yuki looks down at her stone hands. At the cancer growing in her chest. At the absorbed damage killing her slowly. "Because some things are worth dying for. Not because death is good. But because what you protect is more valuable than what you lose. The Sleepers are dying. Slowly. Trapped. If I can free them—if I can fix this broken system—then yes. That's worth it."

The Warden is silent. Processing. Judging. Then he focuses all his infinite eyes on Leo again. "And you, Architect. You who builds. You who controls. Why should I trust you with your sister? You tried to fix her before. You made her worse."

The words hit like a physical blow. Leo staggers. Because it's true. All of it. "I can't control her. I know that now. I was wrong. I was so scared of losing her that I pushed her away. I made her feel like she had to save me by sacrificing herself. That's on me. All of it."

"Then why should you succeed where I have failed?" the Warden asks. "I have maintained this system for twelve thousand years. What makes you think you can do better?"

"Because we're not alone," Leo says. His voice shakes but holds firm. "You've been doing this by yourself. Carrying the weight of reality. Making impossible choices. Becoming the villain so everyone else can live. But you don't have to. We can share the burden. Build something better. Together."

"Impossible."

"Why?"

"Because I have tried!" The Warden's voice cracks. Ancient pain breaking through. "I have offered. Begged. Pleaded with humanity to help maintain the boundary. To share the responsibility. And every time—every single time—they refuse. They demand I fix their problems. They demand I maintain reality for them. But they will not help. Will not sacrifice. Will not collaborate. They take and take and take. And I give and give and give. Until I am exhausted. Until I am hated. Until I am alone."

Silence. Heavy. Painful. Then Trixie speaks. Quiet. Honest. "We're not refusing. We're here. We're offering. Let us help."

"At what cost?" the Warden asks. "The boundary requires energy. Consciousness. Someone must anchor it. If I free the Sleepers, someone must replace them. Will you volunteer? Will you trap yourselves forever? Will you sacrifice your futures?"

"No," Leo says. "There's a third option."

"There isn't."

"There's always a third option," Leo insists. "You said it yourself—you've been alone. Carrying everything. But what if we distribute the weight? What if instead of a few people carrying everything, everyone carries a little? What if being a Gripper means periodically serving as an anchor? Rotating duty. Shared responsibility. Collective maintenance instead of individual martyrdom."

The Warden is silent. Calculating. "That... has never been proposed before."

"Because you never asked," Yuki says gently. "You demanded. Or you sacrificed. But you never invited collaboration."

"Would it even work?" Ghost asks. "Could the boundary be maintained by rotating anchors instead of permanent ones?"

"Theoretically," the Warden admits. "But it would require thousands of people. Constant coordination. Perfect trust. If even one person fails to serve their rotation, reality destabilizes."

"Then we build a system that works," Leo says. "We create infrastructure. Education. Community. We teach Grippers what they are. What they can do. What they're responsible for. And we make it a choice. Always a choice."

"And if they choose not to serve?" the Warden challenges. "If they refuse? If your collaborative system fails?"

"Then we try again," Leo says. "We build better. We learn. We adapt. But we don't go back to this. We don't go back to prisoners. Ever."

"Even if it fails?" the Warden presses. "Even if reality collapses?"

"Even then," Leo says. "Because trying something better is worth the risk. Always." The Warden is silent for a long time. Infinite eyes watching. Calculating. Judging.

Then he laughs. It's a sound like the universe beginning. Like the first thought. Like consciousness itself finding joy. "I have waited twelve thousand years for someone to say that," the Warden says. "Twelve thousand years of humans coming here. Demanding I fix their problems. Demanding I maintain reality for them. Never offering to help. Never offering to share the burden. Until now."

He shrinks. Becomes smaller. More human-sized. More vulnerable. "I am tired," he admits. "So tired. Holding reality together. Watching humanity destroy itself repeatedly. Preventing apocalypses while being hated for my methods. I wanted to be wrong. I wanted someone to prove collaboration works. I wanted hope."

He gestures. The ground becomes fully transparent. The Sanctum appears below them. Beautiful. Crystalline. Alive with captured consciousness.

"Look," the Warden says. "See what you're fighting for." They look. Rows and rows of crystal pods. Each containing a person. Each person suspended in dream-matter. Each one glowing with consciousness. They're not asleep. Not dead. Not absent.

They're awake. Aware. Working. "They're conscious?" Leo breathes.

"Always," the Warden says. "That's the secret. That's the truth I've hidden for millennia. The Eternal Sleepers aren't sleeping. They're building. Creating. Maintaining. They're the foundation of reality itself. And they know it. They feel it. They've been doing it for so long they've forgotten anything else."

Leo scans the pods frantically. Looking for one specific person. There. Third row. Center pod.

Lily. She floats in crystalline suspension. Eyes closed but face peaceful. Hands spread like she's holding something invisible. And around her, through her, woven from her consciousness—threads of dream-matter connecting to every other pod. To every other Sleeper.

She's building something. Even now. Even trapped. "Lily," Leo whispers. Her eyes didn't just open; they ignited. But she didn't step out of the pod—she pulled them *in*.

Suddenly, Leo wasn't standing in a room of glass pods. He was standing in a web of light. He could feel Trixie's heartbeat like it was his own; he could feel Ghost's lingering chill and Yuki's quiet, steady warmth. Lily was at the center, but she wasn't a prisoner. She was the conductor of a symphony.

"It's too heavy for one person, Leo," her voice echoed, not from her mouth, but from the very air around them. "Vance wanted a king. The Warden wanted a god. But the Reverie... it just wants us."

"We're the anchors," Yuki realized, her voice shimmering in the shared space.

"Not just us," Lily said. The web expanded. Leo felt the presence of hundreds of others—the Sleepers—waking up not into the world, but into the *work*. "We don't need a single pillar to hold up reality. We need a net."

Leo reached out, and instead of his father's architectural drawings, he saw the team. He saw that his job wasn't to design the solution, but to hold the hand of the person next to him. As they joined hands, the crystalline pods didn't just crack—they dissolved into light, feeding the new, distributed boundary. The Warden watches. Evaluates. Then nods slowly. "Very well. You have my permission to attempt implementation. Wake the Sleepers. Activate the new system. Prove that collaboration works. But know this—if you fail, if reality collapses, I will rebuild the old system. The Eternal Sleepers will be reinstated. Necessary evil is still necessary."

"We won't fail," Leo says.

"We'll see." The Warden steps aside. Opens the path. "Enter the Sanctum. Speak with the Sleepers. Begin the work. But hurry. You're not the only ones who've come seeking the Sanctum today."

"What do you mean?" An explosion. Outside. Beyond the Sanctum. Reality tears. The boundary fractures. Alarms sound—mechanical and psychic and fundamental.

Someone is attacking. Someone is trying to break through. The Warden's infinite eyes narrow. "Vance's team has arrived. And they're not here to talk. They're here to destroy everything. And reality begins to crack."

[END OF CHAPTER 17]

Chapter 18: The Siege

The explosion rocks the Sanctum. Reality tears. The boundary fractures. Vance's team pours through the gap—armed with technology that shouldn't exist. Weapons powered by dream-matter. Tools that violate the fundamental laws of both reality and Reverie.

"Breach!" the Warden shouts. "They're forcing entry! Damaging the boundary!" Leo runs to the crystal walls. Looks out at New Portside beyond. The city is unraveling. Buildings phase in and out of existence. Streets turn to liquid. The sky cracks like glass. Scale 4 Glitches. Maybe Scale 5. Reality itself is coming apart because Vance's team is attacking the anchor point.

"We have to stop them!" Leo shouts.

"We have to activate the new system first!" Lily counters. "If we don't get it online before the old system completely fails, reality collapses entirely!"

"How long?" Trixie demands.

"Ten minutes to wake all the Sleepers safely," Lily says. "Another five to integrate them into the distributed network. Fifteen minutes total."

"We don't have fifteen minutes!" Ghost is watching the boundary crack further. "We have maybe five before reality unravels too far to repair!"

"Then we work faster," Yuki says. She's already moving toward the pods. "Leo, you and Lily handle the activation. Trixie, Ghost, and I will defend the Sanctum. We'll buy you time."

"How?" Trixie asks. "We're four kids against a trained assault team!"

"We're four Grippers who survived the nightmare zones," Yuki corrects. "We've faced worse." Another explosion. Closer. Vance's team is breaching the Sanctum's outer defenses.

"Go!" Leo shouts. "Buy us time!" Yuki, Trixie, and Ghost run toward the entrance. Leo and Lily race toward the pods.

"How do we wake them?" Leo asks.

"Carefully," Lily says. She places her hands on the nearest pod. Her consciousness flows inward. Connects. Communicates. "They're ready. They've been ready. They're just waiting for permission to wake up."

She sends the signal. The pod opens. An elderly man sits up. Gasps. Looks around confused.

"Where... what year is it?"

"2025," Lily says gently. "You've been serving as an anchor. But now we're changing the system. Are you willing to help? To be part of the distributed network?"

"I can leave?" His voice cracks. "I can go home?"

"Eventually. First we need to stabilize the transition. Can you hold your anchor point for ten more minutes while we get everyone online?"

"Yes. Yes. Anything." He's crying. "Thank you. Thank you for asking."

Lily moves to the next pod. And the next. Each Sleeper waking. Each one agreeing to help. Each one so grateful to finally have a choice.

Leo works on the other side of the Sanctum. Waking Sleepers. Explaining. Asking permission instead of demanding service. Outside, the battle rages.

Trixie infiltrates the minds of Vance's soldiers. Slows them down. Makes them second-guess. Doubt their mission. It won't stop them but it buys seconds.

Ghost phases through walls. Appears behind enemies. Disarms them. Vanishes before they can react. Guerrilla tactics. Hit and fade. He can't beat them but he can frustrate them.

Yuki stands at the entrance. Absorbing attacks. Taking bullets meant for her friends. The stone spreads faster now. Covering more of her body. But she holds. Protects. Endures.

And then Vance herself breaks through. She's not wearing body armor. Not carrying weapons. She's in a lab coat. Holding a tablet. Desperate. Furious. Terrified.

"WHERE IS SHE?" Vance screams. "Where's Catherine? Where's my daughter?"

"She's safe!" Leo shouts from across the Sanctum. "She's in pod forty-seven! But you can't wake her yet! The system isn't stable!"

"I DON'T CARE ABOUT THE SYSTEM!" Vance runs toward the pods. Toward her daughter. "I'm taking her home! Now!"

"If you wake her wrong, she'll die!" Lily moves to intercept. "Please! Give us five more minutes!"

"I've waited six months!" Vance's hands fly across her tablet. Overriding protocols. Forcing Catherine's pod to open. "I'm not waiting another second!" The pod cracks. Opens. Catherine sits up.

But wrong. Too fast. Her eyes are vacant. Her consciousness is fragmenting. She's waking but not waking. Trapped between states. Dying in real-time.

"No!" Vance catches her daughter as she collapses. "No no no! Catherine! Baby! Come back!"

But Catherine can't come back. Her mind is scattering. The forced extraction is killing her. "Ghost!" Leo shouts. "Can you phase into her? Hold her consciousness together?"

Ghost is already moving. He phases into Catherine's body. Into her fragmenting mind. Finds the threads of consciousness pulling apart. Starts gathering them. Holding them. Keeping her from dispersing entirely.

I've got her, Ghost's voice echoes from inside Catherine. *But she's unstable. I can't hold her long. A minute. Maybe two.*

"Lily!" Leo runs to his sister. "Can we integrate Catherine into the network early? Before everyone else?"

"Maybe. If we use her as a test case. But if it fails—"

"It won't fail," Leo says. "Trust me. I'm the Architect. I'll build the connection. You guide her consciousness. Together."

Lily nods. Takes Catherine's hand. Leo takes the other. They reach into the network. Into the distributed system the Sleepers have been building.

And there, inside the consciousness web, Leo finally meets his father. Thomas Finch appears as a presence. Warm. Familiar. Made of memory and mathematics and love.

Hello, son, he says. *I knew you'd make it. Knew you'd find another way.*

Dad, Leo can barely think coherently. *You've been here the whole time?*

Part of me. The part that understands building. The part that knows architecture. I've been helping design this. The distributed system. The collaborative solution. This is my gift. My final architecture. I couldn't implement it alone. Needed collaborators. Needed the Sleepers. Needed Lily. And now I need you.

What do I build?

The connection. Catherine needs to integrate into the network. But her consciousness is too damaged. Build her a framework. A structure to hold her together until she heals.

Leo builds. Constructs scaffolding from dream-matter. Creates supports for Catherine's fragmenting mind. Lily guides her consciousness along the framework. Into the network. Into the collective.

Catherine gasps. Her eyes focus. She's still damaged. Still fractured. But stable. Held together by the network of Sleepers.

Thank you, she whispers into the consciousness web. Then her physical body relaxes. Returns to the pod. To the Sanctum. To safety.

Ghost phases out. Solidifies. Collapses from exhaustion. Vance stares at her daughter. At the pod closing around her. At the consciousness network glowing through the crystal.

"She's alive?" Vance's voice breaks.

"She's alive," Lily confirms. "She's part of the network now. She'll serve as an anchor during the transition. Then she can rotate out. Go home. Live. But she needs time to heal first."

Vance looks at Leo. At Lily. At the Sleepers waking around them. At the system she nearly destroyed. "I'm sorry," she whispers. "I just wanted my daughter back. I didn't know there was another way. I thought control was the only solution. I thought—" She breaks down completely. Human again. Vulnerable. "I'm so sorry."

"Help us now," Leo says. "Join the network. Be part of the solution instead of the problem. We need every anchor we can get." Vance nods. Places her hands on the nearest pod. Lets her consciousness flow inward. Joins the distributed network. Becomes an anchor.

Her team follows. One by one. Laying down weapons. Joining the network. Helping instead of hurting.

The Sanctum fills with light. One hundred and forty-seven Sleepers. Twenty-seven of Vance's team. Leo's crew. All connected. All anchoring. All holding reality and Reverie apart together.

"It's working!" Lily shouts. "The boundary is stabilizing! Reality is repairing!"

"Wait," the Warden says. He's watching the network with his infinite eyes. "There's a problem. The center isn't holding. The distributed network needs a focal point. Something to coordinate all the individual anchors. Without it, the system will drift. Collapse within days."

"What kind of focal point?" Leo demands.

"A center anchor. Someone who serves permanently. Who holds the network together while everyone else rotates. It's the one piece we couldn't solve. The one unavoidable sacrifice."

"How long?" Yuki asks quietly.

"What?"

"How long does the center anchor serve? Forever?"

"No. Once the network is fully established and stable—maybe six months—the center anchoring function can rotate too. But for the initial activation, someone needs to volunteer. Someone needs to hold everything together for about ten minutes while the network solidifies."

"I'll do it," Leo says immediately.

"No," Lily says. "You're the Architect. You need to finish building the external structure. Make sure reality and Reverie stay separated properly. I need you out here."

"Then who—"

Yuki heard the Warden say "center anchor" and immediately knew. It had to be her. Not because the others were weak. Because she was already dying. The cancer from grandmother's healing sat in her chest like a stone. The absorbed Glitches were turning her body to crystal. She had months at most. Maybe weeks.

Why not make those weeks matter? "There's no other way?" Leo asked the Warden. Yuki could have spoken up then. Could have volunteered immediately. But she held back. Let them try to find alternatives. Let them exhaust every possibility.

Because she needed to be sure. Trixie suggested rotating the center anchor function. The Warden explained it needed stability—at least six months uninterrupted. Ghost suggested building an artificial anchor. The Warden showed why technology would fail.

Leo suggested he do it himself. The Warden explained why an Architect needed to stay free to finish building. Every option eliminated. Every path closing. Until only one remained.

"I'll do it," Yuki said quietly. Everyone turned. Stared.

"What? No." Trixie moved toward her. "We'll find another way."

"There is no other way." Yuki's voice was calm. Certain. "You know it. I know it. Someone has to volunteer, and it should be me."

"Why you?" Ghost demanded. "Why not any of us?"

"Because I'm already dying." She said it simply. Factually. "The cancer. The absorbed Glitches. I have months at most. Why waste those months when I can use them to save everyone?"

"That's not—" Leo started.

"It's logical," Yuki interrupted. "It's the right choice. And I'm making it." She looked at each of them. "I'm going to turn to stone. Today or in three months, it's going to happen. At least this way, it means something."

"Yuki, no," Trixie sobs. "We can find another way. We can—"

"There is no other way," Yuki says. Her voice is calm. Accepting. At peace. "This is what I'm for. What I've always been for. Helping people. Even if it costs everything. Especially if it costs everything." She looks at each of them. At her friends. At her team. "Let me do this. Let me matter."

Leo wants to argue. Wants to refuse. Wants to find the third option that doesn't require sacrifice. But there's no time. The framework is destabilizing without a center anchor. Reality is starting to unravel again. They have seconds to decide.

"Everyone comes home," Leo whispers. The promise they made.

"Everyone except those who choose to stay," Yuki corrects gently. "This is my choice. Honor it. Please."

Leo's vision blurs with tears. But he nods. "Okay. Okay. Do it."

Yuki smiles. Her last smile as a fully human girl. Then she places her stone hands on the central crystal. The largest one. The one at the heart of the Sanctum.

Her consciousness flows inward. Into the network. Into the center. She becomes the anchor. The foundation. The heart holding everything together.

The stone spreads instantly. Covers her completely. Face. Hair. Clothes. Everything. She becomes a statue. A monument. A permanent fixture at the center of the Sanctum.

But inside the network, inside the consciousness web, she's alive. Present. Feeling everyone. Holding everyone. Being useful. Being necessary. Being exactly what she always wanted to be.

Worth it,* her final thought echoes through the network. *This was worth it.

The distributed system activates completely. The boundary stabilizes. Reality and Reverie separate properly. The Scale 4 Glitches reverse. New Portside returns to normal. Buildings solidify. Streets become streets again. The sky repairs.

It worked. The new system worked. They built something better. But at what cost? Trixie is sobbing. Collapsed on the floor. Ghost has withdrawn from the network, solidified, and stands staring at Yuki's statue with hollow eyes. Even the Warden looks devastated. Vance, still connected to the network, feels Yuki's sacrifice directly and weeps.

Leo walks slowly to the statue. To what used to be his friend. To the girl who healed everyone and asked for nothing in return. He places his hand on the cold stone. Inside the network, Yuki feels it. Responds. The crystal around her statue glows warmer.

Thank you,* Leo thinks toward her. *Thank you for everything.

You're welcome,* Yuki's consciousness replies. *Now go. Wake the others. Help them adjust. Build the school you talked about. Teach new Grippers. Make this sacrifice mean something. And Leo? Visit sometimes. Tell me stories. I'll be here. Always. Listening.

The Sleepers are waking now. Properly. Safely. One by one they sit up. Stretch. Remember reality. Some cry. Some laugh. Some just sit in silence processing their freedom.

Vance helps Catherine out of her pod. Her daughter is weak. Damaged. But alive. Healing. They hold each other. Mother and daughter. Finally reunited.

"How do we go home?" Trixie asks through her tears. "How do we leave her?"

"The same way we came," the Warden says gently. "Close your eyes. Let consciousness rise. Let the dream release you. You'll wake in reality. In your bodies. Safe."

"Will we remember this?" Ghost asks.

"Every moment," the Warden promises. "Every choice. Every sacrifice. This happened. This was real. And it changed everything."

Leo takes one last look at the Sanctum. At the crystal structure. At Yuki's statue at its heart—glowing, present, holding reality together. "Everyone comes home," he whispers. "Except those who choose to stay. Thank you, Yuki. For choosing to stay. For holding us together. For mattering."

Then he closes his eyes. Lets consciousness rise. Lets the dream release him. And wakes up.

[END OF CHAPTER 18]

Chapter 19: Awakening

Leo opened his eyes. The first thing he noticed was the IV in his arm. The second was how weak his body felt. The third was Ryles' face, leaning over him with an expression of profound relief. "Welcome back," Ryles said. "You've been asleep for seven days."

Seven days. A full week. Leo's mouth was dry. His muscles ached like he'd been lying still for— Well. For seven days.

"The others?" Leo croaked.

"Waking up. Look." Ryles looked exhausted. Like he hadn't slept in seven days. Because he hadn't.

'Thought I'd lost you,' he said quietly. 'Day eleven, when the crystal went red—' He stopped. Breathed. 'But you made it.' Trixie stirred on the couch, an IV in her arm too. Ghost was phasing in and out unconsciously near the window, his body confused about whether it was solid. And Yuki—

Leo's breath caught. Yuki sat against the wall. Not asleep. Not waking. Stone. Her body had transformed just like in the Reverie. Grey stone from her hands to her shoulders, her face peaceful, eyes closed.

"No," Leo whispered.

"She's alive," Ryles said quickly. "Check the Sanctum. She's there. Anchoring. Just like she chose."

Leo's heart hammered. "And Lily?"

"The hospital called your mother three hours ago," Ryles said. He smiled. Actually smiled. "Lily woke up. They don't understand it. Can't explain it. But she's awake. Talking. Transformed like you said she would be, but alive."

Three hours ago. Leo did the math. They'd been asleep for seven days. The deadline was day fourteen. Today was day thirteen.

They'd made it. Barely. "We need to move you," Ryles said. "Can't have four unconscious kids here with IVs when your mother comes looking. Already arranged transport to the hospital. They'll think you all had some kind of shared sleeping sickness. Medical mystery. But you'll be safe."

Leo tried to sit up. His body protested. A week of immobility had left him weak. "Easy," Ryles said. "You're dehydrated, malnourished, your muscles have atrophied slightly. You'll need physical therapy. All of you will. But you're alive. You succeeded."

"Seven days," Leo repeated. It felt impossible. Seven days had passed in the real world. Seven days while they fought through the Reverie. Seven days while Ryles kept their bodies breathing.

"Seven days exactly," Ryles confirmed. "You dove midnight on day six. It's now morning on day thirteen. You made the deadline with a day to spare."

"Did anyone find us?" Trixie asked. She was awake now, pulling the IV from her arm.

"Your mother came by once," Ryles admitted. "I told her you were on a school camping trip. She didn't believe me but she left. The government sent scouts twice. My wards held. And the Glitches from your absence..." He gestured to the window.

Leo looked out. The city was more cracked than before. Buildings leaning. Streets fractured. The damage from their smuggling, from their journey, written across New Portside in structural scars.

"The world survived," Ryles said. "Barely. But it survived. And now, with the new anchor system, it'll heal. Slowly. But it will heal."

Ghost solidified completely. Looked at Yuki's statue with grief in his eyes. "She knew," Ghost said quietly. "She knew what she was choosing. We have to honor that."

"We will," Leo said. His voice was stronger now. "We'll build the school. Train new Grippers. Make sure her sacrifice means something."

Trixie stood shakily. "First, we visit Lily. I want to see her awake. Want to make sure she's really okay."

"She is," Ryles said. "The hospital's baffled, but she's okay. Changed, but okay." They gathered their things. Removed the IVs. Helped each other stand on weak legs. Seven days of sleep had left them vulnerable, fragile. But alive.

And victorious. Outside, the sun was rising on day thirteen. They had one day before the deadline. One day to reunite with Lily. One day to prove they'd succeeded.

They'd cut it as close as possible. But they'd made it.. And Yuki— Leo's breath caught. Yuki sat against the wall. Exactly where she'd been when they entered the Reverie. But she wasn't asleep. She wasn't breathing. She was stone. Grey stone that looked exactly like her dream-statue. Hands pressed together. Face peaceful. Eyes closed.

"No," Leo whispered. "No no no." He crawled to her. Touched her arm. Cold. Solid. Permanent.

"She's gone," Ryles said quietly. "Has been since you succeeded. The moment the new system activated, her body here changed. Became what her consciousness was in the Reverie. I've seen it before. Extremely rare. When a

Gripper sacrifices themselves completely in a dream, sometimes their body follows."

"She's dead?"

"No. She's anchoring. Her consciousness is in the Sanctum. In the network. But her body is here. Stone. A memorial and an anchor point simultaneously. She exists in both places. Forever."

Trixie woke with a gasp. Saw Yuki. Screamed. Crawled to the statue. Pressed her forehead against the cold stone. "No. Please no. Not Yuki. Not her."

Ghost solidified completely. Stared at Yuki's stone form with dead eyes. "We killed her. We let her sacrifice herself and we just let it happen."

"She chose," Leo said. But his voice cracked. "She chose to matter. We honored her choice."

"We should have found another way," Trixie sobbed. "We should have—"

"There was no other way," Trixie said finally, her voice hollow. They sat together for a long time. Grieving. Processing. Existing in the space between victory and loss. The weight of what they'd done—what Yuki had done—pressed down on all of them.

At New Portside General Hospital, fourth floor, Room 412, something impossible was happening. The monitors had gone haywire three minutes ago. Every machine connected to Lily Finch screaming alerts. Heart rate spiking. Brain activity surging. Temperature fluctuating. Nurses rushing in, doctors shouting orders, her mother pushed back against the wall, watching in terror as her daughter's body began to glow.

"What's happening to her?" Mrs. Finch demanded. "What's wrong?"

"I don't know," Doctor Sato admitted, checking monitors that made no sense. "Her vitals are—they're changing. Temperature dropping but she's not hypothermic. Heart rate irregular but not failing. Brain activity is off every chart we have."

Lily's skin began to shimmer. Faint at first. Then brighter. Crystalline patterns spreading like frost across her arms, her face, her whole body. Her hair—dark brown when she'd been brought in six months ago—was shifting. Lightening. Turning silver-white from the roots down.

"She's transforming," a nurse whispered. "How is she transforming?"

"Call security," Sato ordered. "And research. We need specialists. We need—" Lily's eyes opened.

Not human eyes. Not entirely. They held depths. Impossible depths. Like looking into water that went down forever. When she breathed, the air around her shimmered with crystalline dream-matter.

"Mom?" Lily's voice had harmonics to it. Echoes. Like she was speaking from multiple places at once. "I'm okay. I'm awake. I'm—"

Mrs. Finch pushed past the doctors. Grabbed her daughter's glowing hand. Felt the warmth there, the thrum of something underneath. "Lily. Oh god, Lily. You're awake. You're—what happened to you?"

"I was anchoring," Lily explained, sitting up slowly. The monitors shrieked as her vitals refused to make sense. "Holding reality together. And I still am. I'm the bridge now, Mom. Between here and the Reverie. I absorbed dream-matter. I'm part human, part dream now. I can feel the network. I can—"

"You're glowing," Mrs. Finch interrupted. She was crying. Shaking. "Your skin is glowing. Your hair is silver. You look—you don't look—"

"I'm still me," Lily said firmly. She squeezed her mother's hand. "I'm still your daughter. Just... different now. Changed. But I chose this, Mom. I volunteered. I saved Leo. I saved everyone. I matter."

Doctor Sato approached cautiously. "Lily, I need you to tell me exactly what you're experiencing. Any pain? Discomfort? Can you move your extremities?"

Lily flexed her fingers. Toes. Everything worked. "I feel... amazing. Strong. Connected. I can feel hundreds of people. Thousands. All the anchors holding reality stable. We did it. The new system is working."

"What system?" Sato asked. "What are you talking about?" Lily looked at her mother. At the doctor. At the nurses staring in shock.

"There's a lot to explain," she said. "And my brother needs to know I'm awake. Can someone call Leo? Tell him his sister is okay. Tell him we won."

Mrs. Finch kissed Lily's glowing forehead. Felt the crystalline warmth there. Her daughter was alive. Different, impossible, transformed—but alive. Awake. Speaking. Smiling.

"I'll call him," Mrs. Finch said. "I'll tell him to come right away." She stepped into the hallway. Pulled out her phone. Tried to process what she'd just witnessed. Her daughter had been in a coma for six months. And now she was awake. Glowing. Silver-haired. Speaking about anchors and networks and dreams.

The world had changed while Lily slept. And Lily had changed with it. Back at Ryles' shop, the team was still processing Yuki's transformation. Still grieving. Still trying to understand what they'd accomplished and what it had cost.

Leo turned on the TV mounted on his shop wall. News footage played. Reporter standing in front of City Hall. Breaking news banner.

"...unprecedented confession from Director Helena Vance, who turned herself in to authorities this morning. She claims to have orchestrated a decades-long conspiracy to control individuals with the ability to manipulate dreams—so-called 'Grippers.' She's provided evidence of illegal experimentation, forced conscription, and the existence of what she calls 'Eternal Sleepers'—people used as anchors between dimensions against their will." The footage switched to Vance leaving a courthouse, an ankle monitor visible beneath her grey slacks. Released pending trial in exchange for full testimony. She looked broken. Small. Human.

"The Conformity Council has been disbanded pending investigation. All Wellness Centers are closed. And there are reports of people worldwide claiming to feel something new—a connection. A network. Scientists are baffled. Government officials are scrambling. And the question everyone is asking: Are Grippers real?"

Ryles turned off the TV. "You're public now. The secret is out. The truth is spreading."

"How many?" Leo asked. "How many people volunteered to be anchors?"

Ryles checked his phone. Frowned. "I'm getting... reports. Numbers coming in from worldwide. Eight hundred and seventy-three Grippers claiming they can feel some kind of network. All volunteering to serve rotations. The system is working, kid. Reality is stable."

Leo's phone buzzed. A text from his mother: **Lily's awake. Hospital. Come now**. His breath caught. "Lily. She's—she's awake."

A knock at the door. Ryles answered. Catherine and Vance stood there. Vance's ankle monitor blinked beneath her pants—a reminder of consequences even in redemption. Catherine looked weak, leaning heavily on her mother. But alive. Conscious. Human.

"We came to apologize," Vance said. "And to thank you. And to... to ask if we can help. If there's anything we can do to make this right."

Leo wanted to be angry. Wanted to yell. Wanted to blame Vance for everything. But she looked as broken as he felt. "Help us build a school," Leo said instead. "Help us teach new Grippers how to use the network safely. How to serve their rotations. How to maintain the system we created. Help us turn this tragedy into something positive."

Vance nodded. Tears streaming. "Yes. Anything. I'm testifying against the entire Council next week. Full confession. Full consequences. And after—if they'll let me—I'll help however you need."

Catherine stepped forward. Spoke directly to Yuki's statue. "Thank you. For holding me together. For saving my life. I won't waste it. I promise."

They stayed for an hour. Planning. Coordinating. Figuring out next steps. Then Vance and Catherine left to meet with lawyers. To begin the legal process of dismantling the old system and building something new.

When they were gone, Leo turned to his team. His friends. His family. "We need to keep Yuki's statue in the right place," he said. "Yuki belongs with us. Where we can visit. Where we can tell her stories. Where she can be part of what we build."

"Where?" Trixie asked.

"Here." Leo gestured around the shop. "This is where it started. Where we planned. Where we became a team. This should be our headquarters. The place where we teach new Grippers. Where we coordinate rotations. Where we honor Yuki's sacrifice by continuing her work."

"Reverie Recovery," Ghost said quietly. "That's what we should call it. We recover from what the Reverie does. We help people heal. We build something better."

"I like that," Trixie said. "Reverie Recovery. A school for Grippers. A headquarters for the new anchor network. A place where Yuki's statue reminds everyone why this matters."

Ryles looked around his cluttered pawn shop. At the boxes. At the junk. At the kids who'd changed everything. "You're asking me to turn this into a school?"

"We're asking you to be part of something important," Leo said. "You know more about Gripping than anyone. You knew my father. You've been hiding and helping for decades. It's time to stop hiding. Time to teach. Will you?"

Ryles was quiet for a long moment. Then he looked at Yuki's statue. At the peaceful stone face. At the sacrifice she'd made. "Yeah," he said gruffly. "Yeah, I'll teach. Someone has to keep you kids from getting yourselves killed."

They spent the rest of the day moving Yuki's statue to a place of honor. Right in the center of the shop. Where the light hit her. Where everyone who entered would see her first. A reminder. A memorial. An anchor in both meanings of the word.

Leo placed his hand on the stone one more time. Felt the faint warmth that meant Yuki's consciousness was present. Listening. "We're going to build something amazing," he promised her. "Something worthy of what you gave. We're going to teach Grippers to be proud of what they are. To serve without being trapped. To collaborate instead of controlling. And we're going to make sure no one ever has to sacrifice themselves alone again. We'll build it together. Always."

Leo didn't remember the transport ride to the hospital. Didn't remember running through the corridors. Just found himself outside Room 412, breathing hard, terrified and hopeful in equal measure. His mother was there. In the hallway. Face tear-streaked but smiling. Actually smiling.

"She's awake," Mom said. "She's different, Leo. Changed. But she's awake and talking and she keeps asking for you." Leo pushed through the door.

Lily sat cross-legged on her hospital bed, surrounded by confused doctors taking readings. Her skin glowed faintly. Her hair was silver-white. When she turned to look at him, her eyes held impossible depths. "Leo." She smiled—still Lily's smile despite everything. "You did it. You saved me."

"We saved each other," Leo said. He crossed to her bed. Took her glowing hand. Felt the warmth there, the thrum of the network underneath. "What happened to you?"

"I'm the bridge now," Lily explained. Her voice had depth to it. Echoes. "Between reality and Reverie. I was an anchor for so long that I absorbed the dream-matter. I'm part human, part Reverie now. I can feel the network. I can communicate with all the anchors. I'm permanently connected."

"Can you disconnect?"

"I don't want to." Lily's expression was peaceful. "I can feel Yuki, Leo. She's there. In the Sanctum. Holding hundreds of people together. She's happy. She's proud. She doesn't regret it. She'd choose this again."

Leo's throat tightened. "That doesn't make it hurt less."

"No," Lily agreed. "It doesn't. But it makes it mean something. Her sacrifice wasn't wasted. It saved the world. And she knew what she was doing. Honor that."

They sat together in the hospital room. Brother and sister. Changed but together. The world outside had transformed, but this—this connection—remained. "I'm not going home, am I?" Lily said quietly. "I'm too different now. The doctors won't let me leave."

"They're calling it the Sanctum Ward," Leo said. "Special facilities for people who've... changed. You won't be alone. There will be others. And I'll visit every day. I promise."

"Every day?" Lily raised an eyebrow. Still teasing. Still Lily.

"Every single day," Leo confirmed. "You're stuck with your annoying big brother forever."

"Good." Lily squeezed his hand. "Because we've got work to do. The network needs coordination. The new anchors need training. And something's stirring in the deep Reverie. Things older than human dreams. When they come—and they will come—we'll need to be ready."

"Then we'll be ready," Leo said. "Together." He stayed until visiting hours ended. Until the nurses gently kicked him out. Until he had no choice but to leave her there, glowing and changed and more powerful than she'd ever been.

But she was alive. Awake. His sister. And that was enough. Inside the network, inside the Sanctum, inside the crystal at the heart of reality, Yuki smiled.

And knew she'd made the right choice. Worth it. All worth it.

[END OF CHAPTER 19]

Chapter 20: Adjustments

Three days passed. Leo woke each morning to color. Blue walls. Blue sky outside. Blue sheets on his bed. His mother had painted the room while he slept that first day, unable to sit still, needing to do something to mark the change. The grey was dying. Slowly. Street by street. Building by building. New Portside was getting its life back.

He visited Lily every afternoon. She was in the hospital's new wing—the one for Grippers who'd changed. Doctors studied her, fascinated and terrified in equal measure. Her crystalline skin. Her silver hair. Her ability to sense the network.

"How are you feeling?" Leo asked on the third day. He sat beside her bed, watching her glow faintly in the afternoon sun.

"Different," Lily said honestly. "I can feel everyone now. Every anchor. Every Gripper. Eight hundred and ninety-two of us now. The network is growing. And I can feel the Warden too. He talks to me sometimes. Explains things. Teaches me."

"Does it hurt?"

"No. It's beautiful, Leo. Like being connected to something huge and important and alive. I'm never alone. Never lost. Never forgotten. I'm part of something bigger than myself." She looked at him. Her eyes were still her eyes but deeper now. "I know you're scared. That you think I'm trapped again. But I'm not. This was my choice. My gift. My way of building something better."

"You'll never be normal," Leo said quietly. "You'll never just be Lily again. You'll always be the bridge. Always be connected. Always be different."

"Good," Lily said firmly. "Normal was grey and controlled and dead inside. I don't want normal. I want this. I want to matter. I want to help. And Leo? I need you to accept that. I need you to let me choose my own path even when it scares you."

Leo was quiet for a long time. Processing. Learning. Growing. "Okay," he finally said. "Okay. I'll try. But you have to promise to talk to me. To tell me when things are hard. To let me be your brother even when I can't fix things."

"Deal." Lily squeezed his hand. Her touch was warm despite the crystalline sheen. "How's the planning going?"

"Good. Overwhelming. We're turning Ryles' shop into a school. We're coordinating with the eight hundred anchors worldwide. We're fielding interview requests from every news outlet on the planet. And we're planning a memorial for Yuki that's going to be... complicated."

"Public?"

"Very. The mayor wants to honor her. The government wants to show they support the new system. And we want to make sure people remember what she gave. But it's political now. Everything is political."

"She'd hate that," Lily said with a small smile.

"Yeah. But she'd do it anyway. Because it matters." They talked for another hour. About the network. About new Grippers discovering their abilities. About the challenges ahead. When Leo left, Lily was meditating—communing with the anchors, coordinating rotations, teaching newcomers. She was happy. Genuinely happy. And Leo was learning to accept that happiness didn't always look like he expected.

Ghost—no, Marcus now—stood outside his father's office. The Director of the disbanded Conformity Council was packing boxes. Preparing to leave in disgrace. Security had been removed. Press was outside. The mighty had fallen.

Marcus knocked on the open door. His father looked up. Paled. "Marcus? How did you—security should have—"

"There is no security," Marcus said calmly. "You have no power anymore. No protection. No one to hide behind. It's just you and me. And I wanted to talk. One last time."

His father set down the box. Straightened. Tried to reclaim authority he no longer had. "What do you want?"

"To tell you that I remember," Marcus said. "Everything. The Wellness Center. The erasure. The way you watched them wipe me piece by piece until I was nothing. Until I was convenient. Until I was a ghost." He stepped into the office. Solid. Present. Real. "But I also want to tell you that I forgive you."

His father blinked. "What?"

"Not because you deserve it. You don't. But because I need to. Because carrying hate is exhausting. Because I'm building a new life and I don't want you in it. Not even as an enemy. You're just... nothing to me now. A man who made terrible choices. A man I'm leaving behind."

"Marcus—"

"My name is Marcus Harlow. I'm a Phantom. I help people. I'm part of something important. And I exist. Fully. Completely. Visibly. You can't erase me ever again."

He turned to leave. "I'm sorry," his father said quietly. "I know it doesn't matter. I know it's too late. But I am sorry. I was scared. I thought the Conformity Laws would protect you. Keep you safe. I didn't understand what they were doing. By the time I did, you were already—" His voice broke. "I lost you. And I didn't know how to get you back."

Marcus stopped in the doorway. Didn't turn around. "You could have tried. You could have fought. You could have chosen me over your career. But you didn't. And now you have to live with that. Goodbye, Dad."

He walked out. Solid. Present. Free. Ryles was waiting in the hallway. "How do you feel?"

"Lighter," Marcus said. "Like I put down something I'd been carrying for years. I'm not Ghost anymore. Not the disappeared kid. I'm Marcus. Marcus Harlow. And I matter."

"You always mattered," Ryles said gruffly. "Even when you were invisible. Even when you were erased. You mattered. Don't forget that."

Marcus smiled. First genuine smile in months. "I won't." Trixie wasn't handling things well. She avoided the shop. Avoided Yuki's statue. Avoided talking about what happened. She spent her days stealing things she didn't need from stores that deserved better. Pushing boundaries. Testing limits. Seeing if anyone would stop her.

No one did. She was famous now. The Infiltrator who saved the world. Stores didn't prosecute. Police didn't arrest. Everyone gave her space to grieve.

Which made it worse. Because she wanted someone to tell her no. To stop her. To set a boundary. To prove that her actions had consequences.

On the fourth day, Ryles found her sitting on a rooftop. Staring at nothing. "You're spiraling," he said bluntly. Sat down beside her. "And if you don't stop, you're going to hurt yourself."

"Good," Trixie said. "Maybe I should hurt. Maybe I should pay for letting Yuki die."

"Yuki didn't die. Yuki chose. And if you think dishonoring her choice by destroying yourself is going to make anything better, you're stupider than you look."

Trixie flinched. "I should have found another way. I should have—"

"There was no other way," Ryles interrupted. "I was there. I was monitoring. I saw everything. The system needed a center anchor. Someone had to volunteer. Yuki was the logical choice. The bravest choice. The right choice. And you know it."

"It's not fair."

"No. It's not. Fairness is a myth. But meaning isn't. Yuki's sacrifice meant something. The network exists. Reality is stable. Eight hundred people are serving voluntarily instead of being trapped. That's because of her. And if you destroy yourself, if you waste the life she helped save, you make her sacrifice meaningless."

Trixie was crying now. Ugly crying. The kind she'd been holding back for days. "I miss her. So much. She was the best of us and we let her go."

"Yes. You did. Because that's what love is. Letting people choose their own path even when it breaks your heart. Even when you'd rather die than watch them go. You loved her enough to let her matter."

"I don't know how to live with this."

"One day at a time. One choice at a time. You get up. You honor her memory. You teach new Grippers what she taught you. You build something good from something terrible. That's how you live with loss. That's how you survive."

Trixie leaned against Ryles. Let him hold her while she cried. Let herself grieve properly for the first time since waking. When she was done, she wiped her face. Stood. "I'm ready to come back. To the shop. To the team. To work."

"Good," Ryles said. "Because we need you. The memorial is in three days and someone has to make sure Leo doesn't give a speech that's all architecture metaphors."

Trixie laughed. Weak. But real. "I can do that." They walked back to the shop together. Back to Yuki's statue. Back to the work of building something better.

The memorial planning took over the shop. Mayor's office wanted speeches. Press wanted photo ops. Parents wanted closure. The team wanted something real. Something Yuki would actually appreciate.

Leo drafted seventeen versions of his speech. Each one worse than the last. Marcus helped. Trixie edited ruthlessly. Lily contributed from the hospital via video call. Even Vance offered suggestions, though the team mostly ignored them.

"It needs to be honest," Trixie insisted. "Not sanitized. Not political. Honest. She wasn't a saint. She was a kid who helped people. Who made a hard choice. Who mattered."

"The mayor's office wants inspiring," Marcus said. "Something that makes people feel good about the new system. About Grippers."

"Screw the mayor's office," Leo said. "This is for Yuki. We say what she deserves to hear." They worked for hours. Finally settled on something real. Something true. Something Yuki might actually like.

On the seventh day, they stood in City Hall Plaza. Thousands of people watching. Cameras everywhere. Government officials in suits. And at the center, covered in a white cloth, Yuki's statue.

Leo stepped to the microphone. Looked out at the crowd. At his team beside him. At Yuki's stone form waiting to be unveiled. He took a breath. And spoke.

"Yuki Chen was twelve years old when she discovered she was a Mender. She could absorb pain. Take damage meant for others. Heal people by making herself sick. And for six months, she used that ability to help everyone she could. She never asked for anything in return. Never complained about the cost. Never stopped trying to make things better."

He paused. Steadied himself. "Three days ago, Yuki made a choice. When the new anchor network needed a center point to stabilize, she volunteered. She knew it would turn her to stone. She knew she'd never walk away. She knew it would cost her everything. And she did it anyway. Because that's who she was. Someone who helped people. Someone who mattered. Someone who chose to build something better even when it meant sacrificing herself."

He looked at her statue. At the peaceful stone face. "We're going to honor her by continuing her work. By teaching new Grippers to be proud of what they are. By maintaining the network she died to create. By helping people the way she helped us. And we're going to make sure that no one ever has to sacrifice themselves alone again. We'll build it together. As a team. As a community. As builders."

He nodded to Marcus and Trixie. Together, they pulled the white cloth away. Yuki's statue stood revealed. Beautiful. Peaceful. Eternal. And at the base, a bronze plaque:

Yuki Chen

Mender, Builder, Friend

"Let me matter"

The crowd was silent. Then someone started clapping. Then another. Then thousands. Applause that echoed across the plaza. Recognition. Honor. Grief shared among strangers.

Leo placed his hand on the statue one more time. Felt the warmth that meant Yuki was listening. "Thank you," he whispered. "For everything." Inside the network, Yuki smiled. And knew she'd made the right choice.

That night, Leo couldn't sleep. He sat in his blue bedroom. Looking out at New Portside. At the city slowly returning to life. At the lights turning from white to colors. At the transformation they'd started.

Tomorrow they'd open the school officially. Start teaching. Start building infrastructure. Start coordinating the network properly. The work was just beginning.

But tonight, Leo felt something he hadn't felt in months. Peace. Not happiness. Not yet. There was too much grief for that. But peace. The satisfaction of having built something real. Something that mattered. Something that would last.

He pulled out his father's journal. Opened it to the last page. The page that had been blank. Words appeared there now. In his father's handwriting. Impossible. Perfect.

Leo—

I'm proud of you, son. You did what I couldn't. You let go. You trusted. You built with others instead of trying to fix everything alone.

But the work isn't finished. Saving the boundary was only step one. The Reverie itself needs to be freed. Not controlled. Not owned. Free.

I couldn't do it. Vance couldn't do it. You can. Because you understand what we didn't—that freedom requires collaboration, not control. That power shared is stronger than power hoarded.

Tomorrow you begin teaching. In a month, you'll have fifty students. In a year, hundreds. And when the time comes, when the Reverie calls, you'll have an army of builders ready to help.

I believe in you. All of us do. The Sleepers. The anchors. The network. We're watching. Supporting. Believing.

Finish what we started. Free the Reverie. Make it safe for everyone.

—Dad

Leo closed the journal. Looked out at the city. At the future waiting to be built. "Okay," he whispered to the night. To his father's memory. To Yuki's sacrifice. To the team sleeping in the shop below. "Okay. We'll build it. Together. Always."

And somewhere in the deep Reverie, in places humans hadn't yet explored, ancient things stirred. Watched. Waited. The builders were coming.

[END OF CHAPTER 20]

Epilogue: Building Forward

Six Months Later

Leo woke to blue. Not grey. Not regulation-approved neutral tones. Blue. His mother had painted his bedroom walls the week after Vance was arrested, unable to sit still, needing to mark the change.

Six months since the Sanctum. Six months since they'd saved reality and lost Yuki. Six months since Vance's public confession, unable to sit still, needing to mark the change. His room had transformed. Posters covered the walls. Photos of the team. And on his nightstand, glowing faintly, a small crystal from Yuki's statue. It pulsed with warmth—a reminder that she wasn't gone, just different.

Leo dressed and headed downstairs. The city outside his window was healing. Color returning street by street. Red flowers. Green trees. Yellow awnings. The Conformity Council was gone. The Wellness Centers shuttered. And everywhere, people wore ANCHOR badges with pride, serving their two-hour monthly rotations voluntarily.

No prisoners. No forced sacrifice. Just choice. The hospital's Sanctum Ward was on the fourth floor. Lily's room was the one with flowers everywhere—bouquets from strangers, thank you cards, drawings from children.

Leo knocked and entered. Lily sat cross-legged on her bed, surrounded by glowing crystals. Her skin shimmered faintly—part human, part dream-matter. Her silver-white hair cascaded down her back. When she opened her eyes, they held impossible depths.

"Leo." She smiled—still Lily's smile. "Right on time." He took her hand. It felt warm and real, but with that faint thrumming underneath—the network pulsing through her veins.

"Fifteen hundred and forty-three active anchors worldwide," Lily said, her voice holding harmonics now. "The rotation system is working perfectly. Reality is stable. The boundary holds."

"How are you?" Leo asked. "Really?"

"I love it. I can feel everyone. Every anchor. Every Gripper. The whole network." Her eyes met his. "This is freedom, Leo. Real freedom. I chose this. I get to help people. I matter."

She paused, expression shifting. "There's something else. I can feel things in the deep Reverie. Something old is waking up. Things that existed before humans learned to dream. They're jealous of what we've built. When they come—and they will come—we'll need to be ready."

"How long do we have?"

"Months. Maybe a year."

"Then we'll prepare," Leo said. "Together. Like always." He kissed her forehead and left, knowing deep in the Reverie, ancient things stirred and watched and waited.

Reverie Recovery occupied three stories on Salvage Street. The building that had been Ryles' pawn shop now housed a legal, government-approved school for Grippers. The rainbow sign proclaimed: "ETHICAL SMUGGLING TAUGHT HERE." Leo opened the door. At the center of the ground floor, exactly where she belonged, stood Yuki's statue. Stone. Peaceful. Eternal. The plaque read:

YUKI CHEN Mender, Builder, Friend

"Let me matter"

Fresh flowers surrounded her. Every student placed one when they entered. Tradition now. Leo placed his hand on her stone shoulder. "New student today. Just like you'd want."

Inside the network, inside the Sanctum's crystal heart, Yuki smiled. Trixie appeared, carrying books. "The new kid's here. Waiting in your office. Terrified, Leo. Just like we were."

"Then let's show them they don't need to be." Through classroom windows, Leo saw Marcus teaching dream navigation—solid and present, no flickering. In another room, Keiko demonstrated healing techniques. His office was small. His father's journal sat on the desk. And in the visitor's chair sat a kid who looked exactly how Leo had felt six months ago.

Terrified. Lost. Holding something impossible. "Hi," Leo said gently. "I'm Leo. You're Sam, right?"

The kid nodded, voice shaking. "I don't know what's happening to me. This morning I woke up and this was just... here." Sam unwrapped the cloth.

A blue flower. Crystallized dream-matter petals shifting colors. Glowing with inner warmth. Leo's breath caught. The exact same flower from six months ago. The flower that had started everything.

"You're definitely a Gripper," Leo said softly. "And you're definitely in the right place."

"Am I dangerous?"

"No. You're powerful. There's a difference." Leo pulled up a chair. "You won't break reality because we're going to teach you control. Nobody takes Grippers away anymore. You're safe here, Sam. I promise."

"What's a Gripper?"

"Someone who can pull things from dreams into reality. Someone special. Someone like me. Like all forty-seven students here. Like fifteen hundred anchors worldwide." Leo smiled. "You're not alone, Sam. You never were."

Sam's eyes filled with tears. "I thought I was broken."

"You're not broken. You're a builder." After showing Sam around—the classrooms, the library, the training spaces—Leo walked them to the door.

"Keep the flower," he said. "Your first successful smuggle. That's special. And Sam? There's no wrong answer about what to do with it. You get to choose."

Sam left with hope instead of fear. Leo watched them go, feeling that familiar warmth. This matters. This is working. This is right.

That evening, the team gathered at Yuki's memorial in City Hall Plaza. Six months to the day since she'd chosen to become stone. Just the core team remained: Leo, Trixie, Marcus, Ryles, Keiko, and Lily appearing on a screen. They stood in a circle. Seven people who'd changed the world.

"Six months," Leo said quietly. "Since you became our anchor. Our foundation. Our heart."

Each spoke briefly. Trixie about the growing network. Marcus about his Senate testimony. Keiko about learning to be proud instead of destroyed. Ryles about the school. Lily translating Yuki's message: "She's happy. She's exactly where she wants to be."

Leo placed his hand on the statue one last time. "We're opening schools in Seattle, Los Angeles, London. We're building the infrastructure you transformed to make possible. We're creating a world where being different is celebrated. And we're making sure no one ever has to sacrifice themselves alone again."

Inside the network, Yuki listened and smiled.

Worth it. All worth it.

That night, Leo sat at his desk, staring at his father's journal. The last page—always blank—wasn't blank anymore. Words appeared in his father's handwriting. Impossible. Perfect.

Leo—

Six months. You've built something I couldn't imagine. You've let go of control and embraced collaboration. I'm proud of you, son.

But the work isn't finished. The boundary is stable, but the Reverie itself remains caged. Controlled. That must change.

The Old Dreamers are waking. The Nightmare Collective. The Chaos Courts. Things that have lived in the deep Reverie since before humans learned to dream. When they come—and they will come—they'll offer you the choice I faced: control or freedom. Order or chaos.

Choose freedom. Choose chaos.

Not because control is evil. But because true freedom requires trust. And trust requires letting go.

Free the Reverie, Leo. Not by conquering it. By understanding it. By making peace with the ancient things. By showing them that humans and dreams can coexist without war.

That's your mission now.

I believe in you. All of us do.

Finish what we started.

Build something beautiful.

—Dad

Leo closed the journal. Tomorrow he'd tell the team. Tomorrow they'd start preparing. Tomorrow they'd begin mapping the deep Reverie, understanding the Old Dreamers, building alliances with things that terrified them. But tonight, he let himself feel hope.

He fell asleep thinking about his team. About the school they'd built. About the future waiting to be shaped. And the Warden was waiting. They stood in the deep places, far beyond the familiar zones.

The Warden looked smaller here. More vulnerable. "Leo Finch," he said. "The Architect. The one who changed everything."

"What's wrong?"

"They're coming. Sooner than I thought. The Old Dreamers. The Chaos Courts. They've decided you're a threat." The Warden's ancient eyes held fear. "War is coming, Leo. Not months. Weeks, maybe."

"What do we do?"

"Prepare. Train. Strengthen your network. And explore. Map the deep Reverie. Find the ones who can be reasoned with. Build alliances before the war begins."

"We're just kids."

"You're builders. And builders don't fight—they create." The Warden began to fade. "Your father tried to control the Reverie. Vance tried to weaponize it. You tried to liberate it. But none of you asked what the Reverie wants."

"What does it want?"

"Ask it yourself. Explore. Understand." The Warden was almost transparent. "I'll teach you what I can. But the real lessons are down there. In the chaos."

Then he was gone. Leo woke with a gasp. Morning light streamed through his blue bedroom window. He grabbed his father's journal. The message was still there.

Free the Reverie. Choose freedom. Build something beautiful.

They'd saved reality. Built a network. Created a school. But they'd only completed phase one. Phase two was making peace with chaos itself.

Leo stood. Headed downstairs. He'd tell the team. They'd prepare. And when the Old Dreamers came—because they would come—they'd be ready.

Not ready to fight. Ready to build. Ready to show the ancient chaos that collaboration was stronger than control. That freedom was more powerful than force. That humans and dreams could coexist without war.

They'd do it together. He looked out the window at New Portside waking up. At the color returning. At the life blooming. War was coming.

But so was hope. Leo smiled. "Bring it on," he whispered to the ancient things stirring in the deep places. "We're ready." And deep in the Reverie, in places older than human sleep, the Old Dreamers heard him.

They had been waiting twelve thousand years for someone to challenge the boundary. Waiting for humans to grow bold enough to claim the Reverie as their own. Now, at last, the builders had arrived. And it was time to teach them what the deep dreams really meant. The war was coming.

But so was something else. Something the Old Dreamers had forgotten in their ancient rage. Hope.

[END OF DREAM HEIST: BOOK ONE]

Coming in Book Two: The Chaos Courts

When ancient dreams declare war on reality, can a team of teenage Grippers build peace from chaos?

About the Authors

IBRAHIM ROBLE

Ibrahim Roble is a storyteller who believes the best adventures happen when you mix the impossible with the heartfelt. When he's not writing about kids stealing from dreams or monsters invading the Hundred Acre Wood, he's probably scheming up the next wild idea that makes people say, "You can't write that!" (He can. He does.)

Ibrahim lives in Mombasa, usually with his nose buried in a novel or exploring the hidden corners of Old Town. *Dream Heist* is his first young adult novel, co-written with his longtime collaborator Ken Konet, and represents his belief that the best stories are the ones that make you feel something real—even when they're about impossible things.

When he's not writing, Ibrahim enjoys snorkeling in the Indian Ocean, collecting stories like seashells, spending time with friends, and convincing people that yes, zombie Winnie-the-Pooh is absolutely a brilliant idea.

KEN KONET, M.Ed., MBA

Ken Konet is a Corporate Instructional Designer, educational consultant, and author who writes across more genres than most people read. With a Master's in Education and an MBA, he brings a unique blend of teaching expertise and business insight to everything he creates—which explains why his books manage to be both wildly entertaining and sneakily educational. Ken lives in Central Florida with his wife Izzy, who runs ProHandyWoman.com and is infinitely more practical than he is. When he's not writing, he's riding motorcycles, hiking, camping, or explaining to his wife why he absolutely *needs* to start another book series. His writing style—which he calls "Ken Mode"—is snarky, Deadpool-esque, educational, kind, and caring, often all in the same paragraph. He's written everything from science fiction thrillers to children's books to self-help guides, because apparently choosing a lane is for people with less ambition (or better time management).

Dream Heist represents Ken's first foray into YA fantasy, and he promises it won't be his last. Fair warning: he's already plotting Books Two and Three.

BOOKS BY IBRAHIM ROBLE & KEN KONET

Dream Heist Series

- *Dream Heist: The Reverie Heist* (Book One) — 2025 - *Dream Heist: The Chaos Courts* (Book Two) — Coming 2026

Monsterific Series *(Middle-Grade Fantasy)*

- *The Vampire of Pooh Corner - The Zombie of Pooh Corner*

BOOKS BY KEN KONET

Science Fiction & Thrillers

- *Mycelium Chaos* — Alien fungal spores create network consciousness - *Coffin Dodger* — Spy thriller - *The Custodian* — AI science fiction

The Consensus War Trilogy *(Science Fiction)*

- Book One: *The Manipulation Engine* - Book Two: *The Algorithm Wars* - Book Three: *The Final Consensus*

Self-Help & Motivational

- *The Happiness Algorithm* — Personal storytelling meets practical frameworks - *Human Proof: The Skills AI Can't Steal* — Emotional intelligence as career insurance - *Discipline from Zero* — For readers in survival mode, not optimization mode - *The Power of Nope* — Boundaries and people-pleasing - *Still Standing* — Anti-self-help for exhausted adults

- *Don't Work Harder Than an Ugly Stripper* — Productivity guide (yes, really) - *Business Theatre*

— For entrepreneurs stuck in perfectionist planning

Non-Fiction & Analysis

- *The Architecture of Control* — Systemic authoritarianism through networked power structures - *Unfiltered News Network* — Media literacy education (companion to YouTube channel)

Middle-Grade Fantasy

- *Pie-Rats of Tortuga* — Fantasy exploring inclusion and belonging - *Dream Heist* (with Ibrahim Roble) — Stealing from dreams to save reality

Romance *(Various Unconventional Relationship Dynamics)*

- [Titles available upon request]

Coming Soon:

- *Dream Heist: The Chaos Courts* (with Ibrahim Roble) - *The Great Catsby* — Dual-narrative adaptation of *The Great Gatsby* with cats - Additional titles in the Monsterific series

For a complete and updated bibliography, visit

www.ingramcontent.com/pod-product-compliance
Lightning Source LLC
La Vergne TN
LVHW020710110826
845149LV00012B/2194

9781966703211